BEACON GROVE
book two

COUNTING QUARTERS

USA TODAY BESTSELLING AUTHOR
JEN STEVENS

BEACON GROVE
book two

COUNTING QUARTERS

USA TODAY BESTSELLING AUTHOR
JEN STEVENS

Copyright © 2023 Jen Stevens

All rights reserved. No part of this publication may be reproduced, distributed, or transmitted in any form or by any means, including photocopying, recording, or other electronic or mechanical methods, without the prior written consent of the publisher, except in the case of brief quotation embodied in critical reviews and certain other noncommercial uses permitted by copyright law.

This is a work of fiction. Names, characters, places, and incidents either are the products of the author's imagination or are used fictitiously. Any resemblance to actual persons, living or dead, businesses, companies, events, or locales is entirely coincidental.

Cover design: Ashes & Vellichor

Edited by: Nice Girl Naughty Edits

MAP OF BEACON GROVE

CALLING THE QUARTERS

Calling the quarters is a ritual used by magical practitioners at the start of magical or spiritual work. It involves calling on the five elements and their corresponding cardinal direction of the compass to bring these energies into the magical circle to protect and strengthen the practitioner. For the purpose of this novel, the following correspondences are made:

North — Earth

East — Air

South — Fire

West — Water

Center — Spirit

BEACON GROVE

Location: Beacon Grove High Priest: None
High Priestess: None
Elections held: every 3 years
Mayor: None
Sheriff: Kyle Abbot

THE MOVEMENT

A political regime with the goal of removing the Quarters of Watchtower Coven

Founder: Rayner Whittle
Second-In-Command: Demi Kade

THE QUARTERS OF WATCHTOWER COVEN

▽

NORTH - EARTH
Current: Lorenzo (Enzo) Easton
Elder: Andrew Easton
Counter: Unknown

△

EAST - AIR
Current: Lux Alden
Elder: Drake Alden
Counter: Unknown

△

SOUTH - FIRE
Current: Rhyse Forbes
Elder: Silas Forbes
Counter: Unknown

▽

WEST - WATER
Current: Remington (Remy) Winters
Elder: Rowan Winters
Counter: Storie Graves

○

CENTER - SPIRIT
Current: Blaire Granger
Elder: Tabatha Granger
Counter: Kyle Abbot

PROLOGUE

I come from a place most have never heard of and many wish to forget. Nestled deep in the woods, surrounded by steep mountains and dark waters. My hometown follows its own set of rules, laid out centuries ago by the original thirteen families who built it into what it is today. Run by a coven with powers that defy all logic and a government with corruption embedded into its very foundation.

It had always been a stale and unchanging place.

Until it wasn't.

My monsters walk beside me each day, in a town filled with secrets and corruption—with bullies and liars.

But what happens when the most bullied person here ends up being the most powerful? When fury burns through generations and reaches its boiling point?

Catastrophe.

Beacon Grove is all I've ever known.

And I've never wanted out more.

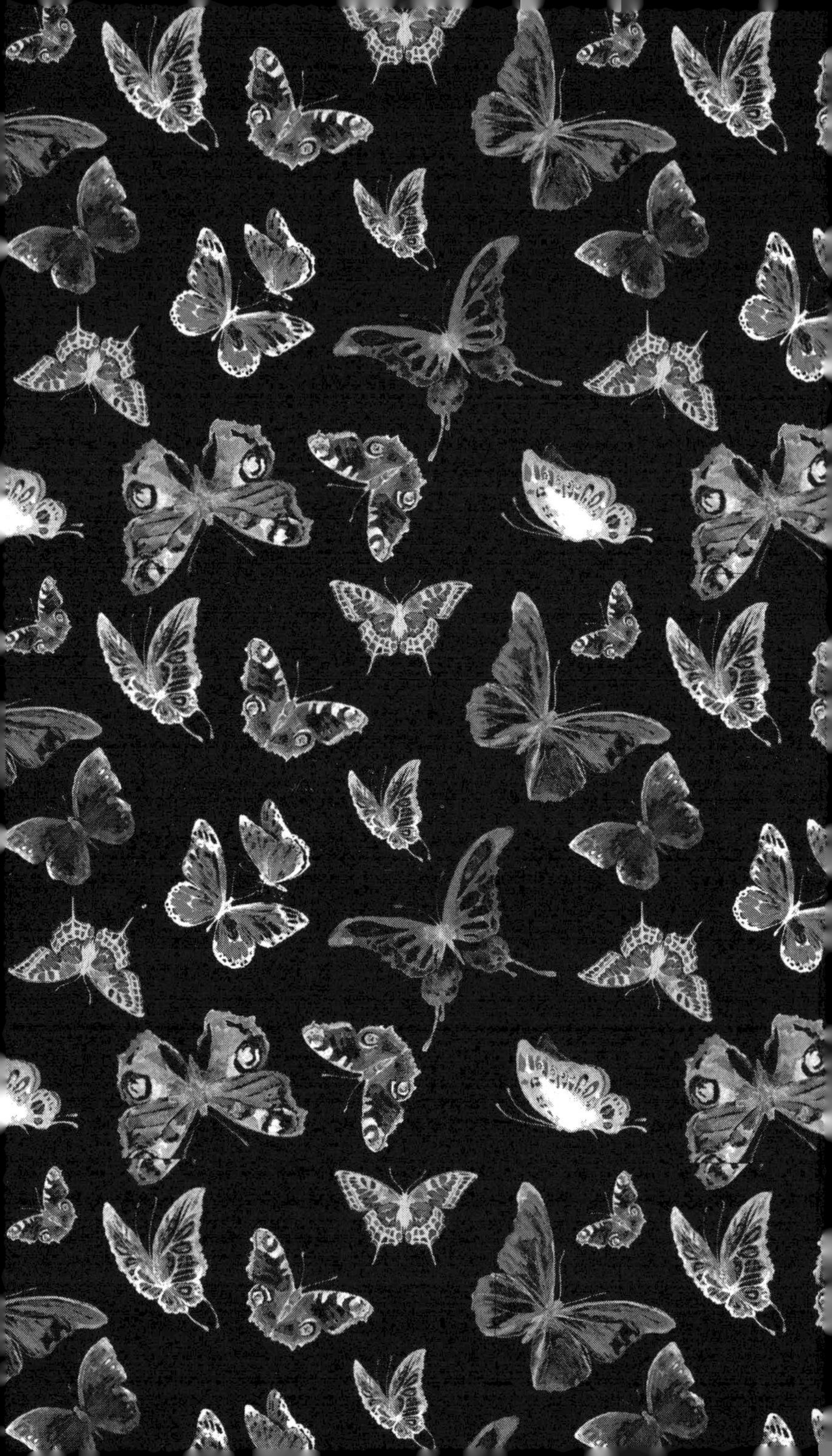

CHAPTER ONE

BLAIRE – NOVEMBER, 2021

Grammy and Mom were sitting cross-legged on the living room floor when I got back from helping Storie sort through the family documents we gathered from the library in the room she was renting from us. For some reason, helping her sort through the details about her family had old wounds from my own coming back to the surface. I went over them in my head as I made the short walk from her hotel room to the main house.

It had been quiet despite the chaotic energy flowing through the streets of Beacon Grove as I made my way home.

Nothing had happened yet. I could feel it coming soon, though.

Something big.

Rayner Whittle was in the town square all day spouting nonsense about his big Movement against the four Quarters of Beacon Grove. They were the four families that essentially ran this town and our coven, Watchtower. And with good reason. The gods had blessed each family with the gift of harnessing one of the elemental powers to protect the rest of the coven:

The Winters could control water.
The Eastons could control earth.
The Aldens could control the air.
And the Forbes controlled fire.

Rayner believed that it was time our town evolved into newer practices and moved away from the way things have been done for hundreds of years. You could guess how far that had gotten him.

The only reason anyone gave him the time of day was because this generation of Quarters was uncharacteristically weak, and that made people feel unsafe. As luck would have it, the gods had decided to split each of their gifts and allow them to flow into a second person, called a Counter. This generation of Quarters had a hard time finding their Counters, though, because so many people were convinced that they were actually weaknesses for the Quarters, set out to steal the gifts and keep them for themselves. That forced many of their families to send them into hiding, if they hadn't already been killed.

In fact, we were only recently learning that wasn't the case, thanks to my grandmother—who was old as dirt and kept immaculate records.

Grammy's old, leather-bound books from her personal library were scattered around them on the worn shag carpet, some opened, and others stacked haphazardly on top of each other.

They invited me to sit with them. Actually, they *insisted* that I sit with them, the way that they always did—and then Grammy pinned me down with her withering stare. The one that made me want to fold myself up into the smallest possible form and roll away from her.

"You've been helping Storie again."

It wasn't a question. Even if it were, she wouldn't expect a confirmation. She was always three steps ahead of everyone.

It was our job to catch up.

Still, I nodded. My crossed legs began bouncing involuntarily, earning me a deeper glare from the old, wretched woman.

Of course, I loved her. She and Mom were the only family I had. Honestly, she was more of a mother to me growing up than my own mom was. I didn't blame my mother for that, though, as one might assume. She wasn't immune to Grammy's constant berating. I just wished she did more to protect me.

Break the cycle.

Instead, she threw me to the wolves and ran off, probably relieved to be free of them constantly nipping at her heels.

Bloodlines are strange, peculiar things, aren't they?

They can tell you who you are and where you come from. They can provide you with privilege and wealth beyond anything you could ever earn yourself. Or they could dig your grave far before you ever even existed.

I'd always known what it meant to be a Granger—the trials and tribulations that were attached to the name. But I'd also been stuck wondering about the other half of me? Where did that path lead?

I don't know who my father is. He was a tourist passing through our boring little town during the annual Mabon celebration. My mother says they instantly connected on a spiritual level and thus led to my conception. They agreed that staying strangers would keep their affair more interesting, opting not to share their real names with one another. He left before a pregnancy test was a thought in her mind.

It was the oldest story in the book, and par for the course with my flaky, eccentric mother, who rarely thought about anything outside of her own colorful aura. My grandmother had never let her live that decision down.

So, without any knowledge of my paternal side, half of me was always missing. I'd sit up at night fantasizing about it. Imagining that while my mother's genetics provided nothing but negativity and mistreatment throughout my formative years, my father's would be the key. That he held an authority and importance in the real world that could get me out of this swampland. That maybe Mom was just trying to be her weird, mysterious self by saying she didn't know his name and she was just nervous to reach out to him for fear of rejection. That she'd hand over a slip of paper on my birthday one year and gift me with the other half of myself.

But no. That day never came.

Reality hit me in the face on my eighteenth birthday when I finally built up the nerve to ask her about him. I'd never forget the look of pity that crossed her face as she repeated the same words she had said to me the first time I'd ever asked. That she truly had no idea who he was and at this point, probably couldn't even pick him out of a police lineup if she had to.

I planned to do things differently for my future children.

My mom noticed my legs bouncing as well. She placed a soft hand on my arm in an attempt to comfort me, effectively bringing my thoughts back to the present.

"We have something pretty serious to talk with you about."

"Okay." I blew out a breath.

They jumped right in, going over the history of the Granger family as it was written in the books they kept stored away in Grammy's office. The books I had always been forbidden from reading. And none of it was what I'd been told while growing up.

Grammy slowly explained that the Grangers were one of the original thirteen founding families of Beacon Grove and the Watchtower coven. We were gifted the ability to control all four elements.

They called us the Center.

Over time, as Quarter families grew greedy and the other original families were being hunted and culled, the Grangers were forced to lie and hide their gifts, claiming the gods ended their powers to feed the Quarters. Naturally, the coven resented them and practically pushed them out, deeming them unworthy of the title.

Since then, they've been forced to hold their power in secret, as the fear of being discovered was far worse than any alternative. If it weren't for the fact that we were also the town's midwives, we would have been cast out altogether.

"If the gift is passed down through the Granger bloodline, does that mean Mom is the one who currently possesses it?"

"That's where things get a little weird. It seems like the gift may have skipped a generation. It very well could have skipped yours as well. There's no way to know," my mother replied.

My eyes swung to Grammy, whose lips were pursed like she was holding something back.

It explained so much.

"So, you're still in possession of it?"

I thought back to what Storie had told me about the other Quarters and their father's refusal to hand off their gifts when their sons came of age. Had Grammy done the same thing to Mom?

Mom answered for her. "Yes and no. Our gifts don't work the way the other Quarters' do. Multiple generations can possess the gift at one time. Grammy's power has been slowly fading away, though. We've been waiting to see if it transferred to either you or me, but it appears to just be disappearing altogether."

I sensed the tension those words invited and smiled nervously.

"All those years of lying seem to have caught up to us," I joked.

"Don't you dare speak ill of our family line," Grammy snapped, her nostrils flaring. Course, white flyaway strands of hair had fallen out of her tight ponytail and surrounded her head in what looked like a crown of spikes. "They made sacrifices you couldn't even bear to think about."

I mumbled an apology and picked away at a speck of dust on my knee.

Mom's soft voice broke the tense silence that hung in the air around us. "We've tried to keep this from you as long as possible. We've watched the way the pressure has eaten away at the Quarter boys and knew it would be a heavy load for you to carry when there were no solutions to even explore. But when Storie came to town and the Winters boy began reclaiming his gifts, we started to feel a speck of hope that maybe the same would happen to us."

"Do we have Counters as well?"

Mom nodded her head, and Grammy allowed her to continue speaking.

"Usually. When the last two generations of Quarters showed their greed for power, things started to shift. That's why they had such a hard time finding your friends' Counters when they were born. Mother Nature did her best to turn the board and ensure no one could cheat. It seems as if our line got tangled in the fray somehow."

"So, all this time we hated the Quarters... when really, we're one and the same."

Mom offered a silent nod.

I looked over to Grammy, and the pieces were finally coming together. "That's why you're so defensive of them. If they fall, we all fall."

"If those boys can't get a grip on this situation and stop the Movement from villainizing them, we're all going to pay the price."

I felt my head bob in a silent nod of confirmation. It didn't seem plausible, though. Grangers were hardly considered members of the Watchtower coven. How the hell can we be the most powerful witches in it?

"Listen to me, Blaire." Grammy sensed my doubtful thoughts. Her tone had dropped so low, I almost couldn't recognize her. She was angry. Or afraid. Or both.

"There's going to be a lot of things that shake up what you thought you knew. You're an ignorant, naive girl..." She inhaled a deep breath, preparing for her next words, which I knew were next to impossible for her to utter.

"That's our fault. Your mother and I have only been trying to protect you, but we've failed at doing that, and now we need you to pull up your big girl panties and follow along."

I wanted to mouth back. To show her that she couldn't speak to me like a child anymore. Instead, I bowed my head and waited for her to go on. I could swear that, as if it were waiting for me to realize its presence, the impossible power they spoke of came to life and tingled beneath my skin.

Waiting to be released. Wanting to retaliate against anyone that doubted or wronged their new owner.

Grammy's words faded into the background as a dark mist crept into my mind. Thoughts and memories flashed behind my eyes of every instance I was ever treated poorly. Each time I'd been wronged by those around me, including the two women sitting before me.

These powers were ancient. They were unsettled and potent and *awoken*. The more my family spoke, the deeper they rooted until I, too, felt the rage at every injustice. Not just against myself, but against every Granger woman who possessed them and was snuffed out by those egotistical Quarters and our spineless coven.

There was an ice that filled my veins.

No, it was colder than ice. Yet, it burned hot at the same time. It was the powerful force of wind creating tsunami waves—of oxygen igniting volcanic flames over barren land. I knew everything and nothing at all. I was the alpha and the omega—the beginning and the end.

The emotions coursing through me were swift and dynamic and not entirely my own. I wanted to scream at the sensation. But deep, deep down, something told me to hold it in. To let them think I was the same girl who walked into this room.

For there was power in ignorance.

I hardly managed to get through the rest of Grammy's lecturing. She was over-explaining and simplifying things that I suddenly knew more about. I wondered if she had ever experienced the shift and if she noticed when it happened to her.

Had Mom ever gotten her chance to wield the Granger gifts, or had Grammy kept it from her somehow? I couldn't imagine she would have ever allowed her mother to treat her this way if she had. It'd been less than an hour and I already wanted to breathe fire down the old woman's throat.

The gods had mercy on her, though, because just as I was about to correct her for yet another skewed fact about our family's history, she rolled her eyes and turned toward my mother.

"I think we should stop. She seems to be checked out," she impatiently huffed.

I didn't have the energy to argue. Instead, I nodded my agreement and stood from the floor, walking off to my room without bothering to offer my help with cleaning up.

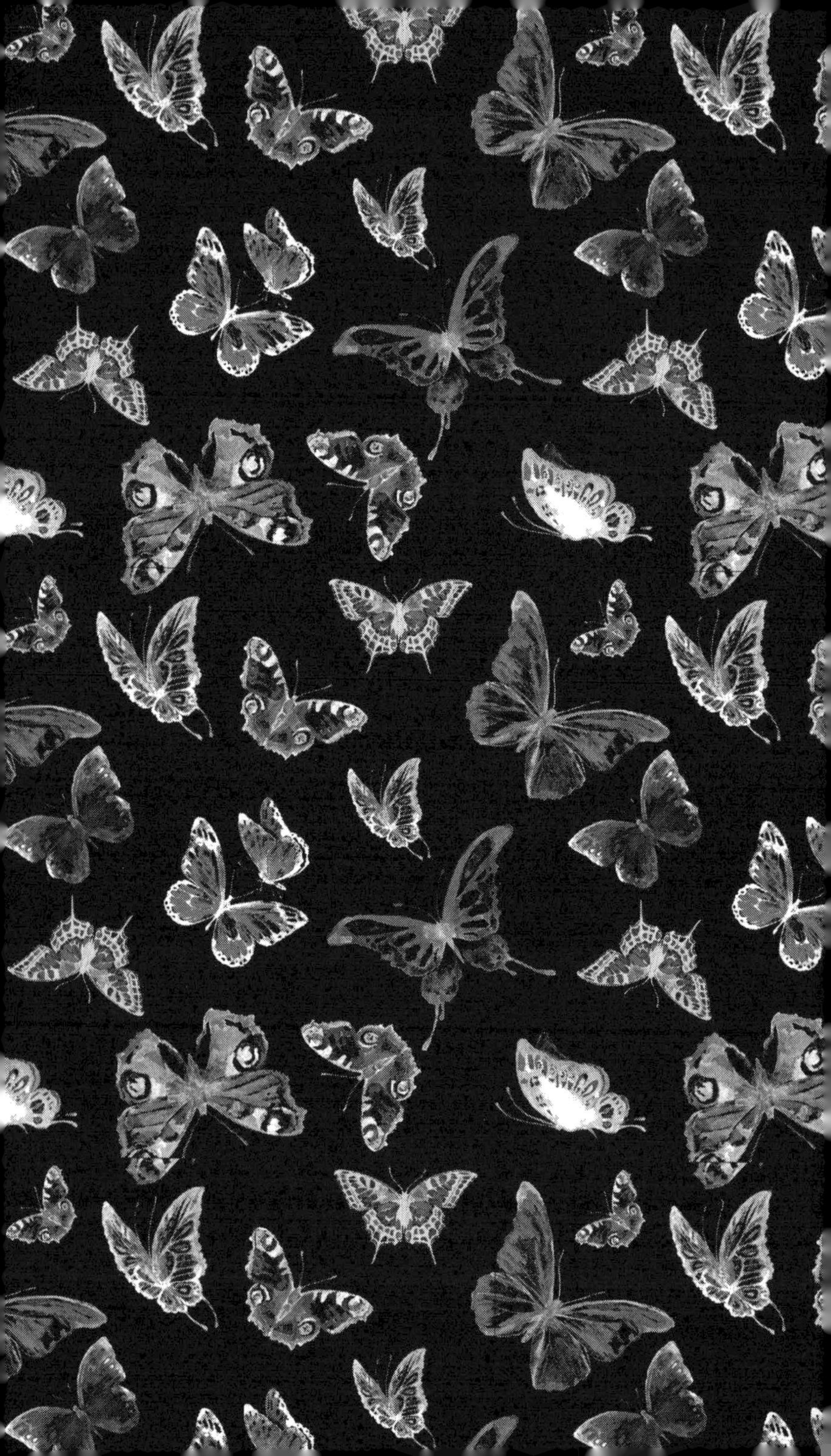

CHAPTER TWO

BLAIRE — PRESENT

I was going to explode.

Keeping my identity a secret in the only place I'd ever known was like chugging gasoline and then throwing a match down my throat. It seared deep into my core—to my very soul. This secret was the only thing that's kept my family line alive, despite being hunted down for centuries by brainless men.

I couldn't be the one to reveal the truth.

But I was so tired of being treated like a lowly member of the society I was raised in. Hadn't I earned my spot? Didn't I deserve the same respect as my peers?

No, because my family's secrets didn't have to be exposed for us to be the town's outcasts. That role fell onto us, regardless. We were used as scapegoats, constantly breaking our backs carrying the weight of the town's problems because we were perceived as the weakest links.

I'd been beaten down and mistreated by children and adults since before I could speak and defend myself. They were the voices in my head, reminding me day in and day out how worthless me and my family were. But I fought against them, just as Grammy taught me to do.

If only they knew our strength.

If only I could show them that I held more power in one finger than they could ever dream of holding as a collective.

Yet, I was forced to stand on the sidelines with my ego bloodied and bruised, while those around me worship the ground that *they* stood on.

The Quarters of Watchtower.

It wasn't fair.

My mother and grandmother constantly reminded me that it didn't *have* to be fair; we just had to survive. They watched me slowly descend into the mental depths of depression as our family burden took its toll on me.

But what kind of life was that?

To merely scrape by. To ignore every gift and shining trait you've been blessed with by the gods, simply because those with small minds couldn't comprehend it. Because they were *afraid* of it.

I say, let them be afraid.

Let them fear us.

Let them worry over every interaction we've ever had with them when they've treated us like lesser beings.

Let them lose sleep over how we decide to enact our revenge.

Let them fear our power.

And if we couldn't do that, then let us be free of this town and all the negativity it holds.

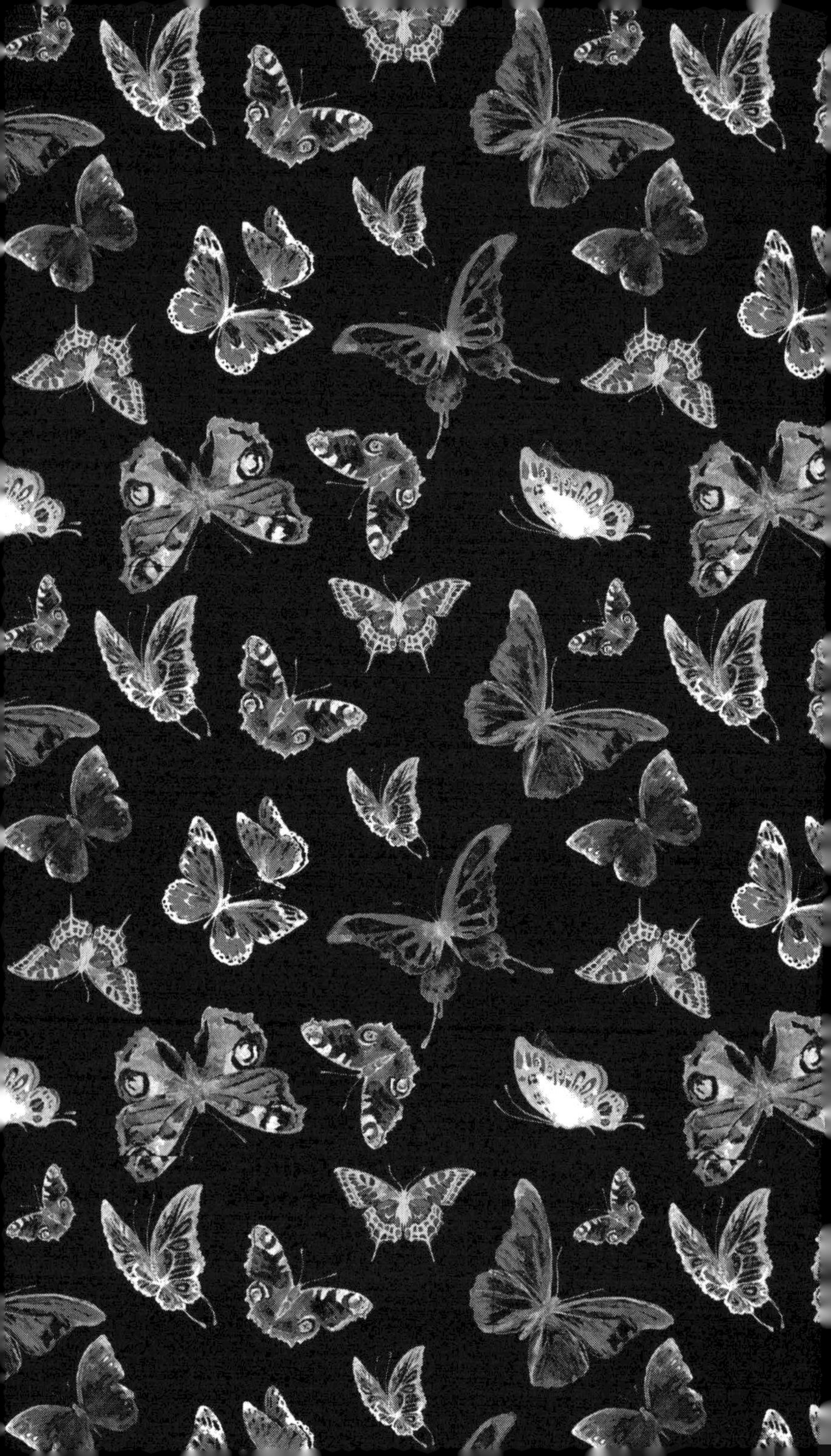

CHAPTER THREE

KYLE — PAST

*R*ayner was rambling again. It seemed like that was all he did anymore. His hatred for the Quarters fueled his passion for a new political system in Beacon Grove. "The Movement," he called it, as if it were the most clever thing he'd ever thought of. It had consumed his entire personality, making him even less bearable to be around than he was before.

If it weren't for his childhood friendship with Mason Graves, we wouldn't have kept him around. But no one else could tolerate the little weirdo, and my best friends, Mason and Bonnie, had a soft spot for him.

"I'm telling you, Mase, it's going to turn these assholes' worlds upside down..." he went on. I drowned him out again, slipping the headphones to my CD player back over my ears.

He was dreaming.

I get it; the Quarters were terrible. The last generation butchered his dad right before his eyes when he was younger and took his brother away to finish the job in private. But Watchtower and Beacon Grove were built on the foundation of having the four blessed families protecting it. It was what the gods intended—why they gave them their gifts.

No matter how powerful Rayner's hatred was, he could never muster enough magic to take them down. It was hopeless. I'm not sure why Mason still let him talk about it anymore.

He and Bonnie would occasionally give their input on things, suggesting he do this instead of that, or agreeing that it would be nice to have some freedom from the four jackasses that we were set to take over when they came of age.

Even my girlfriend and Mason's sister, Asher, would go along sometimes.

I refused to entertain it. That would be like feeding a stray cat—he'd always come back expecting more. Until suddenly, I was on the wrong side of some sort of anarchy.

I flung the headphones off my head and dropped the CD player onto the basement tile beside me.

"I'm bored," I groaned, interrupting one of Ray's tangents.

He looked over at me and rolled his eyes when Bonnie and Mason shyly nodded their agreements. Asher mouthed, "thank you," *from her spot on the chair across from me.*

"What do you want to do?" Mason asked.

Rayner loudly scoffed just as I opened my mouth to answer. I turned my body toward him, smiling when he shrunk back into the couch beside Bonnie.

"Problem?" I asked, flashing my teeth.

"Just because you're satisfied with life so long as you get to hang out in a house with running water and mooch off your friends doesn't mean you can interrupt us whenever you please."

"What did you just say to me?"

I moved to stand, but Mason reached over from the armchair beside me and placed his hand firmly on my shoulder.

"Chill out, Ray," he warned. But the little shit grew braver, with Mason holding me back.

"I'm serious. We have the resources to enact real change here. If you're bored, go count your mom's food stamps or something."

Mason wasn't quick enough to stop me from lunging for him this time, and I'd just barely got one punch in before he slithered away and ran up the stairs. Asher and Bonnie shrieked behind me as I went to chase him, but Mason had recovered quickly and was already waiting at the stairs to push me back by my chest.

"I'll catch up to you when you don't have anyone to hide behind, Whittle," I called up the stairs, then pushed Mason's hands off of me. "I'm cool. Why do we let that little shit around, anyway?"

✴

*P*resent

"It happened again," Stewart mumbled from behind our town's newspaper, The Beacon, as I rounded his desk to get to my office. When I didn't bother to offer him a response, he continued.

"We aren't going to be able to keep them from reporting it much longer. I've already gotten multiple messages from Mark threatening to blow the whole thing open."

I fell into the chair that was older than I was and rolled my shoulders back in an attempt to release the tension burning through my muscles, trying to refrain from stabbing a pencil into Stewart's liver-spotted hand. I hadn't caught a break since the Movement was disbanded, and he did nothing but pile on. I was tired of holding up the weight of this station while he bitched and moaned in the corner over not ever being elected sheriff in his thirty-year career.

"What are we going to do?" he urged, a little too desperately.

Maybe if he ever got his ass away from his desk and actually helped the community, they'd be able to stand him. I could swear his beer belly was wearing an indent into the wood. He considered me as if I were a threat, but I had my suspicions about him, too.

"They'll keep their mouths shut if they want to avoid lawsuits for interfering with an open case."

And they would. I'd already had multiple run-ins with Mark Tackle, the editor of The Beacon, for instigating the horrific events that happened over Mabon and Samhain just over four months ago. By releasing pertinent information about the Movement cases we were dealing with last year, when local girls were going missing left and right, they essentially fed every advantage we had to the leader, Rayner, and kept us one step behind.

My hands were tied in this situation. Mayor Douglas made it a daily task to remind me not to share the most recent events with anyone who didn't absolutely have to know about them.

I had suspicions that Stewart was involved with Rayner's plans from the start, but couldn't call him out on it without hard proof. Which, of course, I didn't have. The Movement Members kept their mouths sewn shut about it all, and aside from the few I'd seen participating in their sick ritual with the Graves girl, there weren't many others that I could pin down and hold accountable.

Storie Graves had only been here for a couple of months when it happened and was hardly a good resource to use for identifying those who took part. She'd been preoccupied with other things—like recovering from almost being burned alive. Nearly every person she named had a solid alibi when they were brought into the station and questioned, so I had no choice but to let them go.

The day I found her little sedan winding through the singular road that led to Beacon's Grove, I thought I'd somehow traveled through time. She was nearly identical to her aunt—and my first love—Asher Graves. Once I got over the initial shock, I realized that her presence in our town meant the worst had happened.

I implored her to leave. To turn her car around and drive away before anyone knew she'd come so close to the very people her family gave their lives to protect her from. These people weren't anyone she wanted to mess with. But a quick dip into her mind—a small gift I'd been given from the gods for some reason—proved she wouldn't listen, so I gave her a warning and sent her to the only people I knew would take care of her.

Storie's parents, Mason and Bonnie, had been my best friends growing up. I was closer to them and Asher, Mason's little sister, than I was to my own family at the time. Born on the wrong side of town to an abusive, alcoholic father and a mother who couldn't even protect herself, let alone her kids, I was willing to do anything to find a way out. Fate put the Graves in my path, and by some miracle, they were willing to see past my address and family's status and accepted me as their own.

Well, I thought they had.

Until Storie was born, and they had to do what was right for their family—their *blood* family.

I wasn't jealous of Storie, though. In fact, I understood. As soon as we found out Bonnie was pregnant, I felt a protective connection to her. I even tried to help them. Practically begged Asher to let me get in the car when they packed their bags and loaded it up. Emotions were running high, and we were all still in shock over Bonnie's death at Rayner's hands hours before. Our own friend had betrayed us beyond belief, and we were left reeling.

When I couldn't convince them to let me go with them, I promised I'd be close behind. That was the only way they were able to get rid of me that day and I think even then, I knew it was a lie.

Asher and Mason had to do what was best for Storie, and that meant cutting off all ties to Beacon Grove.

Which was why seeing her face had my heart ripping apart into a million pieces. It was like I had lost Asher all over again. Even through all the years of no contact after she left, and the miles I drove to find her, I still held onto hope that we would find our way back to one another in the end. But then Storie confirmed her death, and I had no idea what to do.

All I knew was that I had to make their deaths mean something, and that masculine urge to protect flared up again. I watched her from afar, keeping tabs on everything Rayner and the Movement did. But he knew I'd be watching. He threw distractions at me from every angle until I couldn't make any sense of what his next move might be.

The missing girls.

The political rallying.

The black magic.

It was all a way to turn the town against the Quarters—and to stop me from protecting Storie. He had grown a sick obsession with my best friend's daughter, pouring every ounce of hatred and blame for any negative thing that had happened to him into her. And he knew I wasn't going to sit back and watch as he destroyed the last piece of my chosen family.

On the night he tried to kill her, he set up a trap for me. Little breadcrumbs that led to where he was taking all the local girls were left around for me to find, until he left a note on my desk that explained it all. I was given a choice that night; to save Storie, or save the girls. He promised they were all still alive, waiting to be rescued. I had underestimated the power of a Counter, though, and I made the choice that led to the slaughter of innocent lives to save a girl who had the ability to save herself. Now, he was torturing me with the remains of those who didn't, leaving behind gruesome scenes of animal carcasses wearing his victims' clothing all around town for me to find.

And guaranteeing a long, painful death for himself.

The ✻ Beacon

19 MARCH 2022

OSTARA FESTIVAL CANCELED

Mayor Douglas would like to remind the citizens of Beacon Grove that the annual Ostara festival has officially been canceled. He encourages families to celebrate with their household members and avoid large crowds.

When asked to comment, Mayor Douglas explained: "The Spring Equinox is a very special time for us to plant the seeds of our future prosperity, which we believe can be done in the safety of your own homes. We're still trying to avoid the threat that large gatherings pose to the peace we've been able to attain in Beacon Grove. We hope to be able to open the city up for celebrations in the coming months and we thank you for your patience as we calibrate to the changing times."

While the three-day festival has been canceled, there are still ways for us to personally bring in the new season with open arms.

Katy Goff, owner of the Toadstool Flower Shop, has come up with a list:

- Katy says you can sow wildflower seeds in your personal gardens to feed the withering bee and butterfly population or plant your own fruits and vegetables to enjoy throughout the season
- Cleaning your home is a great way to clear out old patterns and start anew
- Decorate your altar to symbolize your manifestations for the next year
- Enjoy a walk through the woods to ground yourself and connect with Mother Nature
- Journaling and meditation

We know the past few holidays on the wheel of the year have been hard on everyone, but the people of Beacon Grove are a resilient crowd. Continue to do your part to ensure the safety of others, and we'll be back to our regularly scheduled celebrating in no time.

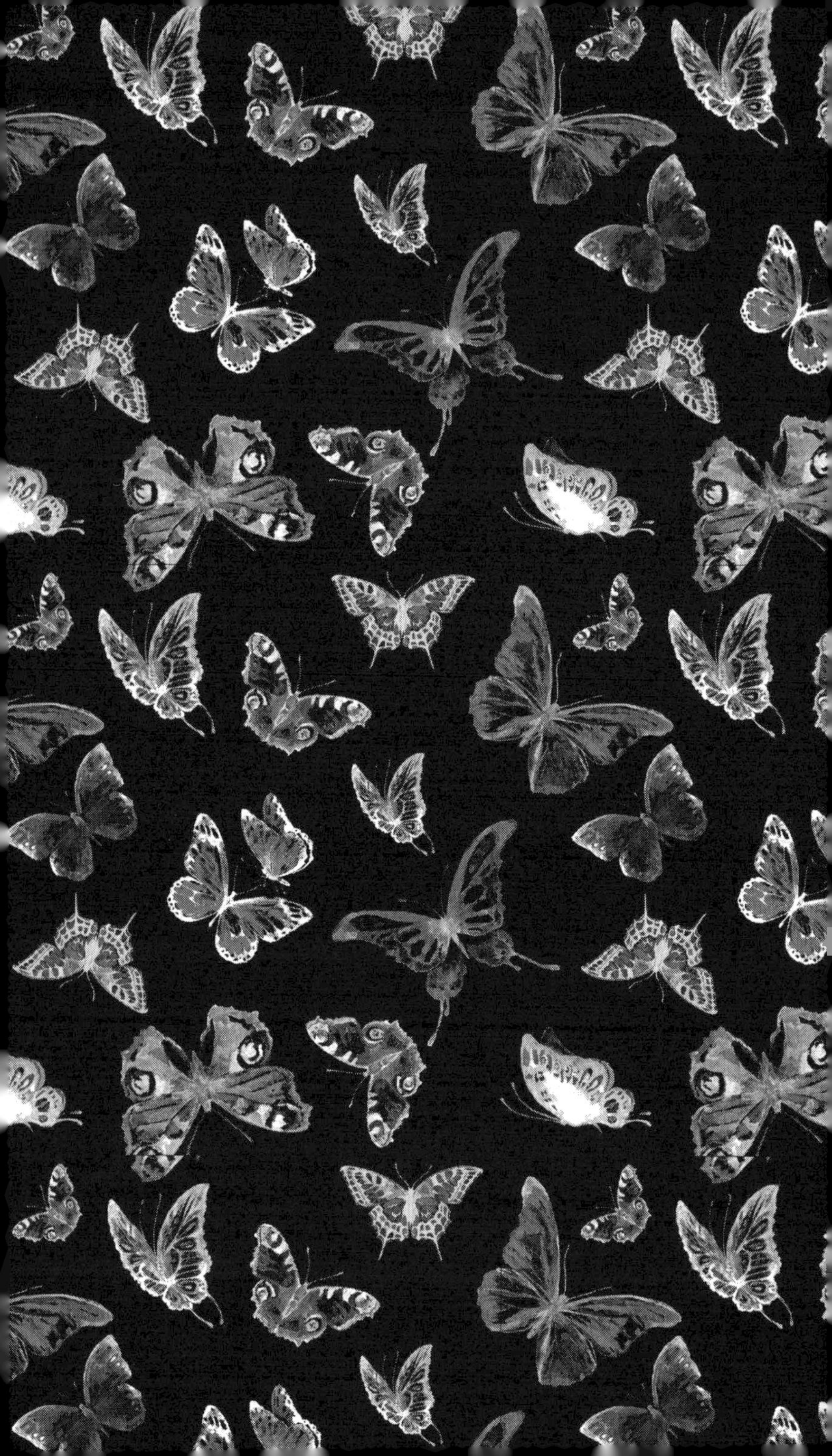

CHAPTER FOUR

BLAIRE

The wind blew its way through the trees, rocking them back and forth against each other overhead as I rested on a fallen log below. The creaking of branches and trunks brushing against one another was somehow both calming and unsettling at the same time. I allowed a few moments to pass as they danced together before slowing the wind and stilling the wood.

I'd never get used to that control over the elements. I tried to use it sparingly, too afraid of the consequences that came with disrupting Mother Nature. I hardly knew how to use these gifts, anyway. Grammy preached about natural balance, yet exercised these powers her whole life that caused nothing but a disruption of that balance.

Who would knowingly choose this life for themselves?

Who would pass this burden onto future generations?

I didn't get it, and I didn't think I ever would.

Shit. I came out here to clear my head and here I was, falling back into the rabbit hole of confusing thoughts.

It'd been this way since Grammy told me about the gift. One minute I was okay, and the next I was breaking down on the bathroom floor from carrying this heavy load on my shoulders.

God, I missed being ignorant.

Steadying my breath, I gave myself five minutes to feel the emotions that took over my entire being. To wallow over what *could* have been. To mourn what once was. Any longer, and they'd consume me. I knew they would because they already had. I spent the last two months clawing my way out of the depression that they sunk me into.

Not again.

Five minutes, and then they had to leave.

But before my five minutes were up, a stick snapped to my left. I whipped my head around and locked eyes with a glowing, petrified version of Hailey Lukas—a girl I graduated with at Watchtower High. A squirrel scurried up a tree in terror at her appearance. I faced forward again and rolled my eyes skyward with a loud growl.

Why the fuck can't I just have five minutes?

"You can see me," her meek voice called out in bewilderment.

Hailey was always the quiet, shy type, though she managed to do better socially than I ever could.

And, of course, I could see her. It was my curse. Still, I shook my head, refusing to look back in her direction.

"No, I can't."

"I haven't talked to a single soul in months. How can you hear me?"

She took a few hesitant steps toward me, stopping about five feet away.

I'm not sure why. It wasn't like I could harm her. She was already dead.

"I can't."

"Yes, you can."

I should have just walked away. It wasn't like she could have stopped me, and I wasn't up for playing twenty questions with a ghost. But I'd learned the hard way that she could follow me and, unfortunately, spirits had nothing but time on their hands.

Time to pester and irritate me until I gave them what they wanted—which was closure.

It would be in my best interest to humor the annoying girl, even if I didn't have the emotional strength.

I stood up from the log and pinched the bridge of my nose, still avoiding eye contact. I hated the hazy, hopeful look their eyes always held when they first realized I could see them. Like I could somehow bring them back.

"Okay, what do you need me to do? Tell your mom you love her? Give your dad a hug?"

It was always something so arbitrary that held them back.

"What do you mean?" I saw Hailey tilt her head from the corner of my eye and finally gave in, swinging my gaze over to her.

"You know, what's going to help you cross over? Go into the light? Follow the big guy's voice or whatever?"

"I don't understand. I just want to go back home. I have an interview for a marketing firm in Seattle and I haven't prepared anything."

Oh, gods. Of course, she didn't know she was dead. That would just be too easy for me.

"I hate to break it to you, Hailey, but that interview is long gone. You didn't get the job. But the good news is that you'll never have to work another day in your life because your life is over. You're free to frolic and play around the spirit world."

Her eyes grew wide, and she stared at me in complete, creepy silence. After a few seconds passed, I turned and bent down to grab my bag from the ground to leave.

I'm sure there was a nicer way to go about this, but I didn't have the energy to coddle her right now. I was already late to my shift at the hotel, and I wasn't looking forward to Grammy laying into me about it.

Hailey went missing months ago, when Rayner, the town madman, started kidnapping local girls to frame the Quarters and turn the town against them. He didn't have to kill them, but Rayner was all about going the full mile. I'd been running into his victims all around town and quickly grew tired of explaining their passings to them.

The police already moved on from their cases, assuming they were victims of the Movement that Rayner ran in an attempt to overthrow the Quarter families and become High Priest of the Watchtower coven. In the beginning, Sheriff Abbot assured each of their parents that he would do everything he could to find them at our town meetings, but eventually, it became clear that they weren't coming home alive.

That wasn't to say they gave up on finding them; they just stopped looking for girls who were alive and reluctantly started looking for their remains instead.

Hailey was pacing back and forth behind me, fumbling over her words. I slung the strap of my crossbody bag over my shoulder and walked off, knowing she'd be close behind.

"Blaire, you have to stop. You have to explain this to me. *Please*. You're the first person I've been able to talk to in months."

Her voice broke when she reached out to touch me, and her hand passed right through my shoulder. I paused to watch the realization burn through her translucent form, my broken heart splintering into a thousand more tiny little pieces.

This.

This was why I was positive I'd been cursed. Because what kind of gift allowed you to look into someone's eyes while they realized they no longer existed? To watch their soul shatter and disconnect from the idea of what they *could have been*.

I couldn't handle it. Grammy was tough-skinned, and Mom was well-trained in avoidance. Me? I was weak and empathetic and tortured with this burden that they severely under-prepared me for.

Hailey's crumpled form fizzled out and disappeared, leaving me alone in the middle of the trees again. I huffed out a breath and continued my trek to the hotel, knowing she'd be back. They always came back. That was the problem. And something told me Hailey was going to be a tough one to break through to and help cross over.

Once I made it to the opening of the forest, I shifted the streets to make a shortcut for myself to the hotel. It was something I'd done a thousand times before and never realized was part of my magic. I truly thought everyone could set a path in their mind and command the earth to bend and conform.

I really should have taken my time to get there to give myself an opportunity to shake off my horrible mood, but it would only make Grammy angrier, and that always made me feel worse. A person could only take so much verbal abuse before they turned bitter. I was quickly reaching my breaking point.

"You're late," her deep voice grumbled from behind the hotel desk.

Does it matter?

The only thing she did whenever I relieved her was sit on the couch and berate me from across the house that was attached to the hotel office. And with the mayor's most recent restrictions on tourists, the hotel was mostly dead.

I chose not to engage this time. Instead, I took the old computer chair that was still warm from her plump bottom and began combing through the schedule for the next twenty-four hours. No surprise; it was basically empty. Grammy took the hint and limped off into the house, slamming the door behind her.

I would love to leave this place. Not just the motel, but Beacon Grove. I often envisioned myself taking the winding, one lane road out and driving as far as I could go. But Grammy wouldn't even let me get my license when I reached the legal age. By the time I was old enough to go on my own, my hopes of leaving had slowly dried out and died off like rose petals, leaving nothing behind but a bitter, thorny stem.

It was easier to handle when spirits weren't haunting me at all hours of the day and I wasn't forced to hide the biggest piece of me from the world. In the past, that wouldn't have hurt so badly, but I was finally finding my footing when my gifts activated and Grammy and Mom admitted that there was more to the Granger bloodline than being hotel owners and midwives.

We were the most powerful witches in our coven.

A coven, I should add, that had ostracized and mistreated us since before I was even a thought.

The bell over the door rang and yanked me from my staring contest with the computer and Sheriff Abbot walked through. He practically had to duck his head to make it under the short doorway, and when he noticed me in the chair, he tucked his chin into his chest in greeting.

We've been seeing a lot more of him since Rayner tried to burn my best friend, Storie, alive to weaken our Quarters, and he was the first one to arrive at the ritual and save her. Of course, she didn't need help by then, but that was a detail the Quarters have decided to leave out of the story whenever it came up with the coven for fear of giving away too much about the power of Counters.

"How can we help you, sheriff?" I greeted in a dry tone.

"Is Tabitha around?" His silver eyes shifted over to the door Grammy had just slammed. If she wasn't in the office, she was usually in the house.

I always thought he was younger than his forty years. Almost as if I could sense that his spirit was more youthful than people his age would ordinarily be, though he didn't reveal that to the outside world. He was typically polite when necessary, but wasn't entirely friendly with anyone.

When Storie came to town looking for answers about her family, I learned he had close connections with the Graves family. Grammy said he hadn't been the same since they all left and passed on, but I never knew what she meant by that. I couldn't imagine our sheriff being anything other than the glum public servant he was today.

His body was definitely not built like a middle-aged man, though. My gaze dropped from his jaw to the gray uniform stretching over wide, muscular shoulders and ventured down to his slim waist and abdomen that I could only imagine was perfectly toned and defined. I'd never seen him eat a single donut—or any junk food, for that matter. And I'd never admit it out loud, but I'd definitely been paying attention.

I turned back to the computer screen before he noticed that I'd been ogling his body like the pathetic girl that I am and mumbled, "She's in the house."

Just then, the door swung open, and my grandmother's stern face appeared behind it, her emerald-green eyes pinning him down in his spot. I knew for certain that she couldn't see how I was just looking at him, yet somehow, I felt like I'd been caught with my hand in the cookie jar.

"Did you bring it?" Grammy asked Officer Abbot, who I only now noticed was zeroed in on me. He blinked, and then walked up to Grammy to hand her a small box I hadn't noticed he was holding before.

"I'm not sure it'll be of much use." Sheriff's voice dropped as he leaned in to say something in Grammy's ear so that I couldn't hear.

I turned away again, irritated at their rudeness. So ridiculously tired of being treated like a child by my grandmother,

She invited him into the house, and they disappeared behind the door, which he closed much more eloquently than she ever did.

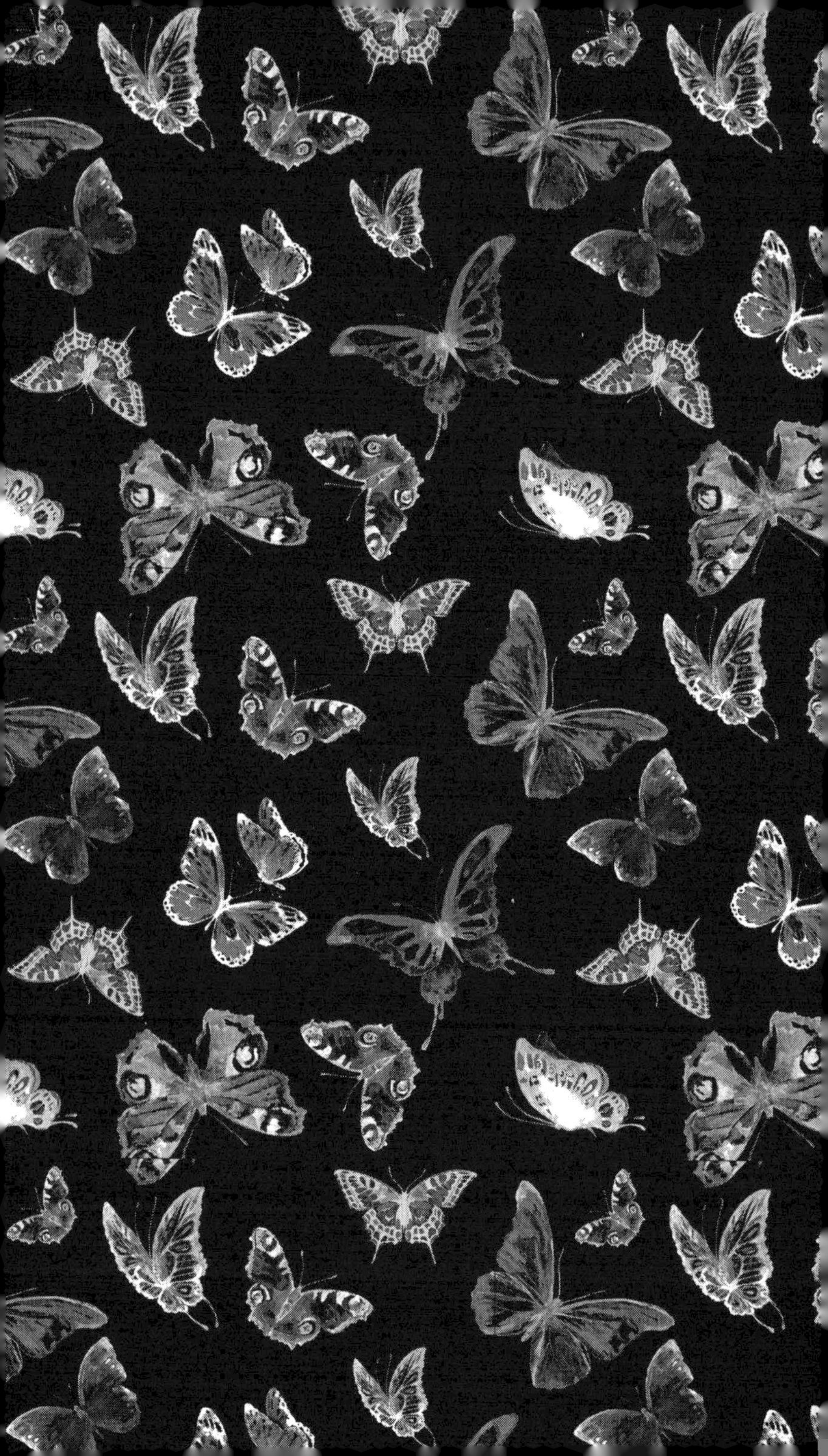

CHAPTER FIVE

KYLE — PAST

*M*y best friends were going to be parents. They shared the news with me and Asher first. Of course, Mason was stressed about what Bonnie's parents would say about them conceiving a child when they didn't even have a place of their own, but Bonnie seemed ecstatic. Not a drop of doubt could be heard in her excited tone as she and Asher gushed over the idea of a new baby together.

Rayner walked into Mason's garage as they were squealing about going shopping for baby clothes and invited himself into the conversation.

"What's so exciting?" he asked.

Mason and Bonnie shared a look, debating whether or not to tell him, and she shrugged.

"I suppose you'll find out soon enough. We're pregnant."

His face lit up with pure joy for our friends. "Congratulations! When are you due?"

"March first," Mason answered proudly.

"That's near Freya Winters' due date."

We all exchanged confused looks. What did that have to do with anything?

"Yeah, I guess so," Bonnie said uncomfortably.

"Bonnie, do you realize how amazing that would be? If your child was a Counter?"

I didn't see the appeal. It seemed like nowadays, a Counter was the most threatening thing against a Quarter, and therefore the most precarious.

"Not really, Rayner."

He clapped his hands together excitedly. "Oh, this is great. We might already have the upper hand. We could destroy them from within..." His voice trailed off as he became lost in thought.

"Well, based on that creepy smile on Rayner's face, I certainly hope it isn't," I said teasingly. My lame attempt to ease the tension that his odd rambling created. He had truly gone off the rails in the past two years.

Rayner cut me a look of pure distaste, but Mason and Asher lightly chuckled. Bonnie still looked a little spooked.

Later that night, when Rayner finally left us to do whatever he did when he was alone, Bonnie turned to Mason with a look of pure horror on her face.

"Whatever happens, no one leaves that kid alone with my baby," she said, and it was almost like she knew what was coming.

✦

*P*resent

Tabitha Granger was a surprisingly useful ally to keep, so long as you managed to remain on her good side. So far, I'd done a pretty good job of that.

She acted as an intermediary between me and the Quarters over the last few months, delivering messages between us to keep anyone else from knowing about our plans. I couldn't risk having Mayor Douglas, or anyone else who was suspected of being on the Movement's side, knowing that the town's sheriff was working with their enemy.

But working with her also meant spending a lot of time at her hotel, which was unusually quiet since Mayor Douglas kept restrictions on all tourist travel and celebrations. Blaire was often the one stuck sitting in the dingy brown office. She never failed to greet me with a frown and a scowl before directing me to the attached home that Tabitha was often waiting for me inside.

If I didn't know any better, I'd guess that Tabitha purposely put the sourpuss in my path as some kind of joke. I knew she never cared much for me or the Graves, especially after the way Storie's parents were run out of town and we were left to clean up their mess.

Today, I was meeting her to discuss the latest animal carcass that had been left behind by the Movement. Blaire and I sat in awkward silence as I waited for Tabitha to invite me inside.

"Do you mind if I hang this here?" I gestured to the bulletin beside me and gave the flier in my hand a subtle shake.

Blaire shrugged, squinting to read the bold words on the paper.

"I'm finally renting out the loft," I explained, wincing as I tacked it on top of a yellowed advertisement for the Broomstick Diner that closed over a year ago. The likelihood of anyone seeing it here was slim, but worth the try.

Blaire noticed me pause and her eyebrows shot up, a teasing smirk playing on her lips. "There's this crazy thing called the internet that's been around for a few decades. It usually gets the word out faster."

"Ha ha," I retorted sarcastically. "I've tried that. I figured if anyone's passing through and falls in love with the quaint charm you lovely Granger women offer, they'll know there's a place to make their stay permanent right down the street."

She ignored the sarcastic jab. "What makes you want to rent it out now?"

I cleared my throat to buy time to make up an excuse. I wasn't even sure why. It was a valid question, given I'd owned the house for two decades now and hadn't rented that space since

I paid the loan off. Blaire was innocent enough, and she wasn't the type to gossip. But I liked to keep my personal life and my professional life completely separate. As sheriff of the town, the lines between the two often got blurred.

"Millie has her hands full with the kids and Ma's health isn't doing too good anymore. I'd like to get a nurse in there to help out and the cost is astronomical." The truth was easier than I thought.

A better man would give his sister a break and take his mother in himself.

But I wasn't a better man.

Millie didn't want to admit it, but Ma's mind was slipping with each passing day. She needed someone who knew how to handle that sort of thing. After I got over my need for space, renting out the loft was a no-brainer.

Blaire just nodded without bothering me for clarification or questioning me, as she would have done in the past. She was known around Beacon Grove as someone who questioned everything to death, but I supposed the last year changed something in all of us.

The door leading to Tabitha's house swung open, and she stood beside it, lifting her brows at me impatiently.

"I have other things to do today, sheriff," her raspy voice said, and I reconsidered that last thought.

Maybe not *all of us* changed that much.

CHAPTER SIX

BLAIRE

Grammy slammed the pots and pans around in the sink while she washed them, as she always did when she was in a mood. Mom and I shared a silent look across the small kitchen table and she mouthed, "not it." Before I could object, she stood up and mumbled something about going to the pharmacy she co-owned as the town's Herbalist, then disappeared behind the front door.

Grammy just shook her head.

I never knew what kind of mood I'd find her in these days. Between her work with Sheriff Abbot, the secret meetings she held with the Quarters, and the lack of business we had from Mayor Douglas' tourist ban, she always seemed to be in some kind of sour state of mind.

Unfortunately, so was I. My ability to feel others' emotions only heightened it.

"You need to turn down the beds in room three. And clean the bathroom in five again. It's filthy."

I took a deep breath, reminding myself that she didn't mean to direct her anger at me. I just happened to be standing in the eye of the storm.

"No one has stayed in room three in months. Why do we need to turn the beds?"

Apparently, that was the wrong thing to say. Grammy slowly turned to level me with a look, green eyes practically glowing with fury.

"Don't question me. Just do it."

She wasn't the only one in a bad mood, though. I was tired of being pushed around by her just for the hell of it.

"I'll do the beds, but I'm not cleaning the bathroom in five. I've done it three times already, and each time it's not good enough for you."

Her body turned the rest of the way, her stance growing wider with the prospect of a fight.

She wanted someone to pick on, and I wasn't going to back down like I always did. I was tired of being on cleanup duty while she kept me out of the loop, yet claimed I held some important role in whatever she was plotting.

"What did you say to me?"

"I said," I began bravely, climbing to my feet to give myself the height advantage. She stood at least six inches shorter than me. "I'm not your bitch. If you want it done a certain way, you can do it yourself."

A growl rumbled deep inside her chest as she took three steps toward me, completely unaffected by my towering stance.

"You would do well to remember not to bite the hand that feeds you," she warned, her voice low and threatening.

I looked into Grammy's eyes and felt nothing but hatred.

Was it mine or hers?

She was right. I was a prisoner, and she was the warden. As long as I stayed under her roof, I'd never have any freedom. A feral, frustrated growl, louder than hers, escaped my lips before I could catch it. That gift inside me—the one I hated so much—purred awake.

"I can't stay here."

I didn't care if I had to sleep in the alley behind the motel; I couldn't stay under this roof any longer. Under her thumb.

Grammy sneered. "Where do you think you're going to go, girl?"

My gaze swung to the bulletin board through the open door Mom left out of, to the flier that was hung up a few days ago. And then, they found Officer Abbot, who was practically cowering in the corner, attempting to blend in with the wall. Neither of us had heard him come in, but his timing was impeccable.

Before I could give it a second thought, I pointed to him. "Your vacant apartment. I'll take it."

His eyes widened, ping-ponging between Grammy, who had whirled around to see who I was talking to, and me, as we waited for his response.

I cut off his jumbled, declining words before they could land. "I'll pay six months' rent up front."

His mouth clamped shut. I knew I had him then. He'd be stupid to decline my offer, especially after what he told me about the other day. *Why* he needed the money.

Grammy just stood there unmoving, no doubt sending mental daggers at him for even considering it. No one crossed Tabitha Granger and got away unscathed, but he needed the money just as bad as I needed out.

She could see the apology written all over his face as he finally tilted his head and shrugged at her in defeat, then turned toward me and nodded.

"Deal."

I couldn't contain the smug smile that spread across my face when my eyes found Grammy again and I saw the fury painted across her features. She had lost. I might regret it later, but I didn't care. I needed space and time to sort this out without her and Mom breathing down my neck and attempting to control me.

"I'll have a check for you tomorrow."

He only nodded, then tipped his head in Grammy's direction one more time before he ducked out the office door and practically jogged to his car, his reason for visiting long forgotten. She would make him pay for crossing him.

When we were finally alone again, I waited for her to break the silence. I could practically see the wheels in her brain turning to find a way to ruin this for me. That was just what she did. But she had no more cards to play.

I'd saved that money since I began working for her at the motel and Mom insisted she pay me *something*. Paying six months of rent would make a huge dent in the savings I had, but it would be worth it to finally have my own space.

To become my own person.

Without a word, she turned away and disappeared down the hall.

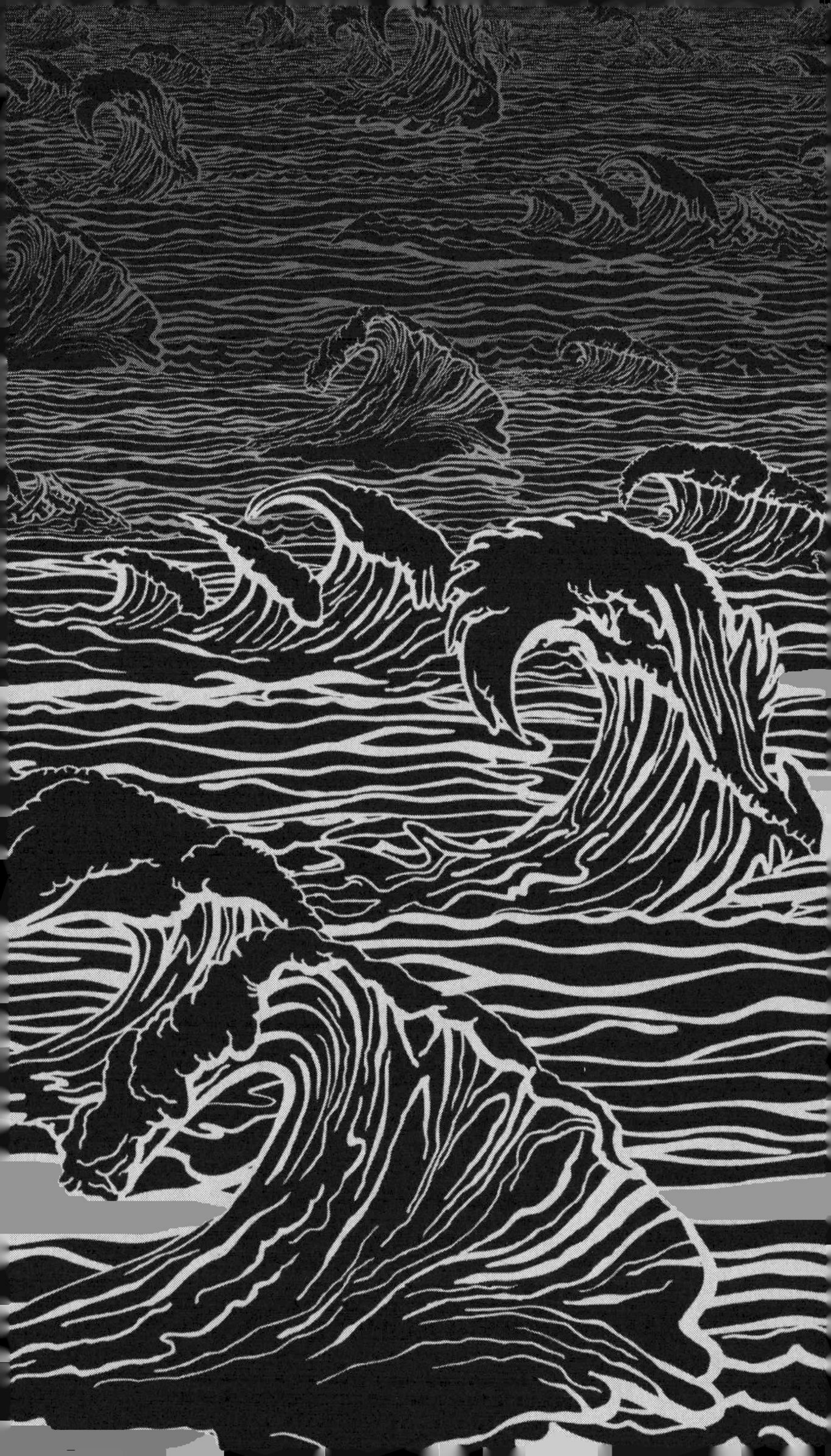

CHAPTER SEVEN

BLAIRE

"When can you move in?" my mother asked from my bedroom floor as she pulled my wrinkled clothes out of my dresser and neatly folded them into a suitcase.

I shrugged from my spot on the floor inside the closet. "I think it's mine as soon as I get him the money."

I hardly had a chance to speak with Sheriff Abbot since he left Grammy stewing in the kitchen three days ago. When I called the number he had on the flier, he responded in a clipped, irritated tone. Even though I offered to bring him the money right away, he agreed to meet with me tomorrow to collect his check and promised to have a contract written up by then. Before I had time to ask any more questions, he mumbled something about having to respond to a call and then hung up.

"I'll help you get moved in. I'm sure Storie can get some of those boys to help us move the furniture out of here."

Her eyes scanned the old, solid wood dresser and bed frame that she sat between.

"You're not taking the furniture." Grammy's voice drifted into the bedroom. Mom's face fell as heavy footsteps made their way through the short hall.

"Come on, Mom," she started, but was shut up with a thick finger pointing at her.

"You might be entertaining this ridiculousness for a shred of affection, but I'm not. That's *my* furniture. I bought it, and it stays in *my* house." She aimed a withering stare at me. "You want to go out on your own, then you can start with buying your own furniture."

Mom rolled her eyes and Grammy stalked off, not even bothering to give me a chance to argue. I heard her grumbling through the hall toward her room. "There's no use moving it, anyway. You'll be back here before it can make dents in the carpet."

Then, she slammed the door.

"Don't listen to her. She's emotional about you leaving."

I gave her a look that said I didn't believe her, and then turned back to the box I was packing.

※

Sheriff Abbot handed the key to my new apartment over as soon as we finished signing our contract. He was going over his expectations as I stared down at the tiny chunk of metal in my hand, an array of emotions coursing through my chest so fast, it ached.

"...rent is due on the first of the month. If you have any trouble paying, just let me know. The porch is a shared space. I don't mind if you use it, just don't leave a mess..."

His voice droned on, hardly penetrating the trail of thoughts that were weaving in and out of my head or the silent victory I felt at what our meeting truly meant.

I did it.

I got out.

And while there was a long road ahead for me, that was a step my own mother couldn't even manage to take.

"I'll help you carry your things up. Do you have anything else?" he asked. His gaze fell to the bags at my feet—the extent of everything I owned—before they moved to the street, looking for a moving van, most likely.

"I'm still working that part out."

It was embarrassing to admit, but not enough to dampen my mood.

He bent forward and lifted the bags into his arms, leading the way through the doorway to my new home.

My front door was positioned right beside his. It opened to a set of white stairs, which led straight into the living room of the loft. The space was completely open, with natural light streaming in from all sides. A galley kitchen with white cabinets sat in the back left corner, the bathroom door sat open beside it, and the bedroom was next.

Everything was surprisingly updated, with light and airy, modern tones, a contrast to the aging exterior. He must have done the work on his own, since he had owned the house for as long as I could remember. I couldn't figure out why anyone would go through that sort of trouble for a space that sat empty, but it didn't matter now.

Sheriff Abbot set my bags down in the center of the loft, kicking up dust that floated around us in a cloud.

"It still needs a good cleaning," he admitted sheepishly. "I haven't had a chance to get up here since we talked. I can send someone in here to do it if you'd like."

"I can do it."

The irony wasn't lost on me that the catalyst for this change was Grammy commanding me to clean a room. But this was *mine*. I smiled to myself at the thought.

Sheriff Abbot didn't linger long. He showed me around, sharing random tips about how to work the faucet or closing a cabinet that was just a little off kilter, before mumbling something about having to get back to work. Within twenty minutes of receiving my keys, I stood in the middle of my new home.

Alone at last.

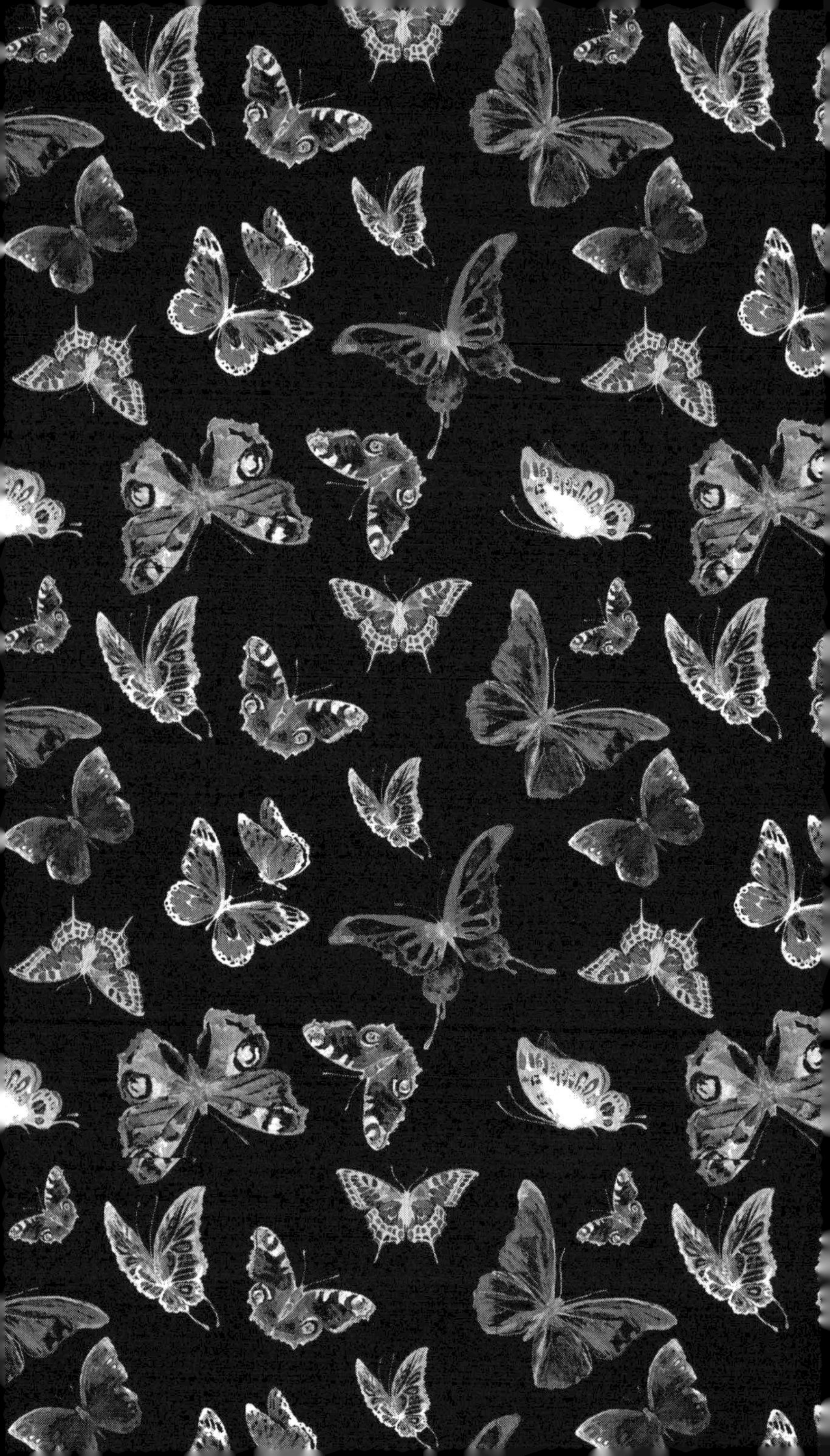

CHAPTER EIGHT

BLAIRE

"You realize I'm the sheriff, right?" His cool eyes rapidly moved between me and the joint in my hand.

I decided after Grammy sent me home from the hotel when I showed up for my regular shift that I needed a release. I could have bought a fifth of vodka and drowned in my sorrows, but that only ever left me with a bad headache the next day. I figured I hadn't smoked weed since high school, and I was feeling reckless. Now was as good a time as any to try it again, so I sent a quick text to Chet Hayes, a seedy guy who lived in the trailer park on the edge of town that I knew could help me. He met me within the hour.

It all happened so easily, I figured it must have been meant to be.

My head tilted, and I lifted the side of my mouth into what I imagined was a sexy smirk. My high had injected me with enough confidence to ask, "Are you going to arrest me, officer?"

I dropped my gaze to the handcuffs looped around his belt, raising a sly brow.

The old Blaire wouldn't have had the guts to be so brazen. He could technically arrest me, and while I'd heard stories about women flirting their way out of tickets before, I was positive that sober Blaire would be mortified at the feeble attempt to seduce a man nearly twice her age.

Or any man at all, really, because *Blaire Granger* flirting with anyone was cringeworthy.

But honestly, who cared anymore?

A shadowy darkness flashed across his features while he considered me for a moment. He didn't try to stop it or hide it, either. We sat there for a space of time, unapologetically staring each other down. It was exhilarating and uncomfortable and exactly the type of thing that I would do to earn an eye roll or some chastising comment. Instead, Officer Abbot welcomed the discomfort. He took it all in stride and threw it right back.

He blinked, and then held his hand out for the joint, shaking his fingers impatiently when I hesitated. Once I passed it over, he tugged his gun out of its holster and unloaded the magazine, then gently rested it on its side on the table beside me.

I watched in shock as he put the blunt up to his lips and took a long, deep pull from it. He inhaled, held his breath, and then smooth, gray smoke billowed out around plump, red lips.

"Don't tell anyone about this," he warned, yanking me from my trance with heavy, hooded eyes.

Okay, I guess I'm getting high with my sheriff landlord.

He didn't pass the roach back to me, and when I balked at him ripping it open and emptying the rest into the ashtray, he mumbled something about me having had enough and him needing to destroy the evidence. Once he was satisfied with his work, he leaned back into the cheap canvas chair and turned his attention toward me.

"So, why is Blaire Granger getting high all alone on a Saturday night?"

I'd been in his loft for two weeks now. Long enough to grow comfortable sitting outside when he arrived home, but not enough to admit openly that the day of the week had no meaning to my social life. I was alone for all of them.

"What is Sheriff Abbot doing getting high on a Saturday night?" I retorted.

His chest rumbled with a deep laugh, one I'd never heard before. "Touché."

After a few moments where time seemed to be a lost concept, he added, "But don't call me that when I'm home. Here, I'm just Kyle."

"Okay, *Just Kyle*," I bit back sarcastically. "Don't call me by my full name, then. Here, I'm not a Granger. I'm just Blaire."

I didn't want the heavy burden of being a Granger infiltrating my safe space. Sheriff Abbot—I mean, *Kyle*—had already done enough of that.

"Deal."

My brain was finally fuzzy enough to turn down the loud buzzing thoughts that weren't mine and block Hailey from popping up anytime soon. Even if she did, I'd be of no help. I obviously didn't smoke very often—or *ever*—so I was hoping to be in a near-vegetative state until I passed out. It was the only way I could think of to find peace.

"Why did you stay here?"

Kyle pinched his brows together. I could tell that I had pulled him from a deep thought, and I fought the desire to know what it could have been.

I had no business inside his head. I could barely stand it inside of my own.

When I could tell that he was confused by the question, I elaborated.

"Why didn't you leave Beacon Grove with Storie's aunt? You were with her, weren't you?"

His mask immediately went back up, and I could tell that I'd hit a nerve. I'd heard him mention Asher Graves multiple times, watched the anguish that crossed his face when he was saving Storie and vowing not to let another Graves die on him. He was clearly still holding a torch for her, and his reaction was only confirmation of that.

I ignored the thorns of jealousy stinging my chest over a dead woman who was twenty years older than me.

Those stone-gray eyes lazily swung over to me, and he slowly explained, "It wasn't my place to burden them. They needed me here more. And I have a family here."

Of course, I knew the Abbots. He had a sister who had to have at least five young kids by now, and as I now knew, his mother wasn't doing very well health-wise. Regardless, I didn't doubt they would have gotten by without him. That was a flimsy excuse. But my life was made on a foundation of flimsy excuses that were just masking the fact that I was controlled by Grammy and constantly seeking her approval.

"I would have left."

"You still could," he pointed out.

"Yeah, and Grammy would hunt me down with the hounds of hell." I huffed out a humorless laugh.

Kyle chuckled a bit, but quickly stopped to level me with the same intense stare he had earlier.

"Seriously, Blaire. Don't let her or anyone else hold you back. You don't want to be sitting on a porch twenty years from now and thinking back on all the what-ifs."

"Is that what you're doing now?"

"No. Right now, I'm thinking about what I have to eat in my pantry."

I laughed a little too loudly, and he shushed me, glancing around to make sure no one was watching us. "I already know my pantry is bare."

"Come inside. I'll make you something."

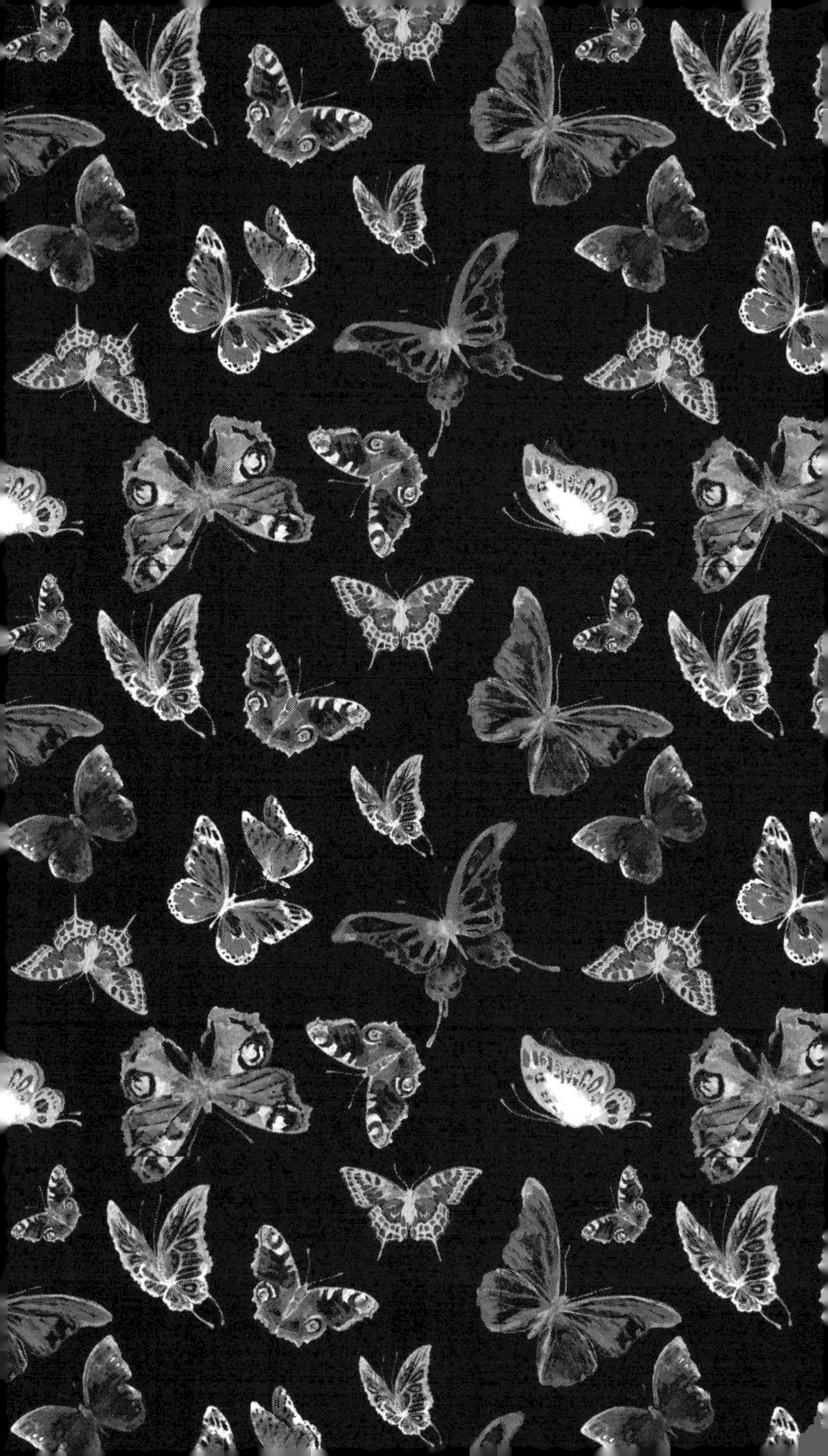

CHAPTER NINE

KYLE

I don't know why I invited Blaire Granger into my home. Or why I offered to cook her a meal. I could blame the weed, but honestly, it was disgustingly dank and nowhere near being strong enough to hinder my rational thoughts from a couple of hits.

Ordinarily, I would have steered clear of her, knowing exactly how annoyingly blunt she could be. But she looked incredibly sad, and I recognized a bit of my own tortured thoughts in her vacant stare, so I decided to take a chance and dance with her demons.

She didn't disappoint.

"I'm used to my grandmother's cooking, so this better be good," she teased from the stool across the island.

There was something about her that reminded me so much of Asher. Just uninhibited by the world around her and how they believed she should behave. It was what made her such a leper in the town. Yet every time she spoke, I was chasing those little specks of familiarity.

I realized that must be why Storie was so drawn to her, too.

"I'll do my best, but all I can offer is some doctored mac and cheese."

"Sounds good to me."

A smile flirted with her lips, begging to be set free, though she was fighting it off. Something had changed about her in the past few months. We all noticed it. I hadn't been committed enough to pinpoint what it was, though.

Blaire sat in silence while I got the supplies together and put the water on the stove to boil. When I was all out of things to busy myself with, I reluctantly turned toward her and was unsurprised to find her openly staring again. She did that a lot. I realized I did, too. That was why I found her so unsettling.

Being fed your own medicine was a bitter, uncomfortable experience.

"I can take you to Fergusons Furniture with my truck and we can get your place furnished."

For some reason, it had been weighing heavy on my mind that she moved into the loft with only one suitcase. I couldn't believe Tabitha and Callista allowed her to leave her home without at least a mattress. Later that day, I saw her walking back from town with a blow-up mattress, but other than that, she didn't appear to have even gathered a chair to sit on up there. That explained why she was getting high on the porch, I suppose.

"I can't afford anything new. I spent most of my savings on my deposit," she admitted bashfully. I felt like an ass.

"Then we can try Secondhand Rose. They usually have furniture there," I supplied, if only to ease my own guilt.

"Okay, I'll check that out."

"I'll help you bring whatever you want up the stairs," I offered awkwardly. She only nodded, then looked down at her hands.

"What are you doing about the girls who are still missing from Rayner?"

She asked the question so casually, I thought I might have misheard.

"We're looking for them." Sort of.

We'd been distracted with finding out more about Rayner than focusing on his victims. The state's homicide unit took over their cases when we had to transfer them over from missing persons. Our station simply wasn't equipped with the tools needed to find them, but we were still expected to keep our eyes and ears out for any suspicious behavior.

"Doesn't seem like it."

She swung her wild red hair over her shoulder, and I watched her wrap it around those long, slender fingers to form her signature braid.

"What makes you say that?"

"Because they're somewhere close, yet they still haven't been found."

My trained instincts began kicking in, pushing away the small buzz I had from the weed. In the blink of an eye, I was stone sober, staring down at the girl before me like a murder suspect.

"Somewhere close?" I repeated.

Blaire just nodded, her doe-eyes wide with confidence.

"Mm-hm."

The water began bubbling over in the pot behind me, so I took the distraction as an opportunity to gather my thoughts. We never considered the Grangers as suspects in the missing girls cases. Although, for some reason, they became closely intertwined with the Quarters around that time, who were everyone's first thought when the girls went missing.

Had I been wrong about them all along?

Tabitha had been helping me try to track Rayner down since everything happened in the woods. Was that just a distraction? Had I been working with the devil this whole time?

Blaire's calm voice slammed the brakes on the wheels turning in my head.

"I wasn't involved in their disappearances. But they won't stop talking about them."

I slowly turned to face her. "Who won't?"

I began assessing her physical appearance before even realizing it. Maybe she was just high and rambling. Maybe she really was as crazy as everyone said. She didn't seem bothered by my examination, either.

Her braid had been secured with the black hair tie she was wearing around her wrist, so her hands sat awkwardly in front of her, as if she didn't know what to do with them.

A slender finger traced circles on the countertop when she explained, "The girls. Most of them want to be found so their families can heal."

"You aren't making any sense. What girls? The ones who have gone missing?"

The timer I set for the boiling noodles went off. Reluctantly, I turned away from her once again to strain them. I made quick work of adding the extras in and fixing her a large bowl, realizing that I needed her to sober up if she was going to start explaining herself more clearly.

"I think I can help you. I don't want to, but they aren't leaving me alone, and I want so desperately for them to go away."

She raised those ethereal eyes to meet mine, and they glowed so bright they practically lit up the kitchen. Once again, she showed me a side of her that no one else in Beacon Grove bothered to look at. One that reached its hand out and drew me into her.

"How do you think you can help?" I whispered.

All my reservations about her disappeared in a cloud of smoke.

What is she doing to me?

Something shifted in her. I could practically see the walls rising back up around her. I watched her expression harden as she shook her head and then turned away from me, giving me the side of her face. Those long lashes fluttered down like a shield as her chest slowly rose and fell while she recovered from whatever had just happened.

"I have to go."

"What? Why?"

She ignored me and started for the door with a small frown, as if I hadn't even spoken.

"Thank you for the food. And the talk."

I watched in stunned silence as she dragged her feet toward the door, slipping through it without bothering to look back.

CHAPTER TEN

BLAIRE

"You bitch!"

The ghostly figure was on my heels the second I closed Officer Abbot's front door. Hailey had been there the entire time, lingering in the corner and floating between rooms. When she wasn't rifling through his things, she was trying everything she could think of to get my attention.

I'd learned to ignore the spirits pretty early on, but none were as persistent and annoying as her. I knew it was time to go when I almost slipped up and told him about my gifts.

Hailey went wild, waving her hands around and begging me to continue. To tell him about her.

It hit me all at once what a mistake I was making. I didn't care if he thought I was crazy. I didn't care if she was mad at me. Nothing would be as bad as Grammy finding out that I got high and exposed the Granger's secret, putting us all at risk.

"I know you can hear me, Blaire. I don't want to be here any more than you want me to be. He could have helped us!"

Still avoiding eye contact, I slid through the front door, slamming it in her face, and climbed the stairs to my apartment. Obviously, it was ineffective at keeping her out, but I could tell it irritated her, and that was all I could hope for.

"You're infuriating," she finally relented from beside the couch with a deep sigh.

I fixed my eyes on her just in time to watch her fizzle out and fade away into thin air, leaving me alone for the first time in hours. I didn't know what had gotten into me tonight. I shouldn't have talked to Sheriff Abbot. If I were smart, I would have walked back inside the second he pulled in.

If you were smart, you wouldn't have moved here in the first place, Grammy's voice berated in my mind.

Probably true.

But whenever he was around, all rational thoughts left my mind. He wasn't judgmental like everyone else in this black hole of a town. He talked to me like a person. Almost like he understood.

The concept of being a black sheep wasn't lost on him.

My thoughts quickly spiraled, leading down to a dark, forbidden place.

Fantasizing about being trapped under the stare of those hooded, stone-grey eyes. To be caressed with those large, capable hands. Would they be rough and calloused, or soft and sweet?

I'd been with one boy in my life. I say *boy* because that was exactly what he was: a rude, judgmental, hormonal *child* who was only after one thing. And I stupidly gave it to him.

After only one month of our secret relationship.

He didn't want people to know he was dating the weird girl, and I was just happy to have someone who was even remotely interested in me. That sort of desperation happened when your peers did nothing but tease you, and your family did nothing but avoid you.

Anyway, he had soft hands. Boyish hands. They were shaky and inexperienced and couldn't even bring me to anything resembling a climax. I had to go home and finish the job myself after any time we were together.

Once the fling was over and he'd effectively deflowered me, he made me promise not to tell anyone. I wasn't even disappointed about that. I personally didn't want my mistake to be shared throughout our high school and have his body stain my reputation any more than it already was.

I could tell Kyle knew exactly what to do. And not because he was nearly twenty years my senior and had time on his side. He just held himself like a man who knew how to please a woman.

I crawled into my bed and slipped my hand under the waistband of my leggings as more and more thoughts of him infiltrated my mind. Silly, stupid, girlish thoughts.

I didn't care. I could entertain this schoolgirl crush on my landlord so long as I never acted on them. And I never would. Not beyond my fantasies.

I closed my eyes and his face appeared in my mind as I slid two fingers in, imagining they were his. My hips formed small circles and a soft man left my lips as I picked up the pace, grinding against my entire hand.

Within minutes, my body was set on fire. I was squirming around in my bed, riding out my release as I ground against Kyle's hands. Once the stars disappeared behind my eyes, I turned over on my side and allowed my lingering high to lull me to sleep.

CHAPTER ELEVEN

KYLE

Mayor Bishop slammed his gavel to bring the flustered crowd back together.

As always, the clacking noise only served to add to the chaos rather than quiet it down. In the past year, these town meetings had become more of a nuisance to me than anything else. The mayor couldn't hold the small crowd that bothered coming anymore together for more than ten minutes without his words igniting some sort of uproar that usually resulted in the meeting ending prematurely to avoid an all-out brawl. For the past six months, I'd had to station at least one officer on the premises to keep some semblance of peace. More often than not, I didn't have the manpower to spare, so I ended up taking it on myself.

Since the Movement's attacks last year, everyone was on edge, and they had very little respect for the puffy, reddened face that stood before them preaching about peace and togetherness. I couldn't count how many times they called him out for hiding out when Rayner and his men launched their attack on Storie Graves and the Quarters.

There was an invisible line dividing the people of Beacon Grove. One that no one dared to admit which side they were on.

Matters of the coven bled into the normal, everyday matters of the town and with the High Priest having been exposed as a player in Rayner's game, no one could be trusted. It all added up to a heaping pile of shit for me to deal with.

The easiest way to remedy all of it was to weed out Movement Members and find Rayner before he could strike again. The problem was that no one outside of the Quarters and Tabitha Granger wanted to help.

With the exception of one other person.

My eyes drifted over the sea of faces and found hers already on me—my new neighbor. I still wasn't sure what she could offer, but I was so desperate, I had to try.

Tabitha didn't speak highly of her granddaughter, if she spoke about her at all. Blaire always acted as an accessory to her—there the moment she needed her and forgotten the rest of the time. It seemed as if she was highly underestimated, though, especially if her high-induced ramblings held any weight.

I held her stare for a few beats, watching her mouth curl up into a secret smirk, before Tabitha grabbed her arm and turned her toward the door.

The mayor dropped his head into his hand, and I knew then that the meeting was over. Ten minutes later, the community hall was nearly cleared out when he turned and offered an earnest smile.

"They don't want to listen."

No, they didn't. Not when they weren't being given honest and clear answers. No one who could do anything wanted to be vulnerable and show their hand, either. They refused to admit that they essentially had no power over the situation.

"Maybe next time," was all I could say, and we turned to walk out the back entrance together.

Mayor Douglas sighed, his pink cheeks puffing out even farther. "I'm afraid these meetings will remain useless until we can offer them some real answers about Rayner and what we're going to do with the Movement moving forward."

"Do you have a plan for what you're going to do?" I probed.

He'd kept his mouth shut about what he and the council were going to do if Rayner ever stepped foot in town. As the sheriff, I had every right to arrest him on the spot. That didn't mean one of those snakes wouldn't slither their way in and find a way to let him roam free.

He shook his head. "None of the council members can come to a decision, either. Wariness is ruining this town like a disease."

Wariness wouldn't be an issue if they had a leader they could trust, but I kept my thoughts to myself. No one was willing to forgive the mayor's inaction against the Movement when they were at their worst, and I saw at least half of that council standing around the open fire the night I caught Rayner trying to sacrifice Storie Graves for his own twisted source of power. I just didn't have any hard evidence to debunk their false alibis, and it was my word against theirs.

He waited until we were standing outside his car, away from any prying ears, before he spoke again.

"Do you have any more information on the recent... incidents?" His round eyes dashed around, looking for any sign of someone eavesdropping.

I shook my head, the image of the deer hanging limply from a tree right outside of town flashing into my mind. It had been slung up by its neck with a pink ribbon. The worst part was that whoever did it had taken the time to dress the doe in the exact clothing that Toni Amster was wearing on the night she disappeared, six months ago. It was the height of the Movement's activity, when we were getting calls for missing girls nearly every day.

Whoever it was either had access to Toni's clothes and was likely involved in her murder, or they had a sick sense of humor. Luckily, one of the few officers I could trust was the one who found it during his morning hike. He called me immediately, and we managed to handle it before anyone else stumbled across the horrific scene. Mayor Douglas believed that if word got out, it would only fuel the fear that the Movement was attempting to create in order to push their agenda. He was adamantly against letting the town in on the attacks.

"The clothes were sent out for testing. Hopefully, whoever we're dealing with was stupid enough to leave something behind for us to trace."

It was all we could hope for at this point.

He nodded, his lips in a tight, grim line. I watched the irritated skin beneath his chin wobble around. He was holding so much information in, it was making him physically ill.

"Keep me posted. And, Kyle?" He regarded me with those bulging eyes. "Don't tell anyone else about this. I can't imagine what kind of a field day the town would have. I'm ready for it all to be behind us."

He crammed himself into the driver's seat of the compact car and closed the door with a final nod. I let out a breath of relief when he pulled away.

I hadn't lied about us sending the DNA in for testing, but I left out that the results were already in. They matched Toni's profile, confirming that they were likely the clothes she wore when she was taken from the Watchtower Tavern on the night she went missing. There were three other DNA samples found, all male, and all of which had no match in their system. Whoever it was, they'd never been caught before.

I couldn't risk sharing that information with Mayor Douglas. Not when there was a chance he could have been involved somehow, and the more he asked about it, the more suspicious he became. I'd tell him the results when the time was right.

My only course of action at this point was to keep my trusted circle tight. I might be making a mistake by putting my faith in Tabitha Granger and the Quarters, but it was a gamble I was willing to take if it meant preventing another innocent life from being lost.

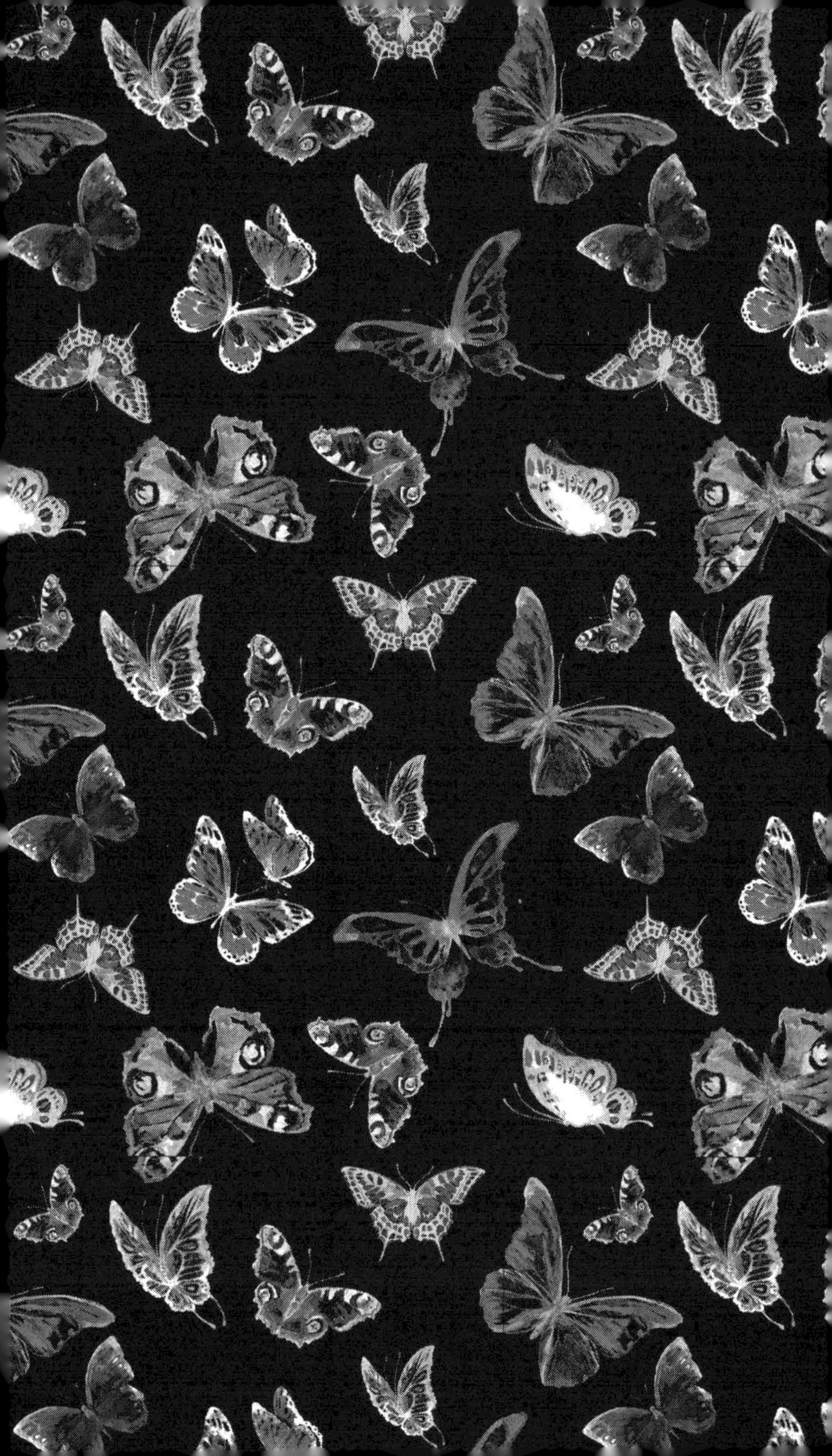

CHAPTER TWELVE

BLAIRE

Meeting Kyle on the porch at the end of the day became an accidental regular thing. I couldn't make any sense of his erratic work hours. He seemed to pop in and out at all times throughout the day, and by some twist of fate, I always wound up sitting in one of those faded Adirondack chairs when his police cruiser pulled into the driveway.

He'd fall into the chair beside mine with a deep sigh and we'd rest beside each other, hardly speaking any words. His silence was comforting—a stark contrast to the constant state of chaos Grammy usually kept me in.

There was something to be said about a person who knew when to shut up.

It seemed to bother him that I moved into my apartment without any furniture, though. It bothered Mom, too, but she was easier to avoid.

He made good on his promise to take me into the secondhand store in town to pick out furniture, and then helped me haul the heavy kitchen table and couch that I scored up the stairs without complaint. When Greer Myers passed away and her family held an estate sale in her home down the street, I managed to find a matching bedroom set, including a beautiful antique dresser and mirror that would have cost a fortune anywhere else. Kyle bargained with the Myers enough to fit it into my budget.

Getting that up the stairs had earned a few frustrated comments about my choices, but nothing too bad.

Today, he plopped into the chair beside me with another deep sigh, but I knew this time was going to be different. He needed to talk, and I was stuck on the receiving end, whether I liked it or not.

"Another animal body was found."

His chrome-colored eyes stared off into the street before us, a frown deepening between his eyebrows. He leaned forward, elbows resting on his knees.

I didn't know what to say. I didn't know there were any bodies found before this one.

"It's always a different animal, but the message is the same," he went on, still avoiding eye contact. "They're slung up with ribbons and dressed in one of Rayner's victims' clothes."

My face scrunched in a scowl. That seemed especially morbid.

He chuckled humorlessly, then leaned back into his seat and slumped down, shaking his head.

"It's like he's toying with us. Trying to get us to look *here* while he does something over *there*. I just can't figure out where *there* is."

I considered him for a moment, unsure why he was bothering to tell me about this. "Maybe it's not a distraction. Maybe he's just biding his time... testing you."

"Is that any better?"

I shrugged. "No. But it sounds like you feel like you're missing something. I'm just saying, Rayner isn't that deep. He doesn't think much beyond himself."

Kyle let that roll around in his head for a moment. We sat in comfortable silence as I gave him the space he needed.

"You said you could help before. You talked about these girls like... like you were talking to them directly."

His shoulders tensed disbelievingly, and I knew exactly what he was thinking. He felt embarrassed to bring it up, but desperation had him considering every possibility. He knew that what he was suggesting wasn't plausible—at least not in his mind—but he was willing to look into it. To see if there was substance in what I had said when I was high, or if it was just another Blaire rambling.

He wanted to help those girls so badly, he was willing to go insane in the process.

For some reason, that made me feel like he could be trusted. Like he wouldn't use the information against me, the way Grammy assumed everyone else would.

I tucked my chin into my chest and lowered my voice when I admitted, "I do talk to them."

A breathy, incredulous laugh escaped through his tightened lips as his brows raised to his hairline.

"You've got to give me more than that, Blaire."

I thought about what he had said before, about the victim's clothes, and an idea sprung on me.

"You said the animals were wearing the victims' clothes. Were those the clothes they were wearing when they were taken?"

He nodded, and my lips spread in a wide smile that had his eyes widening at me like he thought I'd gone mad.

It might work. *Maybe.* But I had to get my hands on those clothes. I had to feel them for myself and see what information came forward.

"Can you take me to them?"

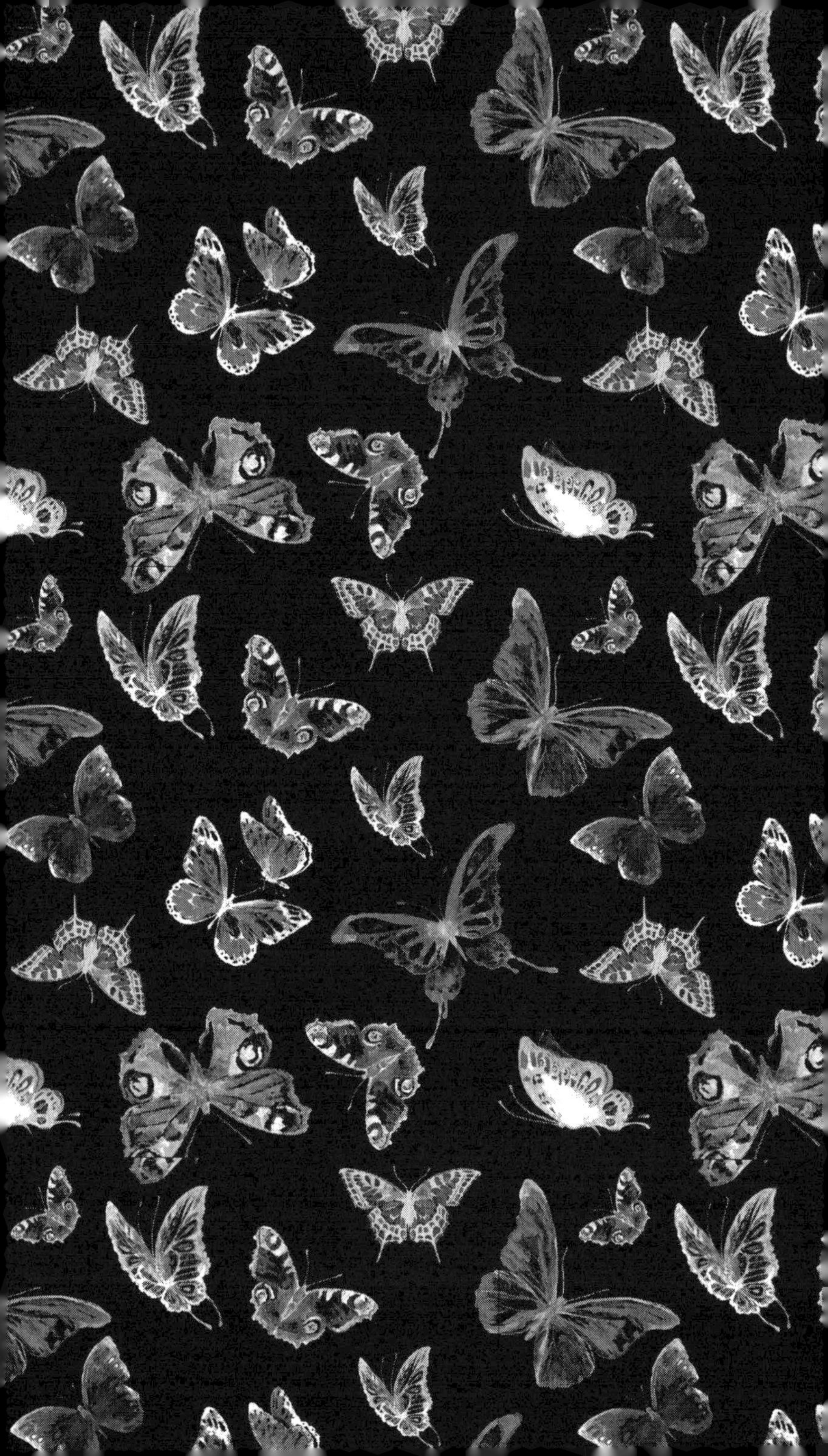

CHAPTER THIRTEEN

BLAIRE

The police station was smaller than I imagined it would be. It was one main room of bland, cream-colored walls and a maze of desks with old desktop computers sitting atop them. To my left, a small office was built out into the space with Kyle's name etched onto the door, but it provided him very little privacy as the walls were completely made up of floor-to-ceiling windows. On the opposite side, there were three identical doors with small windows cut into them, and I knew those were the waiting cells without having to ask.

If this was any indication of how well our town was protected, it made sense why Kyle was so stressed about Rayner attacking again. The forces he was working with were underwhelming.

One officer, who was barely older than me, sat in the open room. He had been reclined in a leather office chair with his feet resting on his rusty metal desk when we entered, but sprung up when he saw Kyle's face walking through the glass doors. I recognized him from around town, but couldn't think of his name off the top of my head.

"Did you forget something, sheriff?" he asked nervously.

Kyle held his composure, pinning the young officer down with a disapproving stare as we weaved through the other desks.

"Didn't mean to interrupt. I'll just be a minute," he said sarcastically.

He led me through a thick metal door along the back wall that opened up to a room hardly bigger than a broom closet. There were lockers of different sizes against two walls and a table against the other, barely leaving room for the door to be fully opened. Neither of us spoke until the latch clicked shut.

"It's soundproofed," he assured me.

It took him two steps to get to the lockers on the far wall, and he had the lock opened in less than thirty seconds. When he reached around me to grab blue rubber gloves, my entire body blossomed into goosebumps at the small contact of his arm against my side. I paused, watching his face for any indication that he felt the same thing, but he just raised his brows expectantly the way he always did and handed me two gloves.

With the gloves on, he reached into the locker and pulled out a large plastic bag adorned with multi-colored labels haphazardly stuck to it. Ever so carefully, he slid out a pile of neatly folded clothes.

I couldn't stop the gasp that escaped me as her spirit entered the room. It was like she sucked all the oxygen from the tiny space, using every ounce of energy she could gather to appear before me.

Before I could look toward Kyle to ask if he felt it too, Toni Amster's spirit form was rushing at me, her hands outstretched to grasp my neck. The sheer force of her energy pushed me back into the other set of lockers. I was frozen in my spot as her hands drifted right through me, leaving a cool chill in their wake.

I shivered as she stared down at me in bewilderment.

I hated this part.

When reality settled in for them.

Toni was quicker than Hailey. She looked around at the room we were in—at Kyle as he stood beside me, eyes wide and mouth agape. At some point, he had thrown his arm between me and the ghostly girl and was still holding it there, against my abdomen.

"You can see her." My voice was raspy, the words quivering on my thick tongue.

Kyle reluctantly turned his head to look at me. "Yeah," he breathed out in disbelief.

Toni just stood there, her gaze flicking between us and the pile of clothes sitting on the table beside us. Clothes she was still wearing in her translucent state—forever stuck to her.

"I need you to explain what just happened, Blaire."

"Blaire?" Toni asked, recognition flashing across her face. She snapped her fingers and pointed at me. "Blaire Granger. I remember you."

"What else do you remember?"

She looked around again, trying to recall. "I remember Beau taking me. He grabbed me from the alley behind the tavern while I was on my break."

Beau Whittle, Rayner's nephew. I hadn't seen him around in a few months, but that didn't mean much. I hardly ever went into town anymore.

"Where did he take you? Was he with anyone else?" Kyle's voice was still laced with shock, but the sheriff in him had finally come out of hiding.

Another pause as she tried to think back. Me and Kyle shared a look just as she looked down at her hands and mumbled, "No, I can't remember anything else."

Kyle shook his head and stepped forward to lift her Watchtower Tavern waitress uniform from the table.

"These are the clothes you were wearing when they took you."

Toni's face contorted into a lopsided scowl. "Nice observation, Sherlock."

She opened her arms to present the matching set on her body and glared. "Do they pay you the big bucks to use that spectacular brain of yours?"

He ignored the sarcastic jabs and continued with his thought. "They have three other DNA samples littered all over them. Whoever did this wasn't worried about leaving a trail behind."

"She isn't the first victim who can't remember what they did to her."

"What do you mean?"

"I've been seeing others. Whatever Rayner did to these girls, he had the forethought to cover up his tracks, even after they had passed."

But how had he managed to wipe their memories on the other side? It seemed like an impossible violation of the balance of life and death.

"I'm wondering the same thing," Kyle replied, and then his eyes widened as he realized what he'd done.

I tilted my head curiously. *Did he just answer my thoughts?*

We stared at each other for a beat too long, where I could swear he silently confirmed, before Toni cleared her throat and reminded us of her presence.

"There are others like me?"

I fought the urge to roll my eyes. They always acted like they were the first to go through this sort of thing.

Still, I answered, "Yes," in a clipped tone.

Toni noticed the attitude and looked me up and down, her lips pursed in disapproval. I didn't care if she was offended—she was dead. And the last thing I needed was another spirit lingering around me the way Hailey insisted.

Kyle ignored the quiet tiff.

"We need to find a way to unlock their memories of their last moments. It's the only way we'll get any answers. No one who participated is talking, and Beau hasn't been seen in months."

"What am I supposed to do while you guys figure it out?" Toni whined.

"What have you been doing?" Kyle asked.

"I'm not really sure. I guess I've been stuck wandering around. It feels like it all happened yesterday."

"Well, sit tight. Hopefully, we'll get some answers soon."

He winked at her, and she practically melted to the floor. I wanted to gag at how easily she was manipulated. She agreed, and then scowled at me right before she disappeared into thin air.

"You could have warned me," he said when we were alone again.

I shrugged. "I wasn't sure if it would work."

He began bagging up the clothes again, and I thought the conversation was over. Once they were securely locked away, he leveled me with a look.

"You've been holding out on me."

"I could say the same about you."

We held each other's gaze once more, challenging the other to spill their secrets. It felt like an eternity passed as I stared into those silver eyes before a calmness washed over me. We each understood that we couldn't. It was almost as if we said more like this than we could ever say with words.

"Let's go home."

Home. My chest ached at the word for some reason. At the idea that we shared the same meaning behind it.

He reached for the door handle, then paused. "Everything that just happened stays between us. No one can know what I just showed you. Not even Tabitha."

Any other time, I would have hesitated. There wasn't much I kept from Grammy, especially because she always seemed to be a step ahead of me. But now that I had my own place and a reprieve from her domineering ways, I knew I could keep this promise.

Not to mention, I couldn't afford for anyone to find out about my gifts, either. It was a risk showing them to him. But he'd returned the favor by showing me one of his, so we were even.

"Agreed."

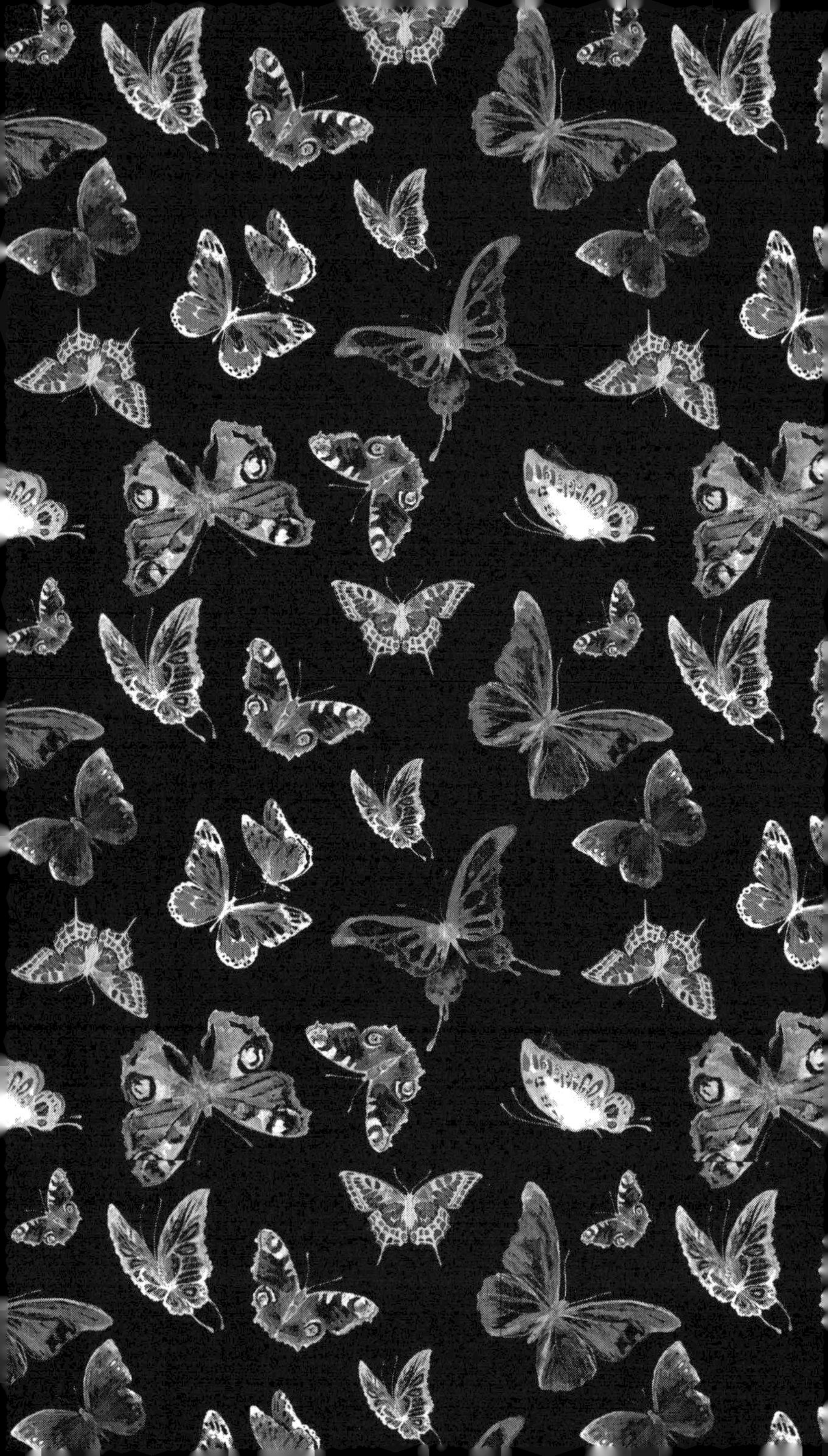

CHAPTER FOURTEEN

KYLE

Blaire Granger just might be the only person in this entire town who stood a chance against Rayner.

She was also the most underestimated.

I couldn't decide if that was a good thing or not.

Why, after all these months of supposedly helping, had Tabitha kept her such a secret?

And why did I feel so strongly like I needed to do the same?

I shouldn't have shown her my gift. If you could even call it that. Reading a person's thoughts sounded exciting in theory, but it often led to knowing things about them that were better left a mystery. The ability came to me around the same time everything else fell apart, and there weren't many people I could confide in then, so I kept it to myself. I usually tried to shut it out, but the shock from seeing Toni Amster's spirit form had me momentarily letting my guard down.

And what the hell was that? I'd never seen anything like it before.

The whole drive home, I questioned everything I knew about the Grangers. I had heard the Quarters talk about a possible fifth in passing, but honestly hadn't bothered to pay much attention when they let something slip in my presence. Their gifts were hanging on by a thread and they were grasping at anything to find answers.

And if by some off chance she were one of them, what elemental gifts did she possess?

I hadn't been able to stop thinking about it since I watched her disappear through her door. Each day, I pulled into the driveway expecting to see her sitting on the porch so we could talk about it, but her chair was empty every time.

It had been a week, and today I stopped at Millie's on my way home. When Blaire gave me her ridiculous deposit, I went straight to my sister's house and told her to start thinking about who she wanted to help her. She was resistant to the idea, claiming she enjoyed taking care of Ma and would rather I come to help more often than have a stranger come around her kids. But we both knew that wasn't possible, and as much as Millie wanted to claim she could handle it all, she was drowning.

"She's out back," Millie's husband, Arthur, greeted me as I stepped out of my cruiser. He was sitting on the porch with one of the kids' bikes tipped upside down on his lap.

We never really got along. Not that there was any tension between me and my brother-in-law, but our personalities didn't click. Especially not in the way Millie wanted us to. We tried in the beginning—for her. But he was a product of the lowly neighborhood we grew up in through and through, and I had dedicated my life to never allowing my upbringing to influence my future.

He was perfectly fine with working a job that laid him off regularly, so he was consistently behind on bills, and cramming his kids into a house that was half the size they needed. I thought my sister deserved better, but I'd never voice that opinion to her.

This was her life—her choices to make. And despite his failures, he was a good husband to Millie and an even better father to my nieces and nephews.

I sent him a nod as I walked past his gangly form crouched over the bike, long fingers struggling to sling the chain back on.

Millie was in the garden, bent over some tomato plants, while three of her kids ran around shirtless in the yard behind her. She lifted her head as I rounded the house and greeted me with a large smile when her kids attacked me, shouting random things over one another. I listened to each story and fact, being sure to give all of them my attention, before Millie interrupted and sent them away again.

"You don't have to do that. I come here to see them, too."

She smiled as if she knew something I didn't. "So, I'm a little jealous. I don't get to see my big brother often, and I want to maximize the time we have."

"Have you thought about who can come help?"

Millie's face fell into a grimace. She wiped her brow with a gloved hand, smearing dirt across her forehead. "I still don't think we need anyone. Work is about to slow down for Arthur, and he'll be home to help more."

"Why don't you want to accept help, Mill? It's too heavy of a load for your family to give her as much medical attention as she needs. I doubt Arthur is stoked about it, either. Just let me do this for you."

I slid my hands into my pockets and glanced up toward the second-story window, where I knew our mother would be sitting.

She was looking down at us with pinched brows. Had she heard what I said? Did she even know who I was anymore?

Millie didn't bother turning around to look. "Why can't you come help out a few days a week after work? I'd feel better about that, and I know she would, too."

"My work schedule is insane right now. I barely have time to eat or sleep with all this Movement stuff."

"That's been your excuse for the past year, Kyle. It's overdone. I know you didn't have the best relationship with her growing up, but there's still time to fix it. She's still in there." When I rolled my eyes, she rushed to add, "You don't want to regret not being there like you weren't with Dad."

I scoffed, biting back my bitter response. The truth was, I *didn't* regret missing my dad's last few months. He had recovered from his alcoholism by the time Millie was old enough to have a childhood with him, often preaching the process of the twelve steps any chance he had. But I was practically gone by then, and I wasn't going to forget any of it.

Not his words. Not the way his fists felt against my skin. Not the way Ma sobbed at night after he punched holes in the wall and jammed insults down her throat.

None of it.

And maybe some of that resentment was misdirected at Ma, and that was why I had a hard time caring for the woman who failed to protect me from it all, but I wasn't ready to admit any of that. Especially not to Millie, who got by unscathed with a near-perfect childhood.

"It's just not possible, Mill. This is all I can offer."

She crossed her arms over her chest and kicked out one foot. "Then, I don't want your help to pay for someone else to do what *you* should be doing."

I just shook my head. It was clear we were at a standstill. She could be so stubborn sometimes.

Before I could say anything I would regret, I turned on my heel and headed back toward my cruiser. "I have to get back to work."

"Aren't you going to at least say hello to her?" Millie called to my back.

"I'll send you a list of qualified people in the next few days. Look it over and pick someone," I replied.

I wasn't giving up my loft for nothing. She'd accept the help, whether she wanted to admit she needed it or not.

CHAPTER FIFTEEN

KYLE

Rayner was moving closer as the days led up to the Fire Festival. I doubted he would make an attempt to re-engage the Movement at the first town event, though. He enjoyed the suspense a little too much. Enjoyed playing with his prey.

And unfortunately, I was his prey at the moment.

No, he'd let us have our festival and live with a false sense of security, thinking the monster had truly gone away. Then, he'd strike. I just hoped he had gotten over his obsession with killing off the Graves line when he realized Storie was protected by the Quarters, and even harnessed one of their gifts. No amount of black magic could stand a chance against the ancient magic that came from the Quarter lines.

Still, I could feel his presence looming. Maybe it was just paranoia, but I could have sworn he was watching me from somewhere. Which is why I stopped talking to Blaire on our porch and invited her inside instead.

As far as I could tell, she held true to her word and hadn't told anyone what happened that night at the station. It was over a week before I ran into her again, and she'd acted as if nothing had happened. I was the first to bring Toni back up, but as soon as I did, I got the odd sense that someone was listening, so I awkwardly invited her inside and she hesitantly accepted.

Once we were settled in at my kitchen table, she was the first to speak. "I haven't been able to find anything in any of Grammy's books about a spell that blocks out a soul's memories."

I sighed. "I'm not going to be able to keep the autopsy results from Mayor Douglas for much longer."

Blaire tilted her head, her nose scrunched in confusion, reminding me just how young she really was. A wave of defeat washed over me at that thought. Here I was, placing my trust and the future of Beacon Grove in the hands of a group of kids and an old woman who would rather die than share her family's secrets. I was a fool to think this would work.

"Whatever just happened, you need to stop."

"Stop what?"

"I can feel your disappointment. I'm not sure what I did to cause it, but you need to stop. It's throwing me off."

I stared at her blankly. "You can feel other people's emotions?"

"Yes." She glared back unapologetically, and I saw it: that Granger fierceness.

Sometime during this past year, Blaire evolved from that innocent, naive girl I'd always known into a woman whose ferocity could rival her grandmother's.

"Why would Douglas want those results?" she asked, interrupting my musings.

"He wants answers just as bad as we do." Although, maybe for different reasons.

"Didn't you tell Toni there were other DNA samples found on her clothes? Do you think he may have been involved with her disappearance?"

I shook my head, already having considered that possibility more times than I'd like to admit. "Mayor Douglas is not the type of man who moonlights as a murderer." I gestured toward my stomach to prove my point. "Though, he is extra involved in these cases," I admitted.

"He could just want this all to be over for Beacon Grove." She shrugged and leaned back into the chair, pulling her braid over her shoulder to inspect her dead ends. "It would be a lot easier if I could just ask Grammy..."

Green eyes lifted to meet mine, and I noticed again how brightly they glowed—the same way the other Quarters' eyes always did. I thought I'd seen it on the night she smoked, but I chalked it up to the weed. Was that a trait of hers that we all missed before, or had it just started happening?

"I'm considering bringing Tabitha in the loop. She's a wealth of information, for sure."

"Sure, if that information served her a purpose," Blaire huffed, and I couldn't argue. Tabitha would only help if there was something in it for her.

But she cared about finding Rayner. She wanted to protect Storie and Beacon Grove, and even if she didn't fully believe it, she would do anything to keep her own family safe. I'd just have to find time to get to her alone.

"Tell me about your gifts."

A chuckle escaped my lips, causing her gaze to fall to my mouth in a way that gave me pause. It took everything in me not to read her thoughts, and I had to focus too hard on my next few words.

"It's not a gift. Just something I picked up along the way."

But Blaire was unphased, completely unapologetic about the discomfort she just caused me.

"Normal people can't read minds. For some reason, you were gifted by the gods, just like the Quarters. Just like me." She sucked in her bottom lip, and this time it was me who was staring.

I shifted uncomfortably in my chair. "I'm hardly as special as you," I said in a near-whisper.

She had me under some sort of spell. I was fully aware of how inappropriate we were being. I was old enough to be her father, for heaven's sake. But none of that mattered as she lifted a coy brow, confidently holding my gaze as she leaned forward in her chair and folded her arms on the table, spilling her breasts out of her shirt. Or when she gently gnawed on her plump lip, and I wanted nothing more than to take its place.

"You're going to have to protect yourself better than this," she warned with a knowing smirk.

Shit. Had she felt all that? Schooling my expression, I took a deep breath and decided not to let her have all the fun. I allowed my eyes to rake over her body slowly—so, *so* slowly—raising my brow in approval, until she huffed out a raspy laugh and squirmed in her chair.

"I'm sorry," I quietly cooed. But Blaire's unease was short-lived. With a shake of her head, she smiled broadly. "I think we're going to have a lot of fun together, sheriff."

CHAPTER SIXTEEN

BLAIRE

"I want to cook you dinner," I proclaimed to Kyle one evening.

He had just gotten home from work, or wherever he went most days, and I was waiting for him on the porch.

He stared at me, confused. "Do you know how to cook?"

I blanched, bending my wrist in mock offense. "Of course, I know how to cook, you ass. Don't be mean to me or I'll rescind my offer."

Kyle raised his hands up in surrender. "Okay, fine. When?"

"Tomorrow. I'll have it ready when you get off work?" I hadn't intended for it to come out as a question.

Would he come home straight from work, or would he stop wherever else he went during the week?

I pushed the jealousy over the possibility that he was with another woman way into the back of my mind. It was truly none of my business.

"Sure. I'll eat anything."

I nodded once, then turned on my heels to head toward my door.

"You aren't hanging out?"

If I didn't know any better, I'd say that was disappointment in his tone. But there was no way that was possible. Not for me.

A lot of our evenings were spent together lately, whether it be us trying to make sense of how to free the spirits that kept haunting me or just because we happened to run into each other on the porch.

And I'd stupidly begun looking forward to it.

I spent my entire life in a place where someone was always around to talk to. Kyle had neighbors, but they mostly kept to themselves. I grew terribly lonely in my short time here, especially since I had already isolated myself from everyone in the months I was wrapping my head around my new reality as a Quarter. I hardly even bothered to see my best friend, Storie, anymore. On top of it, I'd spent the majority of the last couple of weeks alone in Grammy's study, trying to find anything that mentioned erasing a spirit's memory.

I shrugged. "You're home late. I thought you'd be tired."

Kyle looked at his watch as if he had no idea what time it was. "I'm up for company."

Stupid butterfly wings fluttered against my stupid stomach as he stepped aside and let me into his portion of the house.

We've done this before, I reminded myself. He was obviously just lonely, and I happened to be here.

Still, that didn't stop my giddiness as he walked to the kitchen and grabbed two beers. Or when he handed me one, then unbuttoned his police uniform and fell onto the couch beside me. And it definitely didn't stop when he turned his body to face me and asked, "How was your day?" as if he were actually interested.

✦

My smoke alarm went off when I opened the oven and black smoke came billowing out.

"Shit, shit, shit," I grumbled to myself, bravely pulling out the cookie sheet of charred buns.

A firm knock sounded on the door, and I cursed again, flapping a dish towel in front of the alarm so it would stop beeping.

"Come in," I shouted over the ridiculous sound.

"You shouldn't ever invite someone in before you see who it is," Kyle lectured as he climbed up the stairs. Thankfully, I had gotten the alarm to quiet.

"Okay, officer," I snarked.

"It smells great."

He walked right into the kitchen with a teasing smile. His gray eyes found the blackened buns and tightened a little.

"Don't get that look. I only burnt the buns. Everything else is perfectly edible."

"I didn't say anything."

He had changed out of his uniform into his usual plain black tee and dark wash jeans. I bit my lip as I took in his casual appearance. I hoped I didn't look overzealous in my short sundress.

Kyle didn't seem to mind as his eyes slowly raked down my body when he thought I wasn't looking.

"Have a seat."

I gestured toward the dining table he had hauled up here a couple of weeks ago. He politely obliged, and the whole thing felt awkward to me. Maybe I made a mistake doing this.

What is it about this man that makes me so insecure?

I took an extra minute in the kitchen to give myself a small pep talk and remember that this was all no big deal. We ate dinner together most nights, anyway.

"Sure you do, but this display looks a little Desperate Housewives, don't you think?" I turned and saw Hailey sitting on the counter, surveying her nails.

I hadn't realized I was whispering my thoughts aloud. I ignored her, silently willing her out of the apartment, but she stubbornly remained in her spot.

When I brought our plates to the table, Kyle cleared his throat.

"All jokes aside, it looks really good."

"It's chicken parmesan. I mean, obviously. But in case you didn't know." I was a rambling idiot.

I heard Hailey click her tongue from the kitchen and resisted the urge to throw my knife in there.

Kyle lightly chuckled. "I gathered that much."

An uncomfortable silence blanketed us as we began eating our meal. The scraping of our utensils against the plates was the only noise filling the air until he looked up at me and smiled sheepishly.

"Why is this so awkward?" he asked.

I let out a breath and shook my head. "I have no idea. But I'm glad you feel it, too."

"Probably because you're into him," Hailey mumbled from somewhere in the living room. I refused to look over and give her the attention she was seeking.

"I should have you cook dinner more often. This makes my cooking taste like boxed dinners."

"No, I love your cooking."

He snickered and shoved another forkful into his mouth, his eyes roaming around the space.

"This place is coming along. I'm glad we were able to find you a couch and TV. I don't know how you survived so long without them."

My heart fell into my stomach as I realized that the look he kept giving me—the one he usually wore on the rare occasion he came up here and cast his gaze across my space—was pity.

"You don't have to do that, you know."

"Do what?"

"Try to take care of me. I know I didn't come here with much, but I'm not a charity case."

I leaned back in my chair and stubbornly crossed my arms over my chest. I could deal with a lot from him, but I wasn't going to accept his sympathy.

His brows furrowed, eyes taking in the defensive shift in my demeanor. "I never said you were a charity case."

"Sometimes, it seems like you think I need saving." I swiped at a speck of dust on my lap to avoid looking at him.

He leaned forward onto the table, leveling me with a stern look. When he didn't speak for a moment, I lifted my eyes up to his face and realized that was what he'd been waiting for—my full attention.

"If there's one thing I know for certain about you, Blaire, it's that you don't need saving."

And there was something in the way he said it that sent shock waves into my groin. Like, he was proud of that fact. Like, that was part of the reason he kept coming back.

"Then why bother?" I challenged.

Furnishing my apartment, cooking my meals, checking in on me—none of it was typical behavior for a landlord.

His eyes widened, and he gaped at me like I was dense. It took me back to all those years I spent being regarded like the stupid, naive girl everyone in Beacon Grove thought me to be. I was used to it from them by now, but seeing that expression on his face took me by surprise. I had thought that out of anyone else, Kyle saw past that. He was willing to treat me like a human, not a punching bag.

Or so I thought.

"We're friends," he said, slowly shaking his head like he didn't understand how I couldn't see that. "That's what people do when they care about each other."

Friends.

Friends didn't look at each other the way I caught him doing to me. They didn't think about each other as they pleasured themselves the way I did, night after night.

That was why it bothered me so much to think he pitied me, I think. Because whatever was happening between us was anything *but* friendship.

And I may have been wrong, but I think Kyle felt the same way. Even as he said the word, his mouth tilted down in a disbelieving frown.

"Don't act like that."

"Like what?" I pouted.

"Like all this time we've spent together doesn't equate to a friendship. It might be sad to say, but you're probably one of the only people in this town that I know I can trust."

My cheeks heated at the compliment. I couldn't help it. I loosened my arms from my chest and lifted my fork to begin eating again.

"I trust you, too," I mumbled, embarrassed at my outburst.

A smug smile pulled at his lips as he grabbed his own fork. We continued our meal in a comfortable silence as all the awkwardness in the air slowly disappeared, and then finished the evening off as we always did these days—together.

CHAPTER SEVENTEEN

BLAIRE

Beacon Grove became a quiet, desolate place in the weeks following the Movement's attack after Samhain six months ago. The black magic that was cast on our town to fuel Rayner's sadistic agenda took longer to dissipate than any of us would have liked to admit, and its influence bled into every household. I personally shied away from the town's center, too thrown off by the gloomy haze that everyone seemed to be stuck in since then.

Storie wouldn't share what happened to her when Rayner attempted to burn her alive. We truly had no idea how she had managed to snuff out the flames and break herself free from the restraints that Rayner had placed on her. All we could gather was that she mustered up as much of hers and Remy's shared magic as she could to do it.

No one that participated in the strange event was willing to admit what they had done, and since most were cleared out before we got there, we had no way of knowing who was involved. Aside from Beau, Rayner's nephew, who went missing two weeks later, no one was punished. Anyone who dared to point a finger could easily be accused of the same thing, so everyone stayed silent.

And life went on.

Though he promised that the rest of the year would continue on as scheduled, Mayor Douglas canceled Beacon Grove's annual Yule, Imbolc, and Ostara festivals. He claimed the decisions didn't come easily, though they seemed to only keep the knee of depression further dug into the town's back.

"The people need something to celebrate," Grammy had complained at breakfast when she opened the newspaper and read The Beacon's article about Ostara. I was still living with her then.

The Spring Equinox was a time when neighbors came together after a long, harsh winter. It was the last celebration we had before our tourist season kicked back up, when we could just be ourselves. A celebration of fertility and prosperity for the coming season, and it was also Grammy's favorite.

She was a sucker for a good time, apparently.

After about twenty minutes of stewing, she marched the newspaper up to city hall and slammed it down on Mayor Douglas' desk, a mask of pure hatred firmly in place.

I followed behind just to see the bewildered look on our mayor's face as she berated him for keeping our town—our *family*, as she called it—in a depressed state.

He cowered down to her like a small child.

"We don't need any more breaks. We need unity. We need strong leadership. We need to stop allowing fear to fester and open us up to more attacks..."

He sat before her in silence, not even bothering to argue any of her points as she went on for another five minutes straight, hardly stopping to catch a breath. Once she was finished, he agreed not to cancel any other holidays on the wheel of the year.

Grammy nodded triumphantly, straightened her shirt, and walked off.

It was nice not to be her punching bag for a few minutes, and I always liked to watch Mayor Douglas squirm like a pig.

As luck would have it, the first festival Beacon Grove was set to celebrate since the Movement's horrific fire was Baltane—otherwise known as Fire Festival.

The gods truly had a sense of humor.

But we were happy to finally have something to celebrate. A distraction from the dark place our minds had been held captive for the past six months. Any energy that went into planning and setting up for the festival was energy that was taken away from the chaos Rayner left in his wake.

Storie was helping me set up the pharmacy and emergency tent for Mom a few days before the festival. Since it was mostly locals who bothered with it, we wouldn't need to sit here all day as we had for Mabon. But given the nature of things, and the fact that so many people would be wielding fire in many forms, Mayor Douglas thought it would be best to have a tent set up to treat any accidents.

Me and Storie hadn't had a chance to hang out much in the last few months. Not like we did when she lived at the hotel. She was always busy training with Remy or one of the other Quarters, and I was stuck reading the books in Grammy's study, desperately seeking any way we could get ourselves out of the mess we were in. More recently, I was trying to find a way to help the dead girls who haunted me cross over.

It seemed like a lot to unpack on one person.

The Quarters were still unaware of the Granger gifts and Grammy wanted to keep a distance between us until we figured out telling them could benefit us in the long run. She worked with them often, encouraging them to master their gifts while they searched for their Counters. Too focused on holding on to the powers themselves, their fathers never bothered to teach them the basics of controlling the elements they were born into.

When I lived with her, Grammy often came in from a long day with them, swearing she'd never go back, only to wake up the next day and do it all again.

Storie was the only one who knew I was gifted. Not because I chose to tell her, unfortunately. She had figured it out all on her own. The day she asked me about it, things shifted between us.

Caught between being a good friend and her duty as a Counter, I knew I was putting her in a difficult position by not outright admitting it to her.

November, 2021

"*I have something I need to talk to you about.*"

She flipped her keys around in her hands nervously as we waited for our coffees at The Grind. We'd taken a seat at one of the tables along the front window, and I could tell from the moment she walked through the front door that something was off.

"*What's up?*"

She hesitated, her eyes moving around the large mural behind me to avoid my gaze as she began. "*You know you can trust me, right?*"

I only nodded.

"*I mean, Remy is my Quarter and there's this wild connection between us that makes it hard to keep anything from him. But you're my best friend, and I'd never betray you.*"

Her gaze dropped from the wall to the worn-down table and my thoughts immediately went to last year, when she betrayed me and my family to steal the Quarter's Book of Shadows from Grammy's study. They took that turn because that was where Storie's thoughts led them, and for some reason, I couldn't control my gifts around her.

Her guilt was so strong, I could taste it.

I knew now that Grammy actually manipulated that situation herself, but that was beside the point. Storie hadn't known she was being manipulated at the time, and she still made the choice.

More guilt pooled into my churning stomach. It grew so intense, I had to look away from her and recenter myself to stop her reactions from infiltrating my body.

With a deep inhale, I pushed her thoughts and emotions out of my head and focused on only feeling my own.

"I know that I can trust you," *I finally offered, attempting to ease her mind so it would stop torturing me.*

"Well, Remy and the guys came across something recently in the Book of Shadows that I found kind of peculiar. They haven't figured it out yet, but I have."

"Okay. What is it?"

She scraped away at the chipped wood on the table, once again avoiding eye contact with me.

"There's talk of a fifth Quarter. One that can harness the powers of all four elements together. They're supposedly the most powerful…"

My heart sank.

No.

"A fifth Quarter…?" *was the only lame attempt I could make to buy time. But she wasn't having it.*

"Blaire, I know it's you."

A nervous chuckle blew out through my lips as my hand found my braid and my fingers went to work on it—a nervous tick I'd always had.

Storie noticed my discomfort and quickly rushed out, "I don't want you to feel like I'm attacking you. I guess I'm telling you so that you know you aren't alone. And to warn you."

That gave me pause, briefly silencing the storm that was taking over my head, either from her emotions or my own. I couldn't tell anymore.

"Warn me? Against what?"

"Well… they aren't too happy that there's a possibility someone might be stronger than they are. They seem to go between being afraid and being pissed."

My cheeks heated with my frustration.

What did they have to be pissed about? It was my family that was forced to live in the dark to protect their egos. It was my family that had taken every blow to our name and reputation since their ancestors cast us out for being more powerful than them. For being women who shared gifts they believed only men should possess.

I was practically baring my teeth and ready to pounce on her for being so ignorant on the subject, when the barista called out our names and I was forced to shove it down. All of it. The anger, the betrayal, it wasn't her cross to bear.

Storie walked up to the counter to grab our drinks while I centered myself again. It was getting harder to control my anger, but I had to keep trying.

When I was sure that I could speak without venom in my tone, I said, "There's a lot more to it than anyone knows. I'm not surprised you put it together, but I hope I can rely on your discretion until we figure out how to explain it to them."

In a way their pea brains will understand, *I left out.*

"Of course." There was a brief pause as I sipped the cold drink, hoping it snuffed out the embers left over from my rage. "This changes everything," she added.

She had no idea how right she was about that.

✷

S he unloaded boxes beside me quietly as we ignored the awkwardness lingering between us like a third person. In the short time she was here, she easily became a part of our family. Even Grammy treated her like a granddaughter—probably better. She was my best friend. But she also had allegiance to the group of men who stood to lose the most by my gifts, and neither of us could shake that fact.

Right after everything happened with the Movement, she had asked me how to tell who was in Watchtower coven. I didn't really have an answer. It was just something we always knew, and there weren't any telltale signs of a coven member. Now, Watchtower members greeted her like family as they passed, grateful for her role as Counter after all this time without one.

Somewhere along the way, Storie had abandoned the role of tourist and made Beacon Grove her home. I was sad that I missed that transition with her. Sad that I had allowed my own issues to come between us for so long. And I hated this unpleasantness. We'd never been this way before, even when we first met. It was like one day, I was friendless, and the next day, I had her.

"I don't want to let this stuff come between us anymore," I declared aloud, never one who was good with words. I'm sure my words seemed random to her, but I couldn't contain my thoughts any longer.

Storie lightly chuckled at my forwardness. "Okay. I agree. I miss you."

"I miss you, too. I'm sorry I've been so distant."

"It's okay. I understand. I've struggled with all these changes, too."

She stared down at her hands as if they were foreign to her, twisting and turning them.

I knew why. The magic coursing through her veins felt unnatural. Like a parasite feeding off of you.

"Well, now you've got someone to ride the struggle bus with you. But I have to warn you, I only accept the window seat."

She laughed again. "Deal."

CHAPTER EIGHTEEN

BLAIRE

Grammy closed the office the day before the Fire Festival and asked me to come along with her to meet with the Quarters. I hesitated, but she didn't leave much room for argument when she met me at the door before I could step inside, then pulled the door shut behind her, locking me out.

"It won't take long, and you should be there. You're just as important to this town's safety as they are. Maybe more so. It's time you get your nose out of those books and step into your power."

I repressed the urge to roll my eyes at her comment. She had no idea how far I'd already stepped into it. How deeply I'd been thrown into it from the moment they decided to activate all those months ago, when she first revealed them.

She didn't know about the spirits that followed me everywhere or the fury that burned through me each time I was reminded of the injustices made against my family line by the men she chose to spend her days with.

We walked to the cabin in silence, both of us too stubborn to be the first one to speak.

But my curiosity won out.

"Why are you still meeting out here?"

It seemed like a major inconvenience when all four Quarters had their own mansion at their disposal now. And if the cabin was anything like how it was when we first met out here, it wasn't a place I'd find myself regularly coming back to.

"It's a safe space."

"Don't the Quarters have wards cast all around their homes?"

She turned toward me, and I could tell she was already irritated with me. With my curiosity. She hated how much I questioned her.

Still, she answered. "They aren't entirely sure if they can trust their staff just yet. And I don't want anyone seeing us together as much as we are."

I stared downward, absorbing her words. Why wouldn't they think they could trust their staff? Was it because of the Movement, or because their loyalty still lay with their fathers, who were now cast out of their homes?

It felt like eons since we walked this path with Storie on the night Rayner took her, and Grammy forced me to leave her behind. I often wondered what would have happened if we fought him. If Grammy would have just used her gifts and ended him right then and there.

But she was always playing the long game, making sure she came out on top. Using the gifts that night would have exposed us more than she was comfortable with.

"You're late," Rhyse muttered from the couch, not even bothering to sit up.

"Mind your manners, boy. I could have easily not come," Grammy warned, making sure to catch the eyes of the other three Quarters, so they knew her words weren't just directed at the rude pyro.

None of them shrunk into themselves the way I expected them to. I could have sworn I caught a smile playing on Grammy's lips, but it was gone so quick, I convinced myself I had imagined it.

"How nice of you to grace us with your presence, Blaire," Enzo greeted sarcastically.

"Ignore him. He's hangry," Storie said from the kitchen. She pulled me into a hug when I went to stand beside her.

"Anything new?" Remy asked from the other side of her, his eyes trained on Grammy.

She had helped herself to a chair at the kitchen table across from Lux. We all watched as she reached into her bag and pulled out one of her old books, slamming it onto the table with a loud clack.

"As far as I know, there hasn't been a dead animal found for the past week. I'm guessing he's taking a break before the Fire Festival. He probably doesn't want to catch the wrong attention with so many people out and about. But that's why I called this meeting."

"You think he's taking a break?" Enzo asked incredulously.

He had moved to lean against one of the pillars separating the kitchen and the living room, thick arms crossed against his chest.

The space had been cleaned up a lot since I'd last been here. New couches were brought in, and the kitchen had a full set of kitchenware stacked beside the sink, as if someone had just cleaned it. Bunk beds now lined the open upstairs loft, and someone brought in a TV.

Grammy shook her head. Somewhere along the way, she and the Quarters grew comfortable with one another. There wasn't any name calling or finger pointing. They trusted each other. At least, enough to work toward their common goal: to catch Rayner before he could hurt any of them.

I supposed as a fifth Quarter, he could be after me, too. If he knew about the Granger gifts.

"I think he wants us to believe he's taking a break. You all need to be on top of your game in case anything happens. You have to retain the trust of Watchtower *and* Beacon Grove. This is a test for you, and Rayner likely knows it."

"We're still not at full capacity without our Counters," Rhyse said accusingly, glaring at her over the back of the couch.

Ah, so they were still mad about Grammy not telling them who their Counters were.

"There's no way for me to know who they are for certain, especially with everything as mixed up as it is. As I've said before, it's *your* job, as a Quarter, to find them yourselves."

"What do you think we should do for the festival, then? Stay at our alters?" Remy asked, ignoring Rhyse altogether.

Grammy thought about it for a second, looking in her book to buy time. "No, you'll want to show your faces and be on site if anything goes awry. And Blaire can help you, too."

Rhyse snorted out a laugh, and I glared back at him. "What's Blaire going to do?"

Enzo reached over and slapped him in the chest.

"Blaire possesses more power in her pinky finger than you do in your entire body right now, boy. You'd be smart not to make her angry," Grammy warned.

Her emerald eyes slid over to me, brows raised.

I had no idea how to respond. We hadn't talked about this. I had no idea she was going to out me to all of them on the spot like that.

"What do you mean?" Lux finally spoke, his tone calm and detached.

"If you Quarters were any more stupid, you'd have to be watered twice a week," she scoffed, shaking her head.

Storie looked over at me nervously, already aware of where this was going.

When no one dared to mouth back, she went on. "The Book of Shadows suggests there's a fifth Quarter, correct?"

A few nods.

"Why, in the mother's name, do you think I'm wasting my time helping any of you?"

There were a few awkward beats of silence before Lux slapped the table, jarring us all.

"I knew it!"

"You didn't know anything, dude," Enzo retorted, rolling his eyes.

"Blaire's the fifth Quarter?" Remy asked disbelievingly.

I tried not to be offended.

"Yes," was all Grammy said.

My eyes found Storie's again, and she sent an encouraging smile, nodding at me to speak.

"You knew?" Remy's face fell as he and Storie shared a look.

She tilted her head and shrugged wistfully. The intensity of the exchange had me flicking my gaze away from them, over to the other four men who apparently had the same instinct as they all averted their eyes toward me. Grammy continued flipping through her book to whatever page she was trying to find, ignorant to the drama.

"What was your plan then, Granger? Lie to us the same way your family has *always* done? What happened to putting the past behind us and working toward a unified future?" Enzo's rage was a living, breathing beast that stole the oxygen from the room as he threw Grammy's words at me.

My heart thundered in my chest. I fought to shake off the reactions that weren't my own, trying my best to remain level-headed. I had the advantage here.

I don't have to defend anything.

I reminded myself of that fact even as my mouth began moving to share my side of the story. But it was hard not to feel like trapped prey when they were all pinning me down to my spot with their stares. Their ethereal eyes glowed bright, as their anger deepened. I wondered if mine did the same.

"There's not much to say about something I don't fully understand." A partial lie.

I didn't understand the full effect of my gifts, but I'd quickly grown comfortable with them. Like putting on an old pair of jeans, the powers just kind of came naturally.

"Bullshit."

"Watch your tone," I snarled back. The deepening of my voice was eerily similar to Grammy's.

I wasn't the only one left reeling after the outburst. Surprise was etched across all six faces before me as they contemplated their next move. Even Grammy turned away from her book.

"I knew we made a mistake trusting you two," Rhyse deprecated.

As the master of the fire element, his anger seared a hole into my chest. He was calm and collected, but that rage simmered just beneath the surface, ready to begin boiling over at any given time.

He and Enzo were the wildcards of the group.

"Let's all take a second to process what this all means moving forward." Storie attempted to diffuse the situation, but her own Quarter was looking at her with the same disapproval as the rest of them.

"It means that there's someone else around to leech our powers from us," Enzo started again, throwing his hands around animatedly. "Because there's no way in hell the gods would bless one person with the same gifts that were split apart among four families for fear of them being abused."

"Don't speak of things that your brain is too small to understand."

It was Grammy who defended us this time.

This was why Quarters could never know of our powers. They couldn't even wrap their minds around the concept of responsibility. That it actually *was* possible for one person to wield this amount of power and use it for good—for helping others. Instead, Grangers were forced to hide them away and watch people suffer.

All because of the fragile male ego.

I tilted my head and gazed at them, finally seeing each of them for what they were: immature little boys.

And I no longer felt angry or defensive.

I felt pity.

"We don't know where she's getting her gifts from," Lux pointed out levelly.

He was considering me the way one would do a puzzle or a riddle. He wanted to figure me out just as bad as the rest of them, and he had the wherewithal to realize that throwing insults my way wouldn't get him anywhere.

"They aren't coming from anywhere besides my own family line. From the blood that runs through my veins, just like you."

It was no use explaining. They would refuse to believe any word we said, regardless of its merit. I could see it clear across their faces. In how they each held their shoulders back and their stances wide, the way they often did whenever me or Grammy were around. Always ready to fight, even if they were fighting against their own side. I didn't understand why she wasted her time with them for this long.

"I'm out of here, Grammy. They don't deserve our help."

When I turned to leave, it was Remy who called out, "Where are you going?"

"I have no interest in being treated like a criminal for things that are out of my control. We can talk when you're willing to listen, but I refuse to give this any more energy until then."

Storie ran after me and wrapped her hand around my upper arm to stop me from walking any farther. I looked down at it, then at her face, and the coolness of my expression had her quickly pulling away.

She spoke low in my ear, her tone a desperate plea. "Please, Blaire. We need to talk about this."

"We'll listen," Remy added, casting a warning glare back at his brothers.

Grammy watched with an excited, prideful smile stretched across her face.

"What makes you so sure we can trust her?" Enzo asked, and the anger in his voice still hadn't dissipated.

Four doubtful pairs of eyes found my friend and waited for confirmation. My brows shot up to my hairline as she hesitated, and right when I took my next step out the door, ready to be through with all five of them, she confirmed.

"Because I trust Blaire. She's on our side."

Her quivering voice said the exact opposite, though.

"We won't accuse you of anything," Remy promised.

I considered all of them for a moment, weighing my options. None of them had done anything to earn my trust. Even Storie watched me as if she couldn't be sure what my next move was.

They were afraid of me, as they should be.

Isn't this what I wanted?

For them to realize I had value and regret every time they ever mistreated me?

But a flash of light flickered in the corner behind Lux, and I knew what it was before her face could appear. Hailey took in the scene before her with widened, careful eyes, as if she were warned to be afraid of the Quarters, but had never been in the same room as any of them before to know why. I thought back to what she told me she could remember about the night she was taken, and all the other horrible things Rayner and his Movement had done to the people I grew up with.

This was bigger than me. It was bigger than the resentment I held for every single person who wronged me in my life. I couldn't pity the Quarters for allowing their ego to lead them when I was doing the exact same thing.

It was with that thought that I found myself taking a step back into the cabin and allowing Storie to close the door behind me.

✶

Agreeing to put my own feelings aside to talk through our new reality was only the first step. Enzo and Rhyse refused to drop their accusatory attitudes, often sending doubtful sneers my way whenever I revealed more information about my gifts.

Lux continued to watch from the back of the room, peppering his calming thoughts into the conversation when it got too heated. Remy was the most receptive to accepting me as an equal, probably because he had nothing to lose from it. He'd gained the full use of his gifts once he and Storie accepted each other as Counter and Quarter.

The two of them sat across from one another in the small main room of the cottage, occasionally sharing glances that indicated they were having their own silent quarrel.

Grammy finally found what she was looking for in her book. It was a page about securing a powerful protection spell to keep out any dark threats.

"This is ridiculous. We *are* the protection spell for Beacon Grove," Rhyse challenged once she was done reading the page aloud.

She ignored him. "This method works against threats that also may fall within the protection bubble when the spell is cast," she further explained.

"Rhyse is right. How is this better than our method? With Blaire's help, we should be able to lift a shield stronger than ever before." Lux's head was propped on his hand as he leaned over the table to read the spell himself.

"Your shield only offered protection to outside threats. That's how he got away with it last time. I think it's safe to assume that Rayner has members planted all over town. This will neutralize anything that falls under the shield."

"Won't Watchtower be angry about that?"

"They won't know it's in place. No one can be trusted with our plans."

"That makes no sense," Enzo chimed in. "How are we going to keep them from using magic?"

"*We* aren't. I have it on good authority from the sheriff that Mayor Douglas will be issuing a ban on magic for the day of the festival." Grammy raised a sly brow, her mouth twisting into a smirk.

Rhyse and Enzo rolled their eyes at the mention of the mayor. Apparently, me and Kyle weren't the only ones who were skeptical of him.

"Why would he do that?" Remy asked no one in particular.

"Who knows? But if he's in Rayner's pocket like we think, he could be trying to clear the way for the Movement to take Beacon Grove."

I thought back to what Remy had asked Grammy when we first arrived at the cabin. Now that they knew about my gifts, maybe they could help me.

"What do you know about the animals?"

Grammy turned around to look at me curiously.

"There's been a string of dead animals found in the woods wearing women's clothing. Specifically clothing that matches the girls who were taken last year," she explained.

I knew all that, thanks to Kyle.

"Is that all you know about it?"

She eyed me, her curiosity quickly morphing into suspicion. "What are you getting at?"

I held her gaze, silently asking permission to speak freely in front of our audience. She dipped her chin in a subtle nod and squinted at me skeptically.

I thought for a moment, trying to find a way to explain without completely betraying Kyle. "I can see them—the victims."

Hailey perked up in her spot across the cabin, shifting to face me fully.

"You see spirits?" Remy deduced.

"Not all the time. But these girls..." I looked back at Hailey. "They come through strong. And they're stuck."

Grammy considered me carefully. I could tell she had been taken by surprise by the admission. I hadn't told her about the spirits before. Out of every side effect that came with the Granger gifts—the power, the rage, the secrecy—seeing the spirits of Rayner's victims felt the most outlandish and the easiest to keep to myself. They made me feel absolutely insane. There was never a good time for me to confide in her like that when we were constantly butting heads, anyway.

I wondered if she had ever seen them, too. Could she feel other people's emotions the way I did? Did she ever have a Counter?

Suddenly, I wanted all the answers.

Although, Hailey had been lingering in the corners of the cabin for hours now and no one else seemed to sense her.

"They might be able to help us find where Rayner's hiding out. What have they told you?" Lux asked.

I shook my head. "They can't remember anything. It's so weird."

"Nothing?" Grammy's face pinched in confusion. "That isn't right. They should be able to remember *everything*."

"I know. It's like he somehow blocked their spirits' natural progressions."

"Interesting." She gripped her chin with her thumb and forefinger. "He truly doesn't want to reveal his plans until he's ready."

"What kind of magic could block that out?" I asked Grammy and Lux.

I'd been searching for weeks for some sort of clue, but came up short. At this point, they were my best bet for finding the answer and if we were truly supposed to trust each other, this was a good way to start.

Lux turned his attention toward Grammy, and they stared at each other in bewilderment. "It's got to be something dark, right?" he asked her, scratching his head.

"Knowing Rayner, that's all he's got access to. He isn't gifted."

"He must have bound something to their souls," he said, mostly to himself. "I wish I had that black magic spellbook. I bet there's something in there..." He trailed off.

Grammy nodded, snapping her fingers. "I have it. I'll bring it next time."

Silas Forbes destroyed all the records he held about the Quarters. Every last detail was found in ashes in his study after he was detained for his involvement with the Movement.

They were left with nothing. A complete dead end. Unless one of the others had copies of what was destroyed, then Grammy was their only hope for finding information about most everything.

We talked through our theories, the tension easing as they grew more comfortable with me around. We ended the "meeting" with a plan for the Fire Festival and a list of tasks for us to complete beforehand.

The Beacon

15 APRIL 2022

FIRE FESTIVAL IS ON!

Mayor Douglas announced this week that Beacon Grove will be celebrating Beltane and holding the annual Fire Festival. This news comes after the mayor has blocked the celebrations of Yule, Imbolc, and Ostara, forcing citizens to honor the festivities within their own homes instead.

Beacon Grove business owners rejoiced as the news came in, desperate for the chance to catch up on their usual business this year.

It's alleged that Tabitha Granger was the catalyst for making it all happen, and while we at The Beacon are no strangers to the receiving end of Ms. Granger's wrath, we're grateful for the work she's done in ensuring the Fire Festival can be celebrated as it should be.

The festival will begin on April 30th at dusk and will end on May 1st at dusk.

A fair will be set up in the town's square with fun planned for the whole family.

The Quarters will light the bonfire at 6 pm on April 30th. Immediately after, Watchtower High's own theater department will put on the traditional Baltane performance to lead us into Summer.

Please note: While festivities will continue throughout the night, parents are urged to keep their children away from the town square after 11 pm on April 30th and before 8 am on May 1st.

Sheriff Abbot would like to remind the citizens of Beacon Grove that while Fire Festival is a celebration of prosperity and fertility in the coming season, residents are expected to behave appropriately in public spaces.

CHAPTER NINETEEN

KYLE — PAST

Bonnie hissed out a breath and leaned over the inflatable tub, grasping Mason's hand so tightly he winced. Tabitha was behind her, quietly offering words of encouragement as my friend breathed through her painful contractions.

I wasn't sure why they invited me to be here for Bonnie's birth. I guess it was just another part of their lives that I should have been grateful they shared with me. I hadn't given it much thought before, but hearing Bonnie's wails of pain had me wishing they'd just invited me to meet the baby after, when everything was cleaned up.

I turned away, locking eyes with Asher to offer Bonnie and Mason some privacy. I knew it was finally over when Asher's face lit up and Bonnie went quiet. Shortly after, a small cry sounded out, and I spun back around to see Tabitha placing the little human on her mother's chest.

"It's a girl," Tabitha declared happily, tears welling in her eyes.

Mason and Bonnie gazed at their daughter in pure euphoria. Asher joined them after a few moments, gushing over her new niece.

"Welcome earthside, Storie Graves," Bonnie whispered to the little girl. I'd never seen my friend so smitten.

Just as I stepped forward to join them, I caught it: the fleeting, anxious look between Tabitha and Callista. They shared matching worried expressions, brows raised, lips set in a tight line.

Something had just been communicated between the duo, I was sure of it. It was there and gone in a blink, but Tabitha returned to the side of the birthing pool with a sad smile on her face.

It was like Bonnie knew what she was going to say before the old woman had the chance to open her mouth. Her smile faltered, and she dropped her gaze down to her daughter, that same worry etched on her face now. She gently passed the baby over to Callista, who motioned for Mason to follow as she placed her on the couch and began checking her.

"How long ago?" Bonnie asked.

Asher and I shared a confused look. She stepped back into my chest to give Tabitha room to get to Bonnie, then turned back to the baby, a remorseful frown marring her face.

"Twelve hours exactly."

"Shit." Mason hung his head.

"Twelve hours since what?" I asked, confused.

"Since Remington Winters was born," Tabitha supplied dejectedly.

The weight of those words blanketed the space with sorrow and anxiety.

We all knew what that meant.

"Maybe another was born," Asher offered helplessly.

Tabitha slowly shook her head. "I'm fairly certain that's not true."

If that was the case, if Storie was the only child born within the last twenty-four hours, there was a target on her head already.

From the Quarters, who were reportedly hunting and killing Counters for fear of them weakening their next generation.

From Rayner, who wanted to use her as a weapon against his enemies.

They'd fight to be the first to get to her.

If the gods decided that Storie Graves would be Remington Winters' Counter, it would take a miracle to keep her alive long enough to take on the role.

*P*resent

The Fire Festival went off without a hitch, just as I thought it would. Tabitha pulled me aside early that morning to tell me hers and the Quarter's plans for keeping any potentially threatening magic neutralized for the night.

I hung back in the town square and kept an eye on Mayor Douglas while Tabitha, Storie, Blaire, and the Quarters met in the woods and cast their spell. Douglas was none the wiser as I followed him around, pretending to be interested in whatever last-minute projects needed to be tied up before the celebration began. He had unknowingly made the spell easy for them with his ban on magic, though he earned a great deal of grief over the decision from the Watchtower coven.

In the end, they wouldn't push him too far. Not when things were finally going back to normal, and they were still lacking a proper High Priest to defend them.

So, the day began with excited anticipation swirling around in the air. Businesses closed early in the afternoon so the workers could get back in time for the lighting of the bonfire and the small group of volunteer organizers buzzed around to ensure everything was perfect.

As the marker for the beginning of Summer and peak fertility—for humans, animals, and crops alike—the Fire Festival was one that our town preferred to celebrate without much attention from the outside world, given the nature of it. They danced around and celebrated the arrival of life in all its many forms. It usually ended up turning into a display that I spend many nights trying to forget the images of.

When I was younger, I took full advantage of the festival. Though, the early hours were kept appropriate for the children to still be able to enjoy. The High Priestess would light the main bonfire in the town square as she blessed our crop yields, and then she and the High Priest would make their rounds, socializing with their coven.

The high school theater put on a performance of dance and fire-play until the sky turned completely dark and the stars glistened against its inky black. They would fade into the gyrating crowd. Children were taken home for bed, and then the adults began having their fun well into the early morning hours.

As sheriff of the town, it was a nightmare of public indecency. I learned early on from my predecessor that it was best to allow my officers to patrol the streets, but to stay away from the woods or the fields unless we were called on.

Things were a little different this year, as Watchtower didn't have a High Priestess at the moment. It was a detail that they scrambled around for weeks leading up to the festival. The Forbes had betrayed the coven in an act of complete and utter dishonor. They'd served up the Quarters—one of their own children—to the Movement to be sacrificed and butchered so they could hold on to their gift. It was sad, honestly.

As the Quarters blessed with the element of fire, the festival was always a little more magnificent when they were elected. Elections weren't scheduled for another year, so the natural progression would be to have their son, Rhyse, take over, but he didn't want to. None of the Quarters did. And no one dared overstep.

So, as it stood, the coven wasn't led by a single High Priest and Priestess—it was led by all four Quarters, simultaneously.

Which was why they each stood at the base of the bonfire pit that was piled high with strategically placed logs. It was eerily similar to the pit I had found the Movement circling when they took Storie. One glance at her standing tucked into Remy's side told me she was thinking the same thing. Lux called out the ritual as he, Remy, Storie, and Enzo held unlit torches in front of Rhyse, who ignited them one by one. His magic had apparently remained active for the night, though no one seemed bothered by that.

Once the bonfire was lit, the crowd roared in excitement, and the festival began.

I quickly found my family sitting on a blanket in the middle of the field. Mille and Arthur sat side by side as their kids ran around the area with their friends. Ma and her new nurse, Doris, were perched across from them in folding chairs, mindlessly gazing out at the crowd around them.

As expected, Millie proved to be useless in the search for a nurse. I sent her a list of qualified candidates and she found something wrong with each and every one.

Too old. Too young. Not enough schooling. Lives too far.

Each excuse was more ridiculous than the last. I interviewed a few of them myself, and she refused to hear the feedback I had to share.

Every time I visited, though, I could tell she was struggling more. The bags under her eyes grew heavier and darker, her skin paler than the last time. Stuck between the life of her children and the death of our mother, she was withering away. I couldn't stand it.

So, I took it upon myself to choose someone.

Doris Brubaker was as close to perfect as it got. She was a retired nurse from the hospital in the next town and had moved here five years ago, after a visit during Samhain that had her falling in love with Beacon Grove.

She also didn't have any family or obligations that would interfere with the schedule we agreed on. All of that, on top of a full career of working with patients who suffered from dementia, had me offering her whatever salary she wanted to start right away.

I met her at Millie's house early the following morning, fully expecting my sister to turn the woman away at the door. But she surprised me by smiling and inviting us in, warning us not to trip over toys as she led us through the house and into the kitchen, where our mother ate her breakfast.

"Ma, this is Doris. She's here to hang out with you," Millie explained in a loud voice, leaning over so our mother could clearly read her lips.

Doris took the seat beside Ma and jumped right into conversation with her, leaving no room for hesitation or rejection.

I mouthed, "Thank you," to my sister, and she motioned for me to join her in the next room.

"What changed your mind?"

"I guess I was holding on to hope that you'd help more." She ignored my eye roll. "But you bringing Doris here proves that isn't going to happen. And I'm drowning, so if you're going to pay someone to help, then so be it."

It had been three weeks, and Doris melded into Millie's family seamlessly. Ma trusted her, the kids respected her, and Millie was finally starting to gain some color in her cheeks again.

I lingered in the crowd for a moment, watching them all from afar before I infiltrated their family moment. I smiled at the way Ma lit up as the kids ran circles around them, sparklers in hand. She turned to Doris every now and again to comment on what was happening around her, unaware of her disability.

"I'll admit I was wrong," Millie said from beside me, a wide smile on her face as she took the scene in with me. She had noticed me staring and decided to come over.

"Sorry, I must not have heard you correctly. I thought you said you were wrong. Can you repeat that?" I teased. She sent a fist into my shoulder and we each chuckled.

"She's good for Ma. Better than I was. I feel like she's starting to turn around."

I dropped my gaze to my sister, silently warning her not to do that. Not to get hope.

"I know, I know. But I swear, it's true," Millie said defensively.

"Just don't get your hopes up," I warned.

"Come say hi." Millie tugged on my arm before I could refuse.

When we walked up, Ma was in a deep conversation with Doris.

"My son, Kyle, is a police officer. He's probably around here somewhere." She made a show of craning her neck to search the crowd.

Doris greeted me with a smile and Ma finally noticed that I was standing before her. I went to lean in for a hug, when she straightened her back.

"Good evening, sheriff. I hope everything's going smoothly with the festival." She offered a polite smile and crossed her hands over her lap.

"So far, so good," I replied in the most official tone I could muster, unsure where she was going with this.

"I was just telling Doris here about my son, Kyle. I hope he isn't giving you too much trouble at the station." She winked teasingly. "We're just so proud of him."

I stared at her for a moment in complete shock. Then, it hit me.

She didn't recognize me.

Of course, she didn't. I managed to avoid speaking to her for the past few weeks, and my weekly reports from Doris explained that she was losing more and more memory each day, contrary to what Millie thought. But it still hurt.

To see your own mother look at you as if you were a complete stranger?

It hurt.

Millie noticed a moment too late. She wrapped a comforting hand around my arm, but I shrugged it off and stepped away, offering some excuse about having to get back to work.

I was gone before she could stop me.

CHAPTER TWENTY

BLAIRE

Grammy's patience with the Quarters was uncharacteristically high. The way they spoke, the things they did—I wouldn't have ever gotten away with acting in that manner around her, even as a child. Yet she allowed it all to roll off her back without repercussions. It ignited a sort of jealousy toward them, which quickly morphed into full-blown resentment when they took their teasing further and included her in the jokes.

The seriousness and distrust from the first time she and I met them out here in the dilapidated cabin was long gone, and in its place was a comforting camaraderie—a family. Why did she find it so easy to speak with them, to respect them, and it was like pulling teeth just to get her to speak to me with any ounce of consideration?

She brought me back out here to lift the protection shield for the Fire Festival, swearing that I was the most crucial piece to making sure the spell went on without a hitch.

I felt like an outsider as they all teased each other, their moods unusually heightened, especially since the last time I was here. Even Storie laughed and joked with them, her eyes twinkling in a way I hadn't ever seen them do before.

They were happy.

Despite everything going on, they were happy. Why did that bother me so much?

"Loosen up, Little B. Today is a good day," Rhyse said through a smile after catching me scowling at him from my spot in their beaten-down recliner for the hundredth time.

Grammy and Lux were bent over a book, mumbling to each other, confirming they had everything exactly right. Remy and Storie were on the couch across from me and Rhyse and Enzo just finished a pull-up competition off the rafters of the loft.

Rhyse's comment earned me a few curious looks, and I could tell they wanted to agree, but no one bothered to interject.

"I'm fine. I thought this was going to be done by now."

Grammy lifted her head to level me with a look. *There's that ornery old woman I know.* "Do you have someplace else to be?"

Of course, she knew I didn't. I shook my head and looked down at my hands, biting back another sarcastic remark. Storie looked like she wanted to say something, but quickly thought better of it and clamped her mouth shut.

I don't know why I was allowing it all to get to me so badly. I guess it was just off-putting to see them getting along while I'd been isolated and alone.

For the life of me, I couldn't figure out if that was Grammy's or my own doing.

"I think we're ready," Lux declared, making eye contact with the three other Quarters in the room to confirm they were ready, too. I was shocked when his icy blues locked in on mine, and the meaning behind that stare was not lost on me.

He was silently including me in their group.

I tucked my chin down in a stiff nod, and all five of us met at the kitchen table. I took a spot between Remy and Lux while Storie and Grammy lingered a step behind us.

Grammy and Lux instructed us on what to say, and the whole process went a lot quicker than I expected. Once energy in the cabin had been thoroughly cleansed with both palo santo and cedar smudges, we joined hands, chanting in the language I'd always heard but never understood. And just when I thought we were done, having felt none of the usual buzz from my gifts, I was hit with the force of it all at once.

It started in my chest. Like a little spark slowly flickering to life in a dark cave, it hardly stung. But then, it ignited into a full-blown inferno, and I swear I was burning alive. I tried to look to Rhyse to see if he felt it, too, but was shocked again with a cold chill down my spine before I could.

My back arched, nearly breaking my hands free from Remy's and Lux's grip as my body felt like it was frozen in its contorted place. This had to be the wind element. It moved through me in cold waves, like a hurricane or a tsunami.

Next, my muscles tensed up and my limbs felt too heavy to hold. I felt magnetized to the ground. The earth element tried to suck me into its dense layers.

As quickly as the shock from it wore off, my lungs constricted, and I could swear they were filling with liquid—the water element. I sputtered for breath, vaguely hearing Storie's panicked voice behind me as I faded in and out of consciousness.

Something had to be wrong. These gifts—they were owning me. Trying to destroy me.

"Don't interfere," I heard Grammy's commanding voice.

It sounded like she was speaking through a tunnel. There was chaos all around me. A tugging on my limbs. A crack down my back. Whirls of fire licking my skin. Waves of water crashing in my lungs.

Until slowly, it all receded. Inch by painful, agonizing inch, the chaos retreated back into somewhere inside of me. Their voices returned beside my ears and my eyes opened back up to the ceiling of the cabin. I was lying on the floor now, all six faces hovering over mine.

And I knew it was done. All of it.

The protection was in place, as were my gifts.

I blinked, then immediately rolled my head to find Grammy, who was watching me with a wise look on her face. She had known. Her words from before rang in the back of my head.

It's time you stepped into your powers.

That was what this was all about—why she brought me out here in the first place. It was a ritual. She wanted me to complete a spell with the Quarters in order to gain full use of my gifts.

"You could have told me," I finally found the words to say.

She shrugged. "You wouldn't have come."

"I don't know what just happened, but that was freaky as hell," Enzo's strained voice remarked from above me.

The others voiced their agreements and Storie placed her hand on my shoulder to see if I was alright. I gave her a reassuring look and rolled out of her touch to climb to my feet, still feeling a little overwhelmed.

"You needed us to activate her gifts..." Lux surmised. He didn't seem mad or shocked. I waited for the others to voice their irritations at being so blatantly used, but none of it came.

"The shield is in place. Behave yourselves tonight," Grammy said as she packed up her things, ignoring Lux's comment altogether. She looked to me to see if I was willing to come with her.

I took in the mood of the room before me. The way Enzo and Rhyse high-fived. How Remy and Storie shared a victorious kiss. Even Lux replaced his usual disinterested expression with a smile.

And I felt completely out of place here. For some reason, all I could think about was getting back home and telling Kyle what had just happened. If the people I could trust most were here—the ones I could relate to the best—why was the sheriff on my mind at all?

I pushed the thought away and told Grammy I'd stay here, so we could all arrive at the festival together. She only smiled in response, as if that was what she was hoping I'd say, and then left us alone to celebrate.

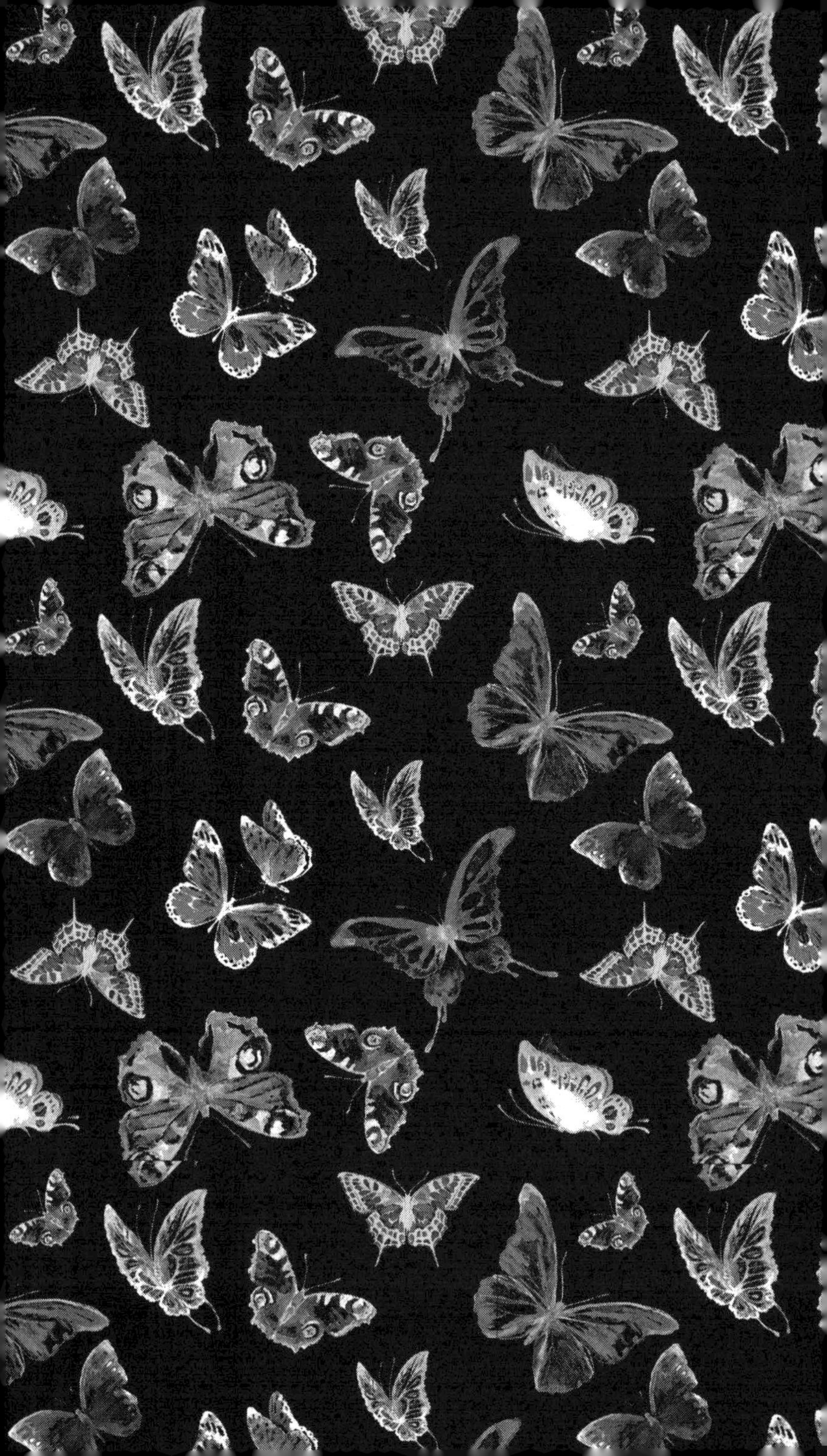

CHAPTER TWENTY-ONE

KYLE

I found Blaire late in the night. The festival was still in full swing as the sounds of music and dancing in the town square echoed through the woods, where it was significantly quieter. She was by the cemetery, of all places.

Tabitha asked me to keep an eye on her after she wandered home for the night. I had no idea why she trusted me with her most prized possession when there were such threats looming around, but I still agreed. Something told me I would have kept an eye on her, anyway.

She disappeared over an hour ago. There one minute, gone the next. I was grabbing some punch from the tavern, but never allowed her to stray too far out of my sight.

Lisa Golden, the owner of the tavern, whispered something crude and unladylike in my ear, temporarily stealing my attention long enough to decline her offer politely. It was like I blinked and missed Blaire walking away. I spent the next hour panicking, slowly trekking through the woods in hopes I'd run into her.

Who knew what Tabitha would do to me if something had happened?

"There you are," I greeted carefully, hoping not to startle her.

She was sitting on a cement bench positioned beside the Graves cemetery plots. Her shoulders lifted slightly in defense at the sound of my feet approaching her through the grass, then relaxed when she heard my voice.

I hated what that did to my heart. The fact that she trusted me so completely.

"What are you doing out here?" I asked in a quiet tone, stopping right in front of her.

I was still wearing my uniform, even though I'd been off duty for a couple of hours now. I hadn't wanted to leave the festival and change—my fear of something happening in my absence outweighing any desire for comfort. On instinct, my thumbs hooked onto my belt loops as I waited for her reply.

"It was getting a little heady over there," she admitted with a teasing smile.

I knew what she meant. By this time of night, the lust in the air was so thick it was hard to breathe through. Fire Festival had to be one of the most inappropriate, primal events Beacon Grove celebrated.

But the poignancy followed me, I guess. Staring down at her from this angle, all I could see were those pouty lips jutting out as she looked up at me.

All I could think about was what they would feel like against mine. Against all of me.

Visions of us together, skin gliding against skin, flooded my mind at once. I almost had to take a step back, when she lightly chuckled.

Realization hit me all at once. Those were her thoughts.

"Don't do that," I warned.

Why can't I block her out?

"Or else what?"

My brow lifted in challenge, and my pants were suddenly too tight.

She wanted to know the consequences?

"You're playing a dangerous game, Granger."

Her smile broadened. God, this girl had no shame. "A little fun never hurt anybody. Why don't you loosen up, sheriff? You're off duty."

I blew out a breath and looked up at the sky, begging the gods to send help. I wasn't going to last against her.

"Is it so bad?"

Her voice had dropped to a near-whisper. When I looked back down at her, she was shyly staring at her hands.

"What?"

"The thought of being with me," she said into her lap.

It was the first time I'd ever heard a hint of insecurity in her tone, and I wanted to kick myself for putting it there.

"No." It came out in a low, insistent growl. "Not at all."

"Then why do you act like I'm torturing you?"

"Because you are."

She lifted her chin and stared back at me, brows knitting together in confusion.

"If I so much as think about touching you, Tabitha is going to have my balls nailed to her mantle before either of us has a chance to get our clothes off."

She rolled her eyes and opened her mouth to protest, but I stopped her before I lost my nerve.

"If I ever take you..." I shook my head. "No, *when* I finally take you, Blaire, it's not going to be in a cemetery on a night when we can write it off as hormones or getting caught up in the festivities."

Her slackened jaw fed my confidence to continue. I took a step closer to her and placed my finger under her chin, tilting her head toward me ever so gently.

"I'm going to take my time with you, properly, in a bed. I'm going to show you exactly how much you've *tortured* me with your little teasing mind games. And I'm going to make Tabitha's wrath worth every second."

Maybe this was going too far. Maybe we were starting something neither of us had the guts to finish. All I knew was that no woman had me feeling this way since I watched Asher's taillights disappear.

I was no stranger to taking women in my bed. Usually, a tourist who was just passing through, but there were times I'd entertain someone from Beacon Grove. Hell, I might have even taken Lisa up on her offer tonight if Blaire wasn't embedded so far into my head. Regardless of who it was, they were always made aware of the rules before a single piece of clothing was shed.

I didn't do commitment.

I didn't do labels.

And any intimacy disappeared the moment they walked back out my front door.

It was just easier that way. I wasn't going to put myself in a position to be destroyed again. But how did the rules change when the woman lived in my house? When we had to interact with each other every day? When she was twenty years my junior and had a family who would kick my ass if they ever found out?

Even when I added all the negatives up in my head, they still couldn't equate to how I felt when she was near. To the constant aching in my chest, the urge to protect her, the desire to please her.

And it most definitely couldn't compete with the way I felt when she stared up at me like she was now, with her lips slightly parted, her eyes glazed over. This close, I could practically taste her—a sweet combination of vanilla and cinnamon—and I wanted to drown in it.

I could fight it as long as I wanted, but it would be futile. Our connection had already been written in the stars.

By denying each other, we were denying fate.

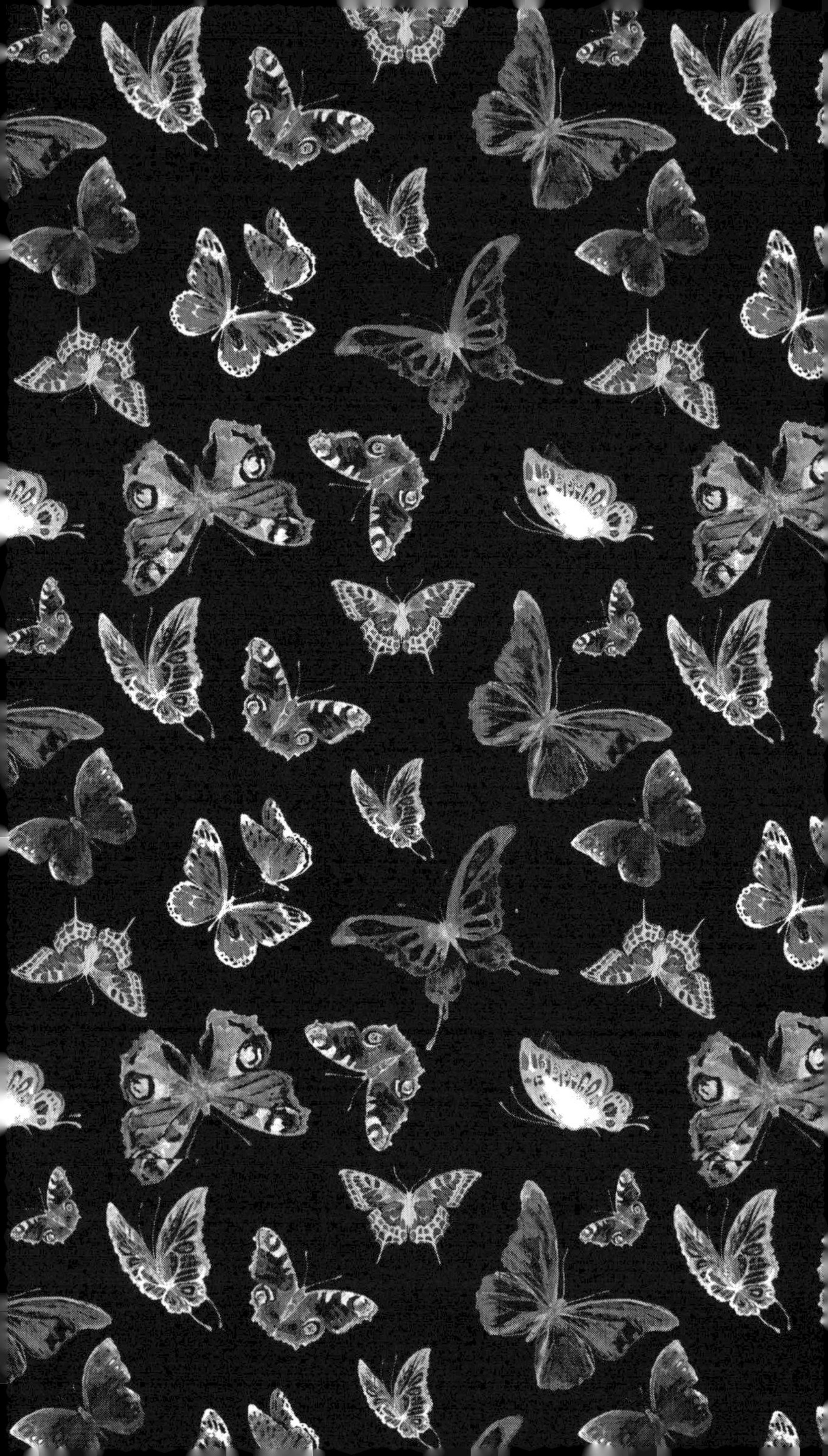

CHAPTER TWENTY-TWO

BLAIRE

I was on the porch when Kyle got home a few days later. His words from the Fire Festival hung in the air between us, a promise that I hoped he was willing to keep. They rang fresh in my mind as if he had just said them. I was only having fun with him at first, but our flirtation had obviously taken on a life of its own.

Was it wrong if I was curious to see where it wound up?

My head rested in my hand as I sat forward in my chair, staring at the potted plant before me. Grammy mentioned to the Quarters that I was more powerful than them. Now that they were fully activated, I realized that I had hardly scratched the surface of my gifts.

I could feel the power flowing through me, buzzing in my veins, and yet, I had little control over it. Aside from the few instances I used it to still the wind or shift the earth, I was mostly afraid to wield it. That seemed foolish considering the threats we were up against, so I made a mental note to talk to the Quarters about how to use each element, and then I noticed the dead plant sitting before me. In my best attempt to harness my inner Enzo, I lifted my hand and willed the tiny flower to stand up.

And it had. Sort of.

Two hours later, I only managed to get one little sprout to bloom fully.

"You shouldn't do that out here," Kyle warned as he walked up the porch steps.

"There's not much happening, anyway."

"Still. Anyone could see you."

I shrugged in defeat, abandoning the plant to sit back in my chair.

Kyle tilted his head toward his door. "Come inside. I want to show you something."

I tried my best to stop the flutter in my chest at being invited into his space again, but failed miserably. For whatever reason, he didn't like sitting on the porch anymore. Whenever he arrived home, he refused to speak about anything related to the Movement or the Quarters until we were inside.

It didn't feel like a big deal to be in his space, given that he made a habit of offering to eat together since my first week here. But then, he made his intentions well known. Now, being alone with him had a whole new meaning.

He led me back to the living room and reached around his side to unlatch his holster, the way he did every night. My eyes followed his movements as he unloaded the magazine, knocked a bullet out of the cartridge, and then gently set it all in his safe before locking it away. This time, I was focused on more than just the gun, though.

I watched the way his long fingers wrapped around the barrel, gliding my tongue over my bottom lip as my imagination ran wild about those fingers on me. He moved from the safe and began unbuttoning his shirt, revealing his usual plain black tee underneath. How had I never noticed how well they hugged his body? How clearly I could make out his abs and biceps through the thin fabric?

I bit down on my lip, lost in thought, when his gravelly voice interrupted.

"Stop."

My eyes snapped up, and I knew I'd been caught. He was frowning, lips pursed in disapproval. The random silver stands in his inky black hair caught the light of the window and glistened. I took a deep breath, filling my lungs with his earthy scent—a mix of leather and cedar and a hint of the musky smell from the police station.

"What do you need to show me?" I asked on an exhale.

His expression shifted, as if he too had forgotten why I was here. He reached into his pocket and pulled out a gold pin, holding it in front of me so I could get a better look.

It was a five-point star with a circle around it. I had no idea what it meant.

"What am I looking at?"

"It's the symbol for the Beacon Grove council. Only members are allowed to wear them. There's a ceremony for being pinned and everything. They take it very seriously," he explained excitedly, pulling his hand back to examine the pin himself.

"I found it on the ground beneath our most recently tied up deer," he added.

My brows shot into my hairline. "You think it's a council member doing this?"

He nodded. "I *know* it is now. Given the circumstances, there's absolutely no chance this is a coincidence."

I shifted my attention back to the pin, my mind reeling at the newfound information. We always suspected the council may be in Rayner's corner, but this made the situation a lot scarier. Just as Silas Forbes had done with Watchtower, they could hand control of the town over to him and his Movement, and there was nothing we could do about it.

That explained why Mayor Douglas was so interested in how the case was coming along. He wanted to know how close Kyle was to sniffing him and his peers out. But if he found the pin at the crime scene, he'd have to document it as evidence, right?

"Won't they come looking for it and know you're onto them when they see it in evidence?"

"I'm not logging this into evidence." He tightly wrapped his fingers around it and shoved it back into his pocket.

"What can we do?" I asked in a near-whisper.

It was all becoming too real. After last year—what the Movement did to go after the Quarters—there was no telling what Rayner had planned next. The lengths he'd go to finish the job. But knowing he had the resources he needed to execute it was terrifying.

"This is good," he assured me.

He took a step closer, lifting his hand to grip my shoulder, and then stopped himself. "Now, we know what we're working against. We can all start making a plan to stop him before he can even begin."

I slowly nodded, but doubt still clouded my mind, curling around my thoughts like black mist. The plant outside flashed behind my eyes, along with my pathetic attempt to force it to bloom. If I was one of the most powerful witches working against him, did we have any hope?

"Don't do that. You've only just found out about your gifts. The others have had their whole lives to learn them," Kyle responded to my thoughts out loud once again. "We'll get them to train with you, just like they have been with Storie."

This time, he allowed himself to grab my shoulders and pull me into a hug without restraint. "I didn't mean to scare you. I thought you'd be happy to finally know what we're up against."

I rested my head against his chest, fully submerging myself in his scent again. He was right, of course. Knowing exactly who our enemies were was the only way we stood a chance. I still couldn't stop that lingering feeling of dread from turning my thoughts negative.

Kyle sensed it and tightened his hold on me. It was probably just an act of kindness, of pity for the girl who thought the weight of the world hung on her shoulders despite the fact that there were four other men ready to do what she clearly couldn't. But it was also the closest he had ever allowed us to be, and I refused to be the first to pull away. If pitying me was the only way he'd let his guard down and get over this ridiculous fear of Grammy, then so be it.

"I don't fear her," he mumbled into my ear. I made a note to make my first lesson on learning how to block my thoughts from him, and he chuckled. "I don't pity you, either. You're going to be the one who saves this town, Blaire, and they're all going to realize what they've been missing out on."

He pulled his head back slightly, and I prepared for him to let go of me. Instead, he surprised me by lowering his hands down my back. I gazed up at him, shocked to see the smug little smirk that was playing on his lips.

"You seem pretty scared for all those dirty thoughts you've been sending my way," he hummed into my ear.

"Scared? Not at all. Just taken off guard. Give me a second to recoup, and then I'll kick your ass."

I fought back my own smile, quickly losing the battle when his hands cupped my rear and gently squeezed.

"I want to kiss you, Blaire," he admitted, his expression pained.

"Then do it."

For some reason, that was all the permission he needed to throw his silly holdups about us out the window. As soon as the words left my lips, he was there to replace them. It was everything I imagined it would be—everything I fantasized about all those nights alone in my bed—and more.

His expert lips moved against mine in a rhythm only we knew the dance to. My chest felt like it was going to explode from pure joy and excitement over the fact that it was finally happening.

All those private conversations, the heated looks... they were finally adding up to something. And if he had any fear of the consequences of Grammy finding out, they had died and withered away with every second our lips touched.

None of it mattered.

The Movement could march into town today and end it all, and none of it could touch us in this tiny bubble we created for ourselves.

Though, it appeared I was the only one who felt that way.

All too soon, he pulled away. A whine sounded in the back of my throat, and he breathed out a tortured, humorless laugh.

"It's taking everything in me not to devour you right here," he admitted, out of breath. "But we have to stop."

"No, we don't," I countered brazenly, too caught up in the moment and frustrated with his constant hesitancy to be embarrassed.

"When are you going to stop allowing the weight of everyone's opinions to slow you down? This thing between us... I think it's worth exploring. Fuck everyone else. They don't need to know anything about it."

He looked taken aback by my honesty, a war waging behind his eyes at the validity of it all.

I shifted my weight onto one leg and crossed my arms. I was right, and I knew it.

The question was: was he brave enough to go along, or would his fear stop him from experiencing something amazing?

I gnawed on my lip, waiting to see which side won out. His brows were pinched together as he warred with himself, and I could feel every emotion pass through him as my words dug their way in.

When I was sure he was going to send me up the stairs with my pride ripped to shreds, his hand reached into the space between us and firmly cupped my chin, tilting my head up so he could easily place his lips against my ear.

"There's no turning back after this," he quietly warned.

"Good," I countered stubbornly.

His lips were back on mine then, desperate and needy. He'd finally given in to the temptation, and now it was his desire that consumed him. I could sense it wafting off him like waves against the shore.

I backed him into the couch and shoved him down so my legs could straddle his hips. His hands were everywhere, running along my spine, slipping into the back of my pants, caressing my thighs. One of them unhooked my bra while the other cradled my head, all while never breaking our kiss.

When he cupped my breast, I stifled a moan, which only encouraged him to continue further. I ground my hips into him, along his erection.

Clothes.

We had too many clothes between us.

I eased away from him and stripped my shirt off, then threw it over my shoulder as he lowered his mouth onto my nipple. My hands raked through his hair and scratched down the back of his shirt, reminding him he was still fully dressed. He grabbed the collar of his shirt and yanked it over his head, then bucked his hips forward, driving himself against me harder, so that he could unbuckle his belt and loosen his pants.

In a few sloppy movements, we were each finally undressed. Kyle offered one last chance for us to end this before it was too late, but I refused. We were already too far gone.

He lifted me into his arms and carried me to his room, then gently laid me on the neatly made king-sized bed. I made a mental note to look around when we were finished, far too curious to see the space he slept in.

But now? Now I was too focused on watching the way his abs flexed as he climbed into the bed and paused, his face grinning between my legs.

He put a hand on each thigh and pushed them farther apart, slowly inching them down toward my heated center. I propped myself up on my elbows and watched as he swiped a finger through my folds, and then placed it into his mouth. Tasting me.

"So sweet," he moaned, then leaned forward and made the same path with his tongue.

I jerked forward, farther into his mouth, and a low chuckle vibrated on my groin at the reaction. He continued rubbing his tongue against me, eventually pushing his finger inside, testing.

I threw my head back when he added another, grinding against his face. When the waves of pleasure began rolling in, I didn't bother muffling the moans that escaped my lips in fast, desperate breaths. They only encouraged him.

Once my heart settled and the high was gone, I looked back down at Kyle's face between my legs and the embarrassment crept in at how quickly I came undone from his touch. He hadn't even been inside of me yet and I was already completely unraveled.

But the heated look in his eyes injected me with another dose of adrenaline. I watched as he climbed up my body, and my center immediately began pulsing again at the predatory gleam he wore as he positioned himself over me and hovered there, his chin still soaked from my juices.

"You're the most beautiful woman I've ever seen," he whispered against my lips.

He didn't give me a chance to respond before his mouth was back on mine, forcing me to taste the tanginess of my own arousal. His tongue darted into my mouth in the same motion he'd just used between my legs, and I grew even needier for more of him.

My hands gripped his hips and forced his erection against me. He bit down into my lip to chastise me for being impatient, but reached between us to align himself with my already-dripping center.

Within one breath, he was inside me. He stilled, allowing me a moment to adjust to his size before he pulled out and repeated the motion.

I ran my nails up and down his back as he found a rhythm, pumping into me as he kissed all along my shoulder, my neck, my jaw. He leaned farther down and took my nipple into his mouth, gently sucking before moving onto the other.

It was an overwhelming stimulation of multiple senses at once, and far sooner than I was ready, I felt the buildup of another orgasm coming. He moved his hands back to either side of my head and drove into me harder, determined to fall over the edge with me this time.

And he did.

It was like we were free-falling into the night sky together. Blasts of starlight appeared and exposed behind my eyes. I was floating and grounded at the same time. It was so similar to the moment I felt my gifts activating—an otherworldly experience that felt so much bigger than me or him.

His name escaped my lips as I cried out, feeling him deep in my soul. Whatever this was, it was intoxicating. Addicting. I'd stay here in this bed and do it over and over again if I could.

But eventually—after quite a bit of time—we floated back down to earth.

He was lying beside me, breaths heavy as we both stared up at the ceiling, when I finally returned to my body.

"That was..." he began, unable to find the words.

"Out of this world," I finished for him.

And I was ready to do it all over again.

A couple of hours later, my eyes openly roamed around his room as I laid my head on his bare chest. It was decorated in the same vein as his apartment, with neutral, airy colors. There were little areas of clutter littered between the open, neat spots.

A hamper exploding with clothes sat in a corner beside his bare dresser. His nightstand was piled with random things that I assumed he pulled out of his pockets before hopping into his neatly made bed. It was a space so at odds with itself, just like its owner.

It fit him perfectly.

"We can't tell anyone about this. Not yet."

My fingers paused on his chest.

"I just don't want to let anything get in the way. I want to explore whatever this connection is before we open ourselves up to the criticism."

The criticism. My insecurities reared their ugly heads one by one. All the insults I lived with came barreling into my mind.

I talked too much. I acted rashly. I was too naive. I lacked social skills.

My skin was just a shade too dark. My freckles were off-putting. My hair was too different. My hips were too wide.

All of it slapped me in the face as I searched through them for any merit. For any chance that he might feel the same as all my bullies had. Did he want to protect himself from being on the receiving end of those insults? Was he hesitant to align himself with such a social pariah?

I never gave life to all the ugly things I'd been told throughout my formative years. I'd just absorb the blow and move on, pretending it didn't affect me at all. Grammy was hard on me, but one thing she showed me was how to own who you are as a person. To flaunt those flaws and make them into strengths. And I tried. I tried so hard to be just like her in that way.

I grew my different-colored hair out long, so there was more of it. I refused to wear concealer to mask my freckles. I didn't use clothes to cover up or hide my skin color.

But hearing someone I truly cared about mention it... that was difficult.

"You've gone somewhere," Kyle said, his brows knitting together in worry. He reached over and swiped a stray hair out of my face, and his fingers left a chill in their wake.

"I'm fine," I lied.

"No, you're not. Talk to me." He sat up, shaking me off his chest.

The move only put more distance between us and fed my negative thoughts.

Why was I acting like this? Why did his opinion matter so much to me?

I wanted to keep the runaway train of thoughts to myself, but it was difficult to keep them guarded from him when I was spiraling so quickly. Unfortunately, he was able to access them all with ease. I watched his face shift into a defensive expression as he rushed to explain himself.

"Blaire, you need to know that every inch of you is perfect. Your hair, your eyes, your body... and your mind is undeniably the sexiest thing about you. I don't care what anyone else thinks. But I've done this before. I've jumped head-first into a relationship with someone who I thought was *it* for me. I don't blame Asher for her choices—I know why she made every single one. That doesn't change the fact that I was left behind, completely forgotten, with my heart ripped out of my chest."

My mouth tightened into a thin line at the mention of his first love.

Why was he bringing her up? I'd never do those things to him.

"Just bear with me for a second, okay?"

He took a deep breath, readying himself to speak again.

"It's been over twenty years since all that happened. I thought what I felt for her was this magnificent, rare thing. One I'd never find again. And I haven't. What we have, Blaire..."

He paused, struggling to find the words.

"It's like I can feel you deep inside in my bones. Whenever you're around, every part of me comes to life again. What I felt for her was only a fraction of the devotion I feel for you. So, yes. I want to take our time exploring this because it feels so much greater than anything anyone out there can comprehend."

I didn't have a response to give him. Not to that admission. It felt like too significant of a moment for me to ruin it with my words. My insecurities.

Instead, I leaned up and placed a kiss on his waiting lips. Then, I moved down to the dimple on his chin. To the freckle on his neck. I made my way all the way down his chest and abdomen, until I reached his waiting erection.

Then, I kissed his tip and used my mouth to show him that his words had landed on their target.

THE ✶ BEACON

4 MAY 2022

COVENSTEAD ANNOUNCED

BREAKING: The Quarters have announced a covenstead tomorrow, May 5th at 5 pm sharp for all Watchtower members.

This will be the first covenstead called by our new generation and the first one to include Storie Graves as Remington Winters' Counter, officially.

Anonymous members suspect they may have answers regarding the future of the coven, updates about the Movement, and which one of them is stepping into the role of High Priest and High Priestess.

The Beacon will report any updates as they come in.

Who do YOU want to be Watchtower's High Priest?

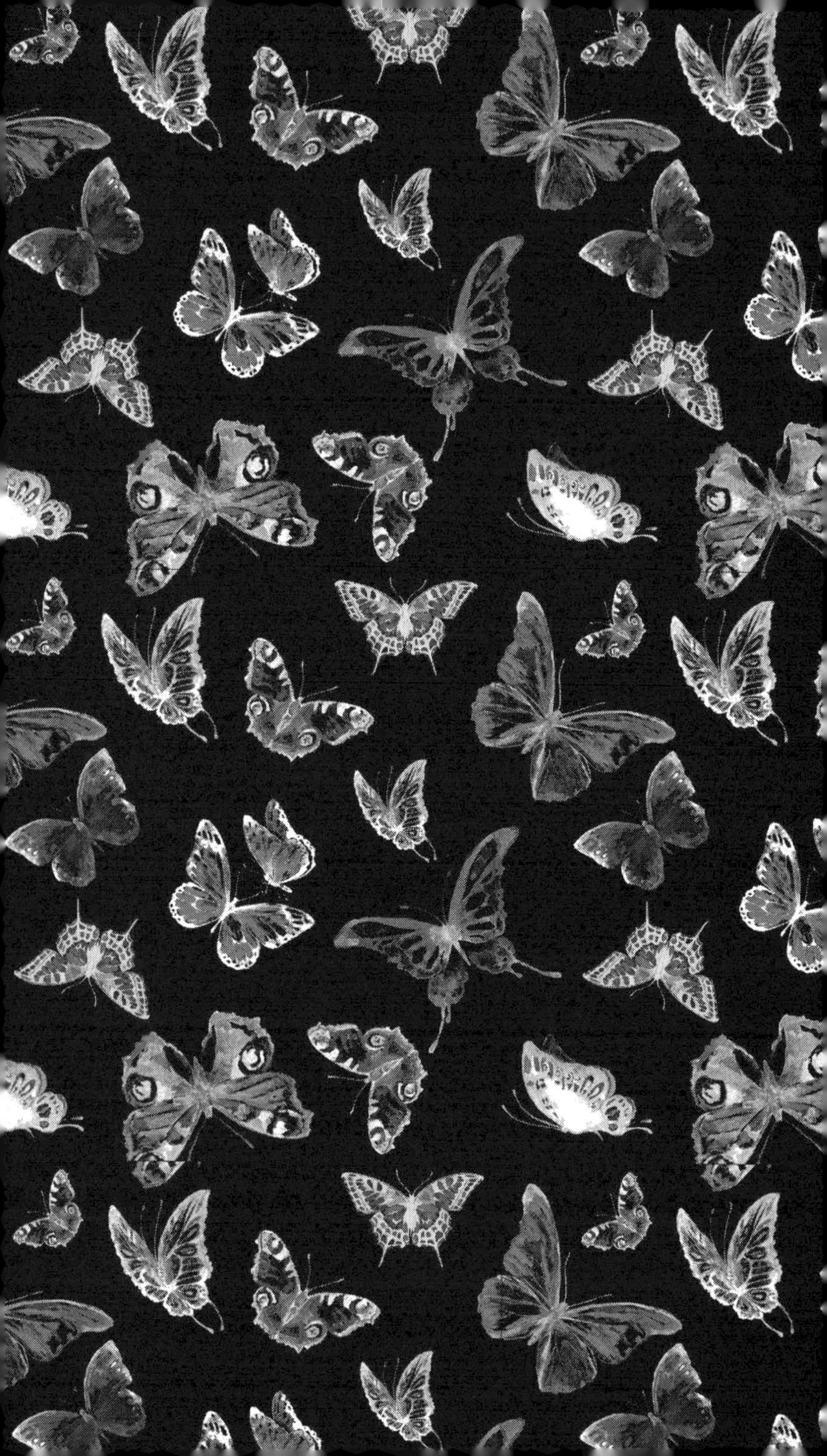

CHAPTER TWENTY-THREE

KYLE

The Quarters called a Watchtower covenstead. It was the first one they officially called as a unit since Silas was stripped of his position. The whole town was talking about it, even those who weren't a part of the coven. Everyone wanted to know what the Quarters had to say. So much so, people who hadn't been to a meeting in years were considering attending.

They were going to share the news about the animals that kept popping up and what they thought it meant for the future of Beacon Grove. Mayor Douglas and his council had no idea. If they did, they would have fought against it with everything they had. But Lux and Remy thought their coven deserved to know about the threat that loomed, and Rhyse and Enzo were ready to begin the war against the Movement.

"I can't wait to watch Douglas' face turn purple when we expose him," Enzo mused as we walked through the woods. Rhyse barked out a laugh, and they went back and forth about how repulsive they found each old, decrepit member of the council.

The covenstead would be held in the community center, just like most of the town meetings. It was the largest space the town had to offer to hold as many people as they anticipated would attend. The last time we planned a meeting this large, Rayner was still openly spewing his Movement propaganda to anyone that would listen.

"What are we going to tell them about Blaire?" Storie asked from the other side of me. She and Remy were holding hands, with Blaire trailing one step behind them.

"Tabitha doesn't think we should reveal her yet," Lux answered from ahead. He was leading the group through the worn-down trail.

I glanced back at Blaire and caught the end of her eye roll.

"I agree with her," I said, earning a sneer from the peppy redhead. I discretely winked and smirked at her and faced forward again.

"At this point, she's one of the only secret weapons we've got," Remy added in a low voice, darting his eyes around for any sign of someone trying to listen in.

They raised a privacy spell around us, but there was no way to know for certain if it worked against whatever magic the Movement was using.

The other three muttered their agreement, and it was Storie's turn to look back and offer her friend a remorseful look.

I felt out of place walking with the pack of twenty-somethings. Tabitha asked me to escort them to the meeting so she could get to the community center ahead of time and look for any potential traps or surprises. Of course, she asked for the favor without any of their knowledge, fully aware how offended they would be if they ever found out she thought they needed a babysitter.

Truthfully, all of them were far better equipped for protection than I was, but I agreed nonetheless. At the very least, it gave me the chance to keep an eye on Blaire, who I was growing more and more protective of with each passing day.

The memory of the feel of her skin against mine last night flashed through my mind. I let it go too far. I knew it. But nothing about it felt wrong at the moment, and there had to be a reason for that. I pushed the thoughts away before I could beat myself up over it any more. Or before I had to adjust myself in front of a group of four guys who would know exactly what I was doing.

"Well, I'm not much of a weapon if I don't even know how to use my gifts," Blaire complained.

"We'll train you," Remy assured gently.

"Yeah, Granger. I'll spar with you," Rhyse said with a wicked smile.

"No thanks."

Rhyse lifted his hand to his chest in mock offense. "Why not?"

"Because you just want an excuse to throw flames at me, and I might not be able to control my gifts, but I'll still kick your ass."

Rhyse and Enzo laughed again, slowing their pace to wrap their arms around Blaire's neck, and I fought the urge to rip them off.

"We'd never try to hurt you, Little B. We just want to have some fun," Enzo razzed.

"Yeah, it's been a while since we had someone new to spar with. Enzo turns into The Hulk too quickly these days. I hardly have a chance to practice before he's an all-out animal."

Blaire made a disgusted face and shook them both off of her. "You're insufferable."

"Why don't you start by shifting the streets so we can get there on time," Lux offered over his shoulder. "Since Enzo is so distracted."

She huffed out an irritated breath, and the path changed before us. It was like we'd jumped forward at least five hundred feet. I had seen Tabitha do the same thing, but I didn't realize it was part of the gift.

"I'm not that inexperienced," she mumbled, and then did it again.

Mayor Douglas looked like he wanted to disappear from his spot in the front of the crowded gymnasium. He requested to sit on the stage with the Quarters, as he had always done when Silas Forbes was in charge of these meetings, but they unanimously refused. Instead, he was stuck between the four men who were going to expose his secrets, and the crowd full of people who would want answers from him.

As a result, I was forced to put an officer beside him in case anyone attempted to get physical. I chose Stewart, the perfect little rat for the job. Rhyse looked like he wanted to knock me out when he heard me make the command over the radio, but they weren't the only ones playing this dangerous game. I had to keep up a facade, too.

"Thank you for giving us your time on such short notice." Lux was the first to address his coven. "We know this has been a long time coming, and we apologize for the delay as we've gotten things organized. We didn't want to come forward until we could do so as a unified front."

"As we're all painfully aware, my father committed the most dreadful act of betrayal against this coven. He herded us up and fed us to the wolves for his own personal gain," Rhyse said, knowingly locking eyes with Mayor Douglas, who had been consorting with Silas as those events were unfolding, yet somehow managed to come out unscathed. He was also explaining exactly what Douglas was potentially doing to our town.

There were a few murmurs from the masses as they were forced to recall the events from last year.

Rhyse went on. "We're here to tell you that won't happen again. We've come up with a plan for the future of Watchtower, which we'll get to in just a moment. We hope these changes will better us for the next generations to come and provide a more diverse leadership than what we've had in the past."

Remy stood to say his piece. I knew this was it. He wanted to be the one to expose Mayor Douglas for working with the enemy that had attempted to kill his Counter just months before. To deliver the fatal blow to Douglas' career.

There was no way of knowing how they would react to finding out they've been lied to all over again. That another man in power was keeping secrets, especially where the Movement was involved. And to Douglas' credit, it would have been a noble effort to keep them shielded from an attack so soon after the last. It *could* have been—if he hadn't been only doing it to cover his own ass and working with Rayner.

"The fight against Rayner and his Movement isn't over. They've been leaving messages for Beacon Grove. Dead animals strung up with ribbons and dressed in Rayner's victim's clothing—in *your* family's clothing." He paused, allowing them to absorb the severity of his words. "They're sending the message that they aren't finished with us, and the leadership in this town has conveniently kept it from you."

As expected, the quiet murmuring turned into angry arguing, mostly directed at Mayor Douglas and the council members standing before them. The Quarters made sure they would be easy to spot for this part.

The uneasiness of the crowd had me instinctually reaching for my weapon, my eyes scanning for any threats. They were teetering on the line between peace and chaos, but the Quarters knew what they were doing.

"Before we allow this to unravel our meeting, let's all take a beat and talk this through, as a group," Lux said, taking a theatrical, deep breath.

Something happened to the antsy crowd then. Like a wave of calm had suddenly washed over them, their mumbling died down and silence fell across the room. Instinctually, my eyes found Blaire, standing off to the side with Tabitha, and I knew it had been her doing.

She could feel and control emotions.

"The Movement has affected each and every one of us. Our daily lives were interrupted, our families threatened—hell, even our social lives were put on hold. After the bonfire..." Remy paused to take a deep breath and Storie squeezed his hand for encouragement.

"Beacon Grove has been changed forever. Now, there's no true way to know which side anyone stands on in this fight. I'd like to believe that all of you are on ours, but I know that our fathers have made that hard for you. There's no way to know how Rayner plans to make his return, either. But I'm telling you right now, if you side with the Movement, you're going to suffer immensely."

"How are we supposed to trust anything you boys say when we just found out our own mayor has been hiding things from us?" Ben Davis, a pudgy, middle-aged man, asked.

He owned the party store off of fifth street that had been robbed by Movement Members the night of the bonfire.

"I suppose you aren't, but the alternative is to trust Rayner," Lux simply said.

"Or we could stop trusting any of the people who want to *lead* us and think for ourselves," Ben replied.

Enzo smiled at that, then cracked his knuckles as if he would welcome the challenge.

"The last thing we need is a third side," Lou Roberts commented from the back.

"There aren't any sides," Mayor Douglas dared to interject, earning a room full of glares.

"Easy for you to say. You appear to be on the wrong one," Ben sneered.

"Yeah, Mayor, care to explain why we weren't aware that Rayner is back?" Lou added.

Douglas held his hands up in front of him. "Let's be clear, Rayner is not back. We've been working closely with law enforcement to ensure that's the case. This is just a misunderstanding. It's the result of a silly prank."

He was floundering. The council members who stood beside him nodded their agreement, and I knew they'd do anything to save face, including throwing me under the bus.

"A prank? You can't be serious. These are innocent people's lives that have been stolen from them, and instead of allowing their spirits to cross over and rest, they're taking it a step further and using their remains to send a message." As Rhyse spoke the words, temporarily shedding the calm, collected demeanor he'd been successfully holding on to, my shoulders stiffened.

I hadn't told them about the spirits.

The only way they could have known about them was if Blaire told them. And if Blaire revealed that to them, what else had she shared?

I found her once again, the question burning in my stare. Had she betrayed me? Did she tell them about my gifts?

As if she were the one who could read thoughts, she adamantly shook her head, her eyes pleading. For the first time ever, I intentionally opened up the path between our minds.

I would never, she insisted mentally.

There was a conversation happening in the background, but I wasn't paying attention to it anymore.

I only told them about the spirits. We need to figure out why they can't remember, she reminded me.

I considered her for a moment, hoping she was telling the truth, and then nodded to let her know I had heard.

"...Sheriff Abbot has been making sure to notify the proper authorities. If they thought it was more than some silly game, he would have told me," Mayor Douglas was saying, turning their attention toward me.

"With all due respect, Mayor, I've taken these incidents very seriously. I'm certain they're more than just *silly games* at this point."

He squinted those round, bulging eyes at me, surprised I wasn't willing to take the fall for him.

"What do you think you're going to do that's so different from your worthless fathers?" Matilda Kent asked the Quarters, diverting their attention.

I was surprised to see her standing there in the thick of it. She was nearly Ma's age.

The Quarters each looked to Lux to explain. "We're going to hold elections, like we usually do. But we think it's time we took a step back from being High Priests of the coven and allow one of you to take on the role. Our lives are still dedicated to Watchtower, and as such, we'll all have a say in any coven matters. But it's time we consider your voices when making decisions for the whole, don't you think?"

"You want to make Watchtower a democracy?" Matilda asked, her lip curled in distaste.

Lux nodded.

"What's so bad about that? It's about damn time," Ben argued, noting Matilda's look of disagreement.

"It's not how this is meant to be. The gods blessed *you* for a reason. They wanted the Quarters to run the coven.

She crossed her arms stubbornly and one of her curls fell out of her loose bun as she nodded her head, agreeing with her own words.

She would be in for a rude awakening when she discovered everything she thought she knew about the Quarters was a lie. That there were five of them and only two held any real power.

"That's not entirely true," Lux gently retorted. "The Quarters were given our gifts to protect the coven, but there's nothing in Watchtower's bylaws that states we're meant to run it. In fact, the very existence of the elections suggests otherwise."

They volleyed ideas back and forth, not quite reaching any decision. They often brought the attention back to Mayor Douglas, who maintained the stance that he didn't think Rayner was a real threat. An hour later, the Quarters called the end of the covenstead and promised there would be another in the near future to iron out the details.

If Mayor Douglas thought he could slither away unnoticed and that they had forgotten about what he did, he was badly mistaken. As soon as the meeting was ended, nearly half of them rushed forward to speak to him personally. Stewart had his work cut out for him, keeping them at a far enough distance to step in if he had to. I took my time walking over to them, making sure he knew he made a mistake by trying to take me down with him.

There would be a shift in Beacon Grove after this. A clear line had been drawn between those who stood with Rayner and those who remained loyal to the Quarters—to Watchtower. Movement Members would no longer be able to hide in plain sight the way they have been, not if Quarter Supporters wanted to move beyond this.

Which is exactly why Douglas didn't want them to know. It was easy to keep the discontentment stifled when the majority were ignorant to the threat that loomed. He gave them a false sense of security for nearly six months, and the Quarters just ripped that away from them. But now that they were given a reason to fear—to defend what was theirs—there wasn't going to be anywhere for the Movement to hide.

And when they were forced to step out of the shadows, we'd be there to make them pay.

The ✳ Beacon

A QUARTER COMEBACK!

BREAKING: The Quarters are officially making their comeback!

In the largest covenstead turnout in decades, the Quarters updated Watchtower members on what they believe the future of the coven will look like. In the meeting, they discussed the possibility of electing other members into the High Priest and High Priestess roles, with the Quarters acting as council. This would be a huge shift to how their fathers wanted to handle things, and some members aren't happy about the prospect of a democracy within the coven.

The Quarters also revealed some gruesome details regarding the victims of Rayner Whittle's Movement. They stated that someone has been leaving the clothing that the victims were wearing when they were taken on dead animal carcasses in the woods surrounding the town, suggesting that Rayner and the Movement might now be gone, after all.

Mayor Douglas denies these statements, claiming that it was all just a "silly prank" being used to scare the people of Beacon Grove.

The Beacon is still gathering the most accurate and up-to-date information on this story.

CHAPTER TWENTY-FOUR

BLAIRE

Things were coming together for our plan against Rayner, but it still felt like we were missing something. Like there was a piece of the puzzle we still hadn't found, and that would be the one he used against us.

The covenstead went better than we expected it to, though. Doubt was placed on Mayor Douglas and the Quarters managed to get a few more people on their side, while proving they wanted to run things differently than their fathers had.

I wanted to stay back and make sure Kyle got out safely after Mayor Douglas tried to bring him down with him. He just subtly shook his head and sent a wink that told me he'd meet me at home later.

Before I could argue with him about it, Mom offered to walk me home and finally see my new place. She managed to keep her distance over the past few weeks, since the last night I lived with them at Grammy's. Between her midwifery clients, the pharmacy, and covering shifts for Grammy and me at the hotel while we trained with the Quarters, she really didn't have a lot of time to get out.

At least, that's what she claimed.

"It's such a *Blaire* space," she mused as we entered the main room, taking her time to absorb the tiny loft.

It felt smaller with her in here, like her big personality took up more space than the usual person's would.

"Is that a bad thing?"

"Not at all." Her lips spread in an easy smile. "I love it. I love that you did it."

I followed her to the couch, and we each took a seat. "Did what?"

"The one thing I couldn't ever find the strength to do: you got out." She turned to face me, tucking her leg underneath her body. Soft hands reached between us to grab my own. "I'm so proud of you."

I shrugged, looking down at a spot on the carpet. "I didn't have much of a choice. Things weren't good between me and Grammy."

"I know. I wish I could have done more."

And maybe it was the victory of the night, but something had me bravely asking in an accusatory tone, "Why *didn't* you? She listens to you."

Her smile faltered, morphing into a sad, contrite expression. There was a quiet moment where she debated what to say next. I almost convinced myself she was going to dance around the subject again, awkwardly dodging the elephant in the room. But instead, she surprised me by releasing a deep sigh, and then began explaining.

"I was so young when I had you. Younger than you are now. And I didn't have any idea who your father was, which invited a lot of nasty opinions of me. My mother was hounding me about the gifts... It was just so much at the time, and I think I fell into this pattern of allowing her to take over with you because it meant she wasn't pushing down on *me*. Like, I could breathe for a moment.

"And then I blinked, and that moment turned into years and she might as well have taken over the mother role completely." She looked down at our connected hands and sniffled. "I know it sounds horrible. It's such a cowardly excuse."

It wasn't, though. "It's exactly what I would have done."

"No, it's not. You're different than me. I've always felt like... like my mother is the vessel that delivered me into the world, but maybe she isn't my *true* family. We're truly nothing alike. Maybe that's why the gifts skipped me... I don't know." She swiped her finger across the bottom of her nose.

I couldn't imagine growing up and feeling that way. Like, the one person who should have accepted her for exactly who she was, was the one who shamed her for it. For all the things she may have handled wrong, for all of her flaws, Mom never made me feel like I was anything less than spectacular.

"Enough about me. I want to hear about your new landlord." She wiggled her brows.

"What does that mean?"

"Oh, please, Blaire. I saw the way he watched you across the room today."

I shook my head, biting my lip to hide the smile that was fighting its way through.

"He's a good man. A little old for you, but good nonetheless."

There was a moment I debated sharing the whole truth with her. To tell her about his odd gift and the way we bonded over it. How he understood being an outcast and never seemed to treat me the way everyone else in Beacon Grove always had. I wanted to gush with my mom over my first *real* experience with a man. But that openness I'd always felt with her seemed to have dried up somewhere along the way, stopping the words before they could pass through my mouth.

"I doubt it means anything," I disparaged.

"You can't fight the fates."

"I feel like us being together *is* fighting the fates."

All her amusement from before was instantly gone. "You know, Blaire, these gifts... they've been jumbled up the past few generations. Quarters and Counters have been shifted around, and just when we thought we knew the rules, they changed on us."

I knew all that.

"Okay. What are you saying?"

"I'm saying... there wasn't another child born within twelve hours of you, and as tradition suggests, there should have been. We checked into it."

She was referring to the rule set by the gods that Counters were always born within exactly twelve hours of their Quarter. It was how Rayner and the old Quarters attempted to hunt the current generation of Counters so they could weaken Remy, Rhyse, Lux, and Enzo by cutting off half their power source. The sick game forced families to hide their children if they ran the risk of being suspected, hence Storie's family taking her out of town at less than a week old.

It was also why Storie was the only Counter identified so far.

"So, I don't have a Counter at all, then?"

Mom squinted her eyes, contemplating her next words carefully. "Grammy and I have gone over this so many times. More so in the past few weeks, since you moved here."

"Okay... what is it?"

She scooted closer toward me and stretched her arm across the back of the couch, as if she wanted to be closer to me as she delivered her next words. "There wasn't a child born within twelve hours of *you*, but there was only one child born within twelve hours of *me*."

She didn't have to say who it was for me to know.

Kyle.

He was supposed to be Mom's Counter, had she inherited the gifts.

But she never did.

She nodded as my face morphed, the truth dawning on me.

"That undeniable connection you feel... it's there for a reason. So, allow yourself to go with it."

Mom stayed longer than I had expected her to. Long past when we heard Kyle's door open and close with his arrival back home. He must have known she was still here, though, because he didn't attempt to come up the stairs the way he suggested he would at the meeting.

I was grateful for the reprieve she provided.

I needed a chance to catch my breath after what she had told me. Time to wrap my head around the fact that this fling that me and Kyle had was so much more than we thought it was. That it was somehow decided by the gods long ago.

So, we drank wine and caught up. And when the alcohol pushed away the cloud of doubt that was hanging over my head, I actually felt like I had before any of the weight of being a Quarter was dropped on my shoulders. I felt like the carefree Blaire that no one seemed to like.

For the night, we were simply Callista and Blaire. Mother and daughter, sharing laughs and swapping anecdotal stories from the past few weeks.

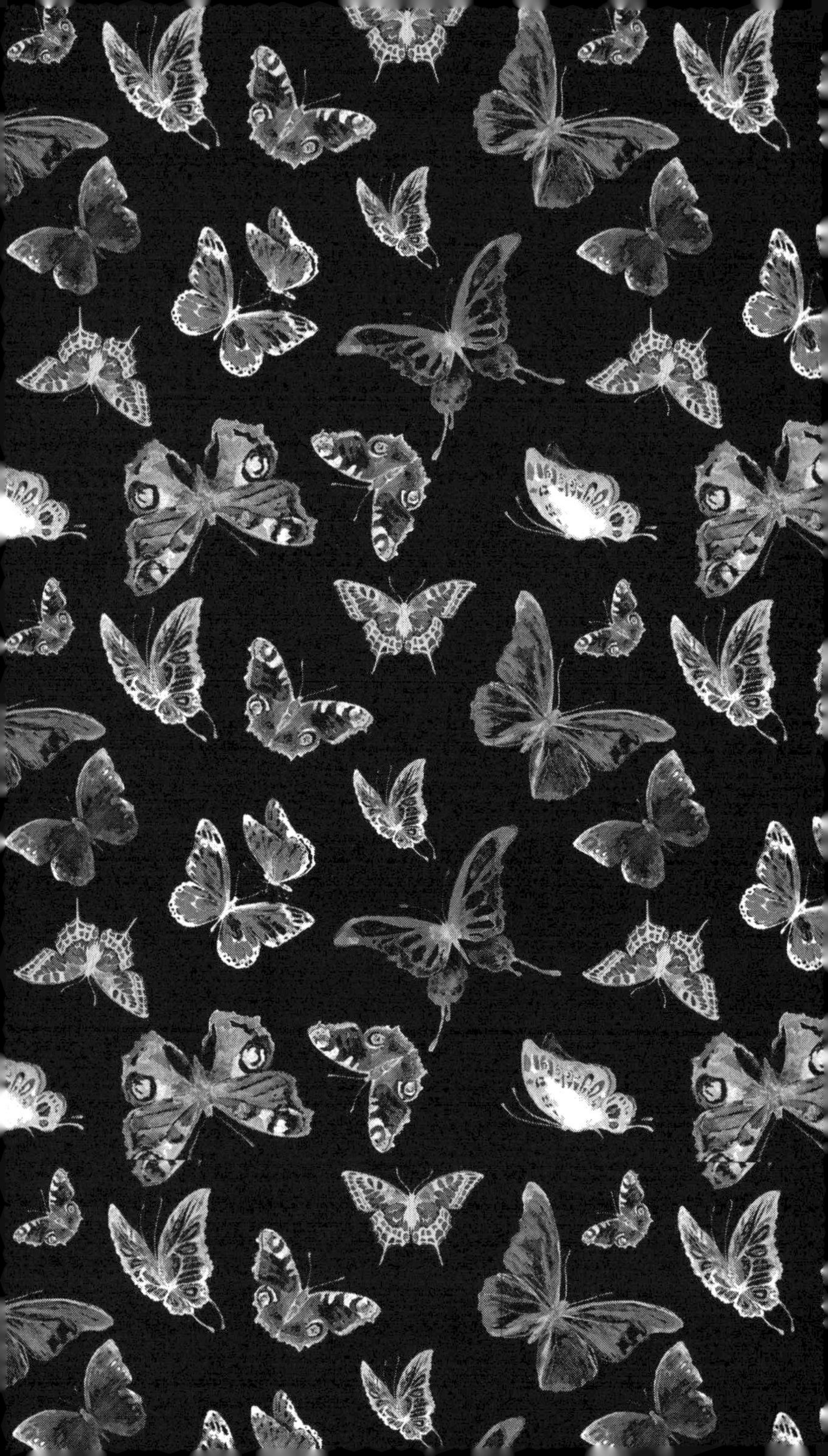

CHAPTER TWENTY-FIVE

KYLE — PAST

Police and emergency vehicles were haphazardly parked across Mason and Bonnie's lawn, in the driveway, and lining the street. I lifted the yellow caution tape over my head to go to the side door and a strong hand pushed against my chest, stopping me.

"This is a closed crime scene." Officer Cotteral's voice was rough and tired.

"Come on, Cotteral. You know I'm basically family." I stepped forward again, only to be pushed back.

"Go home, Kyle. You don't want to see what's behind that door," he warned, leveling me with a stern look.

He was trying to protect me. To spare me from a lifetime of being haunted by the images I was about to see—the grief I was about the experience. I wouldn't understand that for a few months, though. Instead, I was stubborn and irritated. I began loudly calling out for Mason from my spot on the lawn.

His head peeked through the door after a few moments of my shouting. He nodded for Cotteral to let me through, and the officer relented with a deep sigh.

My friend's face looked like he had aged ten years in the few hours since I last saw him. I had no idea what I was walking into. I was cutting through town to get home from the tavern when I heard the sirens, and then someone mentioned Bonnie's name and

I came running. In the heat of the moment, I hadn't even looked to see who said it.

From my spot in the kitchen, I could see paramedics quietly setting up a black bag on a stretcher that took up the entire living room. I couldn't see the couch from this angle, but I heard Bonnie's mom, Lunet's, guttural cries coming from somewhere behind the stretcher.

Mason led me into the nursery, where Asher was sitting in the rocking chair with Storie tightly tucked into her arms. She was quietly sobbing, her tears falling freely onto the swaddled clump.

I rushed over to her and kneeled at her feet, and my hands grasped each side of her head as I surveyed her for any injuries. When I couldn't find any, I used my thumbs to swipe away her tears as they flowed.

Mason watched the exchange with a detached expression, his eyes hollow.

"What happened?" I breathlessly asked.

Where is Bonnie?

Mason shook his head and looked over at his daughter, his face softening the tiniest bit when she stirred.

It was Asher's cold voice above that explained, "Rayner."

I looked back at her, my eyes searching her face for any clarification. Just as I was going to ask for more, the paramedics in the living room each counted to three and a loud thud sounded out. Lunet's cries grew louder, and my feet took me back down the hall before anyone could stop me.

They were zipping the bag over her face as I rounded the corner. If I were one step behind, I would have missed it.

I half expected her head to turn toward me at the last second. For those odd, violet eyes—staring lifelessly up at the ceiling—to blink. But none of that happened.

Lunet had thrown herself over her daughter's body as the paramedics finished zipping up the black bag, refusing to move when they politely asked. After allowing her a few more moments to say her goodbyes, they gently peeled her away and began wheeling Bonnie's body away.

And when the room had been cleared, I finally saw it: the blood.

Splattered all around the room, mostly concentrated on the white couch that Bonnie and Mason argued over for weeks. He thought it was a ridiculous color to choose with a baby coming, and she argued that it pulled the space together.

The homey space she worked so hard to create, which was now covered in crimson. In her.

I wanted to look away, but something kept me rooted in my spot, helplessly watching as they wheeled my best friend's body out the front door.

It didn't make any sense. We were just together, laughing about Mason's blunders as a new dad. Comparing the beautiful little girl's face to her parents—Bonnie insisted she was a carbon copy of her father, and Mason pretended he didn't notice.

It all just happened. I swear, I could still hear her voice, and her quiet giggles echoing off the splattered walls.

She couldn't be gone.

Present

"What the hell was that, Abbot?" Mayor Douglas shouted as he entered the double-doors of the station. The two junior officers sitting at their desks jerked up to attention, their hands instinctively reaching for their weapons from his outburst.

"Nice to see you, too, Mayor Douglas," I purred sarcastically through my office door, not bothering to stand and greet him.

His round figure practically rolled through the station, just barely fitting through the gaps between desks.

By the time he reached me, his breathing had already grown labored.

"What game do you think you're playing with those boys?" His loud voice boomed off the cinderblock walls.

He lasted a whole two days before hobbling his way in here to find me.

The two officers stood up, silently asking me if they should step in. I shook my head, then stood to usher the mayor into my office so I could close the door.

Not that it mattered. They'd likely hear every word if he continued shouting.

"I don't know what you're referring to, Mayor. The Quarters and the coven asked their questions, and I gave them answers."

"How did they know about the clothes?" he asked, seething.

I knew this was coming. I had considered long and hard what I would do when he questioned me. There were whispers about the animal carcasses, but as far as he knew, no one was aware of the detail of the clothing—just a few of my officers and the mayor.

My initial instinct was to lay all the blame on Tabitha. No one would think twice about it, and no one would bother going after her, either. In fact, they'd expect it.

But we were on the edge of war in Beacon Grove—the city I swore an oath to protect. And the people I care about were going to be caught in the crossfire. They had been for years, since I watched Bonnie get wheeled out of her home in a body bag. Since I watched Asher and Mason drive out of town.

When this story was told to future generations, I wanted to be on the right side of history.

"I told them."

My admission fueled his anger even further. He flailed his hands in the air, creating a spectacle. "Why would you do that?! We agreed..." He stepped closer toward me, and I offered him one warning look to step away before he started something he couldn't finish. Realizing his disadvantage, he obliged and backed into the office door, then tried again.

"We agreed you'd keep this under wraps until we could find answers."

"With all due respect, Mayor..." I shot him a look that said the opposite. "Something tells me you've done everything in your power *not* to find answers."

"You don't know what you've started, Kyle. I've done my best to hold them back. There's no stopping what's about to come."

"What are you saying?"

I wanted him to admit it. I wanted to hear him say that while Beacon Grove was suffering at his hand for the sake of safety, he had been priming us to be an easy target for our enemy.

He quickly realized his mistake, though. His mouth tightened into a tight line as his words resonated. He lifted his hands in surrender.

"I don't know what I'm saying. I've just been blindsided by this whole thing," he backtracked.

His left hand reached behind him then, twisting the doorknob so he could make his escape.

"Just remember, Mayor," I said in a low, warning tone. "There's going to be a winning side and a losing side in this fight. You're dangerously teetering on the line between the two. I'd suggest you pick a side before one gets picked for you."

He stared at me for a beat, brows raised high onto his forehead. Then, without another word, he turned on his heel and waddled back toward the doors he came in.

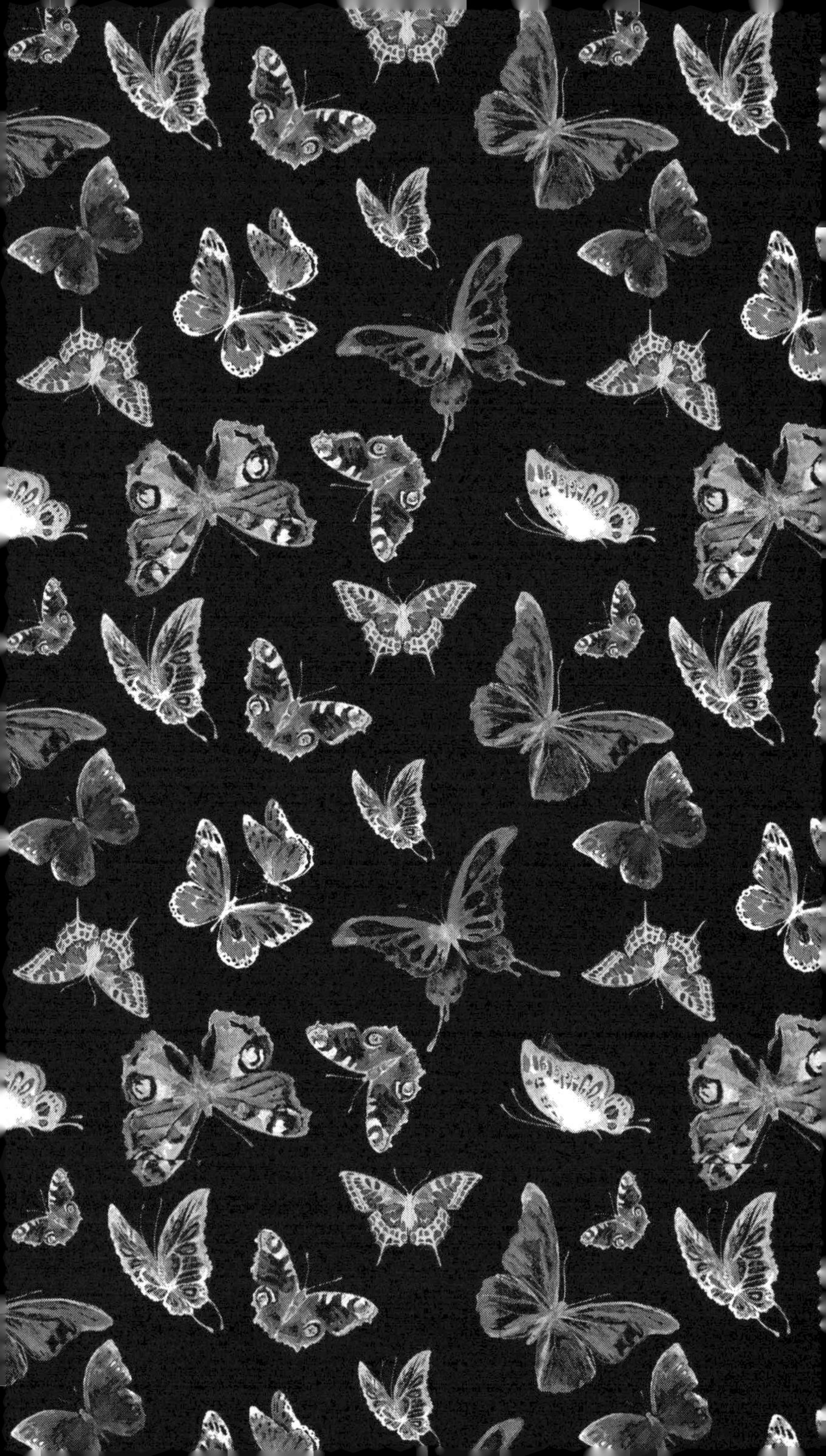

CHAPTER TWENTY-SIX

BLAIRE

Kyle had another set of victim's clothing to show me, so we could attempt to make contact with their spirit. I was losing hope that any of them would remember the horrible things the Movement had done to them. The ways they defiled their bodies. But Kyle clung onto the idea that we only needed *one* to remember. To give us some semblance of an idea of where to look.

He led me through the station as he'd done three times before, only this time, no other officers were at their desks. It was well into the early morning hours by the time he peeled himself away from me to drive us through town and into the station. The lights were only on halfway, and save for Randy, the town drunk, mumbling in one of the holding cells, we were mostly alone.

Amy Bishop's spirit appeared with less force than the others had. Her small figure fizzled into the room, eyes wide and bouncing around.

"What's going on?" she asked, glancing at the table where her clothes lay.

Rayner's favorite spot to grab women was the Watchtower Tavern. I knew because most of his victims were either waitresses there, or were clad in skimpy clothing that suggested they were enjoying a night out when they were captured.

Amy was the latter, wearing a black cropped tank top and tight leather shorts with fishnet stockings. Her feet were clad in a pair of combat boots that apparently weren't a part of the Movement's disgusting animal display because they were the only part of her outfit that wasn't sitting on the table before us.

Once we got past the awkward, 'you're dead and we're trying to figure out why,' talk, Amy proved to be the most useful spirit we'd encountered.

And the most annoying.

"Do you remember anything about where you were taken?" Kyle asked, his usual optimism lacing his tone.

Amy thought for a moment, then nodded. "Yeah, I do. It was somewhere in the woods. Near the Forbes property. I remember thinking it was weird he took us out there, given how much he hated them."

"Us?"

"Yeah, there were three of us taken. Me and my two friends were celebrating their bachelorette party. They had just gotten engaged."

Me and Kyle shared an excited look. She actually remembered. This was huge.

"I wish I'd paid more attention to you when it mattered," she purred, standing as close to Kyle as she could without misting through him.

I scowled at her. "Put your tongue back in your mouth."

"I'd rather put it somewhere else." She dropped her eyes to his crotch and smirked.

"Yeah, that's not how that works."

"We'll make it work somehow."

I looked to him for help, my eyes widening at her brazen attitude. "Why do they always flirt with you?" I whined.

He shrugged, his brows lifting as he started to answer before Amy cut him off.

"I think it's the uniform." She dragged her hand over his chest, and it disappeared. "It doesn't leave much to the imagination."

I quickly ended things with her after that. Kyle politely sent her on her way to wherever they went, and we closed up the evidence locker, making sure to leave everything just as we found it.

When we left the room, one of the younger officers sat at his desk with his back to us. I glanced over to Kyle's office and tugged his hand, not giving myself a chance to rethink my decision.

He stopped and turned to see what I was trying to say, then glanced back at the officer to remind me we weren't alone. I sucked my bottom lip into my mouth and raised a brow, challenging him.

His resolve didn't last long before he allowed me to lead him over to his office. With a quick glance back at the officer, who still hadn't bothered to turn around, we slipped inside and quietly shut the door behind us with a soft, nearly inaudible click.

Three of the walls were made up of floor-to-ceiling glass windows looking into the station, while the back wall had a large window overlooking the empty parking lot. Blinds covered two of the interior walls and I assumed it was to stop the evening sun from shining on him, only leaving us exposed on two sides.

I looked over and saw the door to the evidence room we just came from, but the officer's desk had been on the other side of the station, currently blocked from view, as was Randy's cell.

"What are you doing?" Kyle whispered as I slowly shut the paper curtain to the small window on his door—the only spot we could be seen from.

I didn't bother answering. Instead, I walked back to where he stood and grabbed the back of his neck, pulling his lips down to meet mine.

It didn't take much coercion for him to reciprocate the kiss and before I knew it, the backs of my thighs were hitting his desk.

"We have to be quiet," he warned as I worked on the buttons of his shirt.

I nodded half-heartedly, but he stopped my hands and forced me to look at him.

"Fine," I hissed.

Impatient with the buttons, I opted to abandon the mission halfway down and untucked his uniform shirt, then pulled it over his head.

He loosened his belt, and then slammed his mouth back into mine, as if he couldn't wait any longer.

His hands cupped behind my knees and lifted me onto the desk. A few random knick-knacks tipped over and crashed onto the ground, and he hissed out a string of cuss words as he scrambled to grab the rest. He paused, listening for any sign that the officer was coming to investigate. When it was clear he wasn't, he blew out a relieved breath.

With careful hands, he set the remaining items down onto a table behind him, and then turned back to me to rip my leggings off in one swift motion.

I yelped, and he covered my mouth with his, biting down on my tongue as punishment. I smiled against him, and our teeth clanged against each other as he used one hand to shove his pants and briefs down enough for his erection to spring free while the other pushed my shirt above my breasts.

Once that was done, his hand reached between my legs and gently swiped his fingers against my center, gauging my readiness.

He snickered into my mouth as he discovered I was dripping wet, and I slapped his shoulder bashfully. There was something about the prospect of being caught—of being so out in the open—that turned me on. And after seeing Amy so close to him, I couldn't wait for us to get home. I had to have him now.

Thankfully, he was more than willing to oblige.

He made quick work of lining himself up against me and pushed inside, torturously slow. When I glanced up at him with a question in my eyes, he flicked his brows up and smirked teasingly.

He was punishing me again.

I grabbed the back of his neck and pulled him back to my mouth, then leaned back onto the desk so he had to hover over me. It forced him deeper inside, and all his teasing was gone.

The air filled with quick, heavy breaths as he pumped into me. He shifted, then grabbed my left leg and draped it over his shoulder, so he had better access when he rubbed his finger against my swollen clit.

I inhaled a sharp breath and arched my back, so close to reaching euphoria. It stopped when Kyle's movements suddenly stilled. He turned his head to listen outside of the office again.

There was distant murmuring between the officer and Randy, but it didn't seem like either of them had realized we were here yet.

His body leisurely began working against mine again, and he turned his attention back to me with a wicked, mischievous smile as he realized we weren't going to be caught. His right hand returned between my legs, and he drove into me harder, caressing my inner thigh with his other as he peppered kisses along the spots his fingers brushed.

Worshiping me.

My orgasm came swiftly and powerfully, coursing through my body in red-hot waves. I swung my arm over my mouth to stifle my moans as I tensed up beneath him. The sensation reached all the way down to my toes.

Kyle leaned forward again, stretching my leg as he pulled my arm away and replaced it with his mouth. He swallowed my whimpering and picked up his speed as I pulsed around him, until I felt him twitch inside me.

His warm liquid filled me, and he pulled away far enough to stare into my eyes. A lustful haze surrounded him as stars danced around in his swirly grays.

Once our breathing calmed back down, he placed a kiss on my nose and then backed off of me.

"That's probably going to be my favorite image of you," he rasped, taking another step back to fully absorb the vision of me sprawled out on his desk. "How am I ever going to get work done in here without imagining you?"

I scoffed and rolled my eyes at his pig-headedness, and then hopped off to get dressed again.

By the time we were finished, the officer had disappeared, and we walked out unseen. When we got back to the house, Kyle tugged me through his door, and we got started on round two.

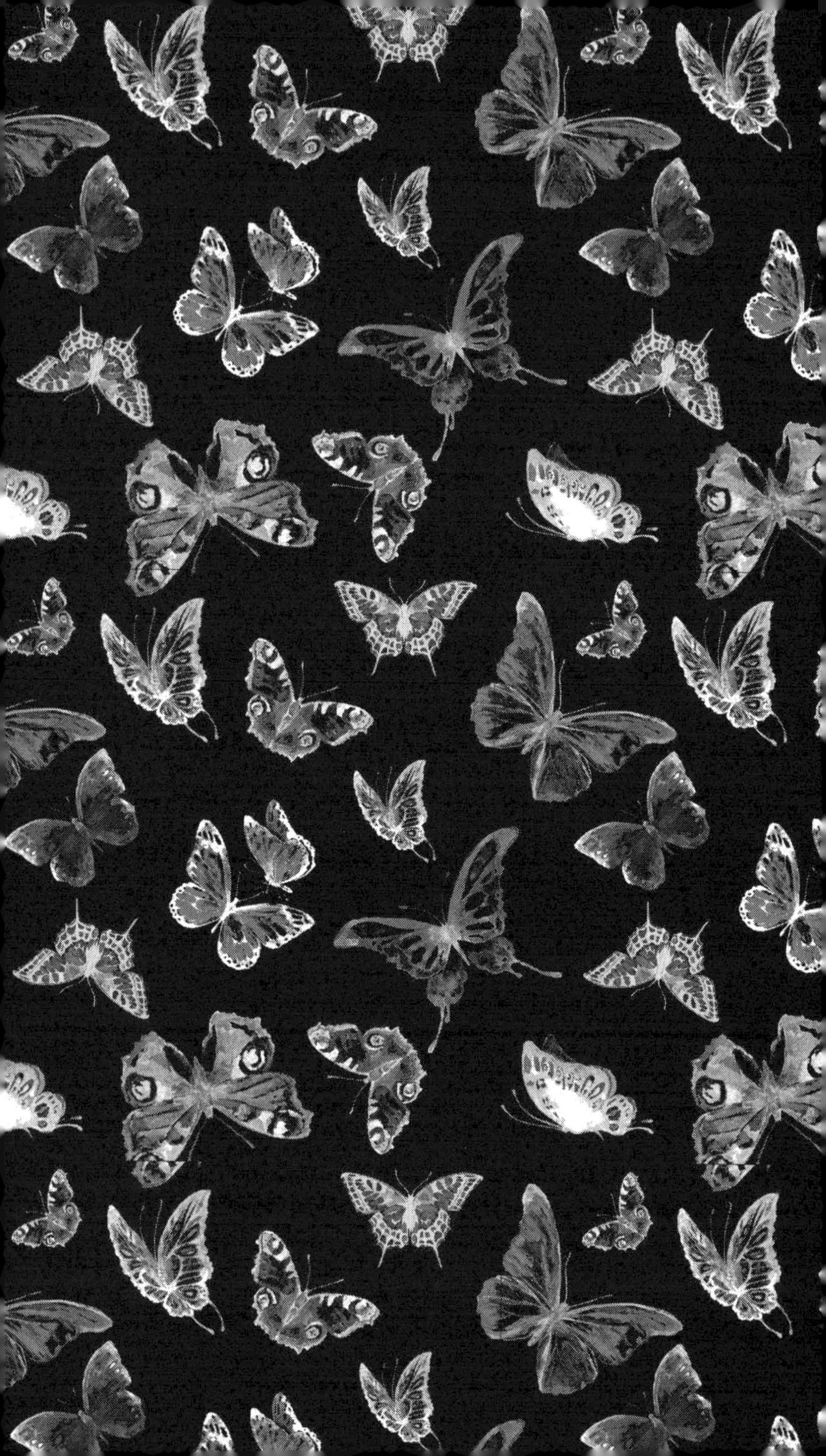

CHAPTER TWENTY-SEVEN

BLAIRE

Movement Members were being exposed by Quarter Supporters in droves.

It became a sport for some. Neighbors turned on each other overnight. Business owners were reported, resulting in their businesses being closed and looted. Each day began calm and orderly, only to turn into chaos by dinnertime as more were revealed.

People who were a part of our everyday lives had proven to be untrustworthy, and no one was safe from accusation.

Maisy Sanford, the owner of my favorite diner in town—although, Storie had already sworn she saw her at Rayner's bonfire. Her strong alibi got her out of police questioning, but we knew it was fake.

Esther Newberry, our ancient librarian—also someone Storie had named after the bonfire. Somehow, she had an alibi, too. Until her daughter-in-law reported her with evidence to back it up.

Shane Gardener, the new post office worker.

Someone even nailed a list to the gazebo in the town square, updating it each time a new Member was caught. They called it the Member Manifest.

Those who were guilty had to answer to the Quarters.

The mystery surrounding where they were taken after someone from one of the four Quarter's estates wheeled them away was a beast that had grown a life of its own.

I was torn as I watched my home be ripped to shreds from the inside out. The disorder was worse than when Rayner and the Movement were at their strongest. At least back then, we could blame it on the black magic stirring up the town.

Now, it was all our own doing.

Grammy and the Quarters promised it would all be worth it in the end. That with so many of his Members being exposed and unable to carry out whatever plans he had, Rayner would be forced to leave hiding.

At first, they watched each Member get hauled away with vicious smiles on their faces, happy to see the result of months of work come into fruition.

But I saw the worry wearing them down as each day ended with more and more people being accused. Many of them screamed and wailed that they were innocent, thrashing around in the bodyguards' hands. Though, no one listened.

I felt their anxious anticipation each morning from afar as I watched them walk to that list and check whose name was added overnight.

Kyle probably beat himself up about it the most, caught between his obligation to keep the town safe and his desire to push Rayner out of hiding.

They were all afraid the tiny slice of power that was given to the people of our town had gone to their heads. That they would destroy each other before Rayner ever got the chance.

And their fear was justified.

Those who I grew up idolizing had proven to be nothing but monsters. Some were even traitorous Members. And my anger from before roared back to life.

I wasn't allowed to be seen with my allies. Not yet. We were waiting for the right moment to unveil my gifts.

Even Grammy kept her distance from the four men who walked through town like grim reapers. They didn't want to risk Rayner or the Movement catching on to the fact that I possessed enough power in one finger to crush his heart to pieces without more than a thought. Especially now that I knew Kyle was my Counter.

Sitting back and watching the fray from the sidelines was no fun, either.

Rhyse and Enzo continued taking turns giving me lessons on mastering the physical aspect of my gifts. I'd meet them at the cabin with the sun, and we'd spar into the late afternoon. Sometimes, Remy would take some time for us to bounce ideas off one another about the spirits that haunted me without my consent, but he and Lux were usually the ones who went to town to pick up the newest batch of traitors for the day.

Hailey had remained by my side most of the time, peppering in her annoying insults here and there. But I think the spark that once kept her hopeful and alive was fizzling out. She was realizing what a daunting task we were taking on and losing hope that she'd ever be found.

"You're leaving your left side unguarded," Enzo reminded me for the tenth time that morning.

I let out a frustrated growl and threw my gloves on the ground, reaching for my water. "This is useless. When am I ever going to be fighting someone like this? Shouldn't we be focusing on training my gifts?" I complained.

Enzo stared at me unblinkingly, his gaze far off. "I used to ask my dad the same question."

He closed the distance between us and fell onto the ground beside my feet, gesturing for me to sit with him. When I obliged, he went on. "He used to tell me that I might not always have my gifts to lean on if something ever came up. That it was better to be prepared than to be sorry."

I squinted at him. That was a crock of shit. We'd always have our gifts.

But as soon as the thought entered my head, I knew that wasn't true. Last year, when Storie came into town and Rayner was at his strongest, the Quarters had been nearly depleted of their powers.

"I used to think it was bullshit, too. I hated training with him. The others always bragged about practicing their gifts, while I was stuck using my hands like some sort of ape. But I think he knew, even back then, that something like this was coming. And despite his greed, he wanted me to be prepared."

We allowed his words to marinate for a moment. I still thought training like this was a waste of time that we didn't have, but maybe Enzo was right. I might not be able to master the power to control the earth like him in this short span of time, but I could certainly learn to block my left side in case I had to go up against a Movement Member in a fight.

"What's going on out here?" Rhyse called from the doorway of the cabin. Smoke filled the air as the grass beside us caught on fire and we both leaped up to our feet, cursing the crazy pyromaniac.

"You're supposed to be training, Little B," he taunted.

Enzo swiped away a flame that had caught on his pants, a string of curse words leaving his mouth as his skin burned from the contact. "We were taking a break, you prick. You're replacing these pants. I'm sick of repairing burn holes from your temper tantrums."

Rhyse barked out a laugh, and the two went back and forth, throwing insults at each other. I couldn't stop thinking about what Enzo had said, though. It sent a string of nervous energy straight through me that had me standing back up and abruptly interrupting their bickering, so we could resume.

Rhyse even joined in, and they both became determined to help me strengthen my left side's defense.

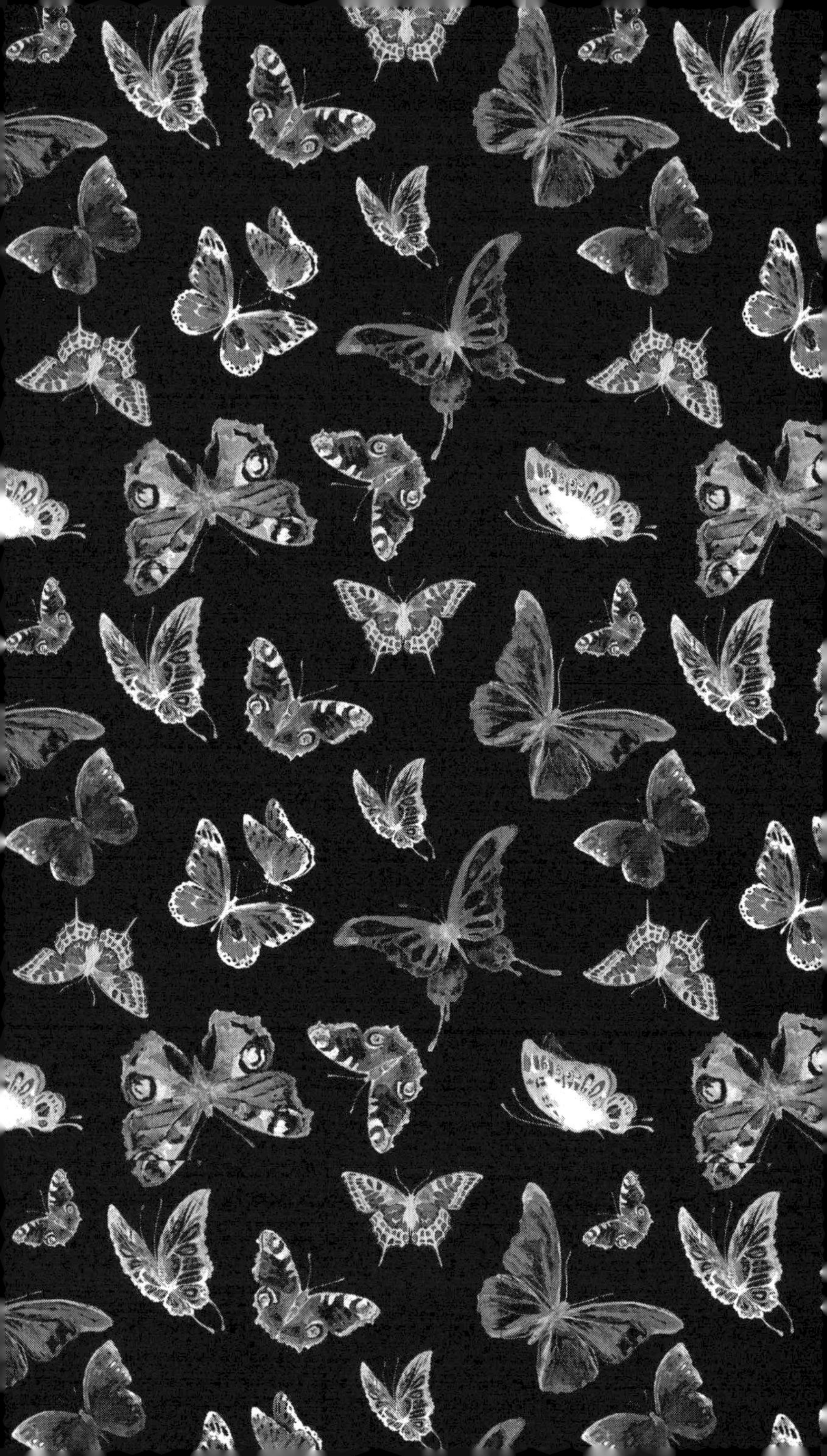

CHAPTER TWENTY-EIGHT

KYLE — PAST

I stayed with Mason and Asher long into the morning. Police took their statements, combed the house for evidence, urging us to find some place else to stay for the night. When Mason refused, a couple of the officers who were closest to us in age—who knew Bonnie personally—hung back to help clean up.

Once they had all cleared out, the four of us remained on the floor of Storie's room, the rhythm of her tiny breaths filling the silence.

"We have to leave," Mason croaked. It was the first time he'd spoken in what felt like hours.

I went to object, when Asher nodded her agreement.

"What? No. We have to make that fucker pay for what he's done," I argued. I still wasn't even sure what, exactly, Rayner had done here, but he was as good as dead, nonetheless. "We can't let Bonnie's death go unpunished."

"He came here for Storie. Bonnie sacrificed herself to save her," Asher gently explained.

"Bonnie gave her life to save our little girl. I can't let that be in vain."

My friend had changed. Not just since he found the love of his life dead mere hours ago, but in the past nine months. He was different now—a true family man. Nothing meant more to him *than his girls, and now that one of them was gone, I could tell he was floundering.*

"We'll make sure he doesn't touch Storie." I'd stand guard outside this house myself if I had to. Let Rayner try this again with his Movement bullshit.

"We have to go, Kyle," Asher's tired voice said. There was no room for argument in her tone. They made their decision well before I walked through that door.

"Okay, fine. When do we leave?"

"We're going. You have to stay here."

Mason stood from the floor and started packing the diaper bag with random things. A pacifier. A stack of diapers. A package of wipes. He paused when one of Bonnie's hair ties fell out of the diaper caddy, staring down at it like it had grown a head and come to life.

Asher gently leaned over to set Storie in the crib, then walked over to her brother and wrapped her arm around his shoulders. They shook under her grip with the quiet sobs he was finally letting free, and I decided it wasn't the time to argue.

Whatever they had planned, I knew it would be what was best for Storie. That's really all that mattered at this point.

I lifted my body off the carpet and pulled Asher into my chest. I don't know how long the three of us stood there like that, mourning the loss of our friend. She was the glue that held us together. A future without her seemed bleak and gray, but we'd get through it. We'd make things right, for Storie.

✦

Asher and Mason didn't change their minds about me staying back. They spent the early morning packing up Mason's car with anything they could think of, working together in silence.

When Storie was secured in her car seat and Mason was in the driver's seat, Asher pulled me off to the side.

"I can come with you. We don't even have to stop at my house. Everything I need is in that car," I begged one last time, gesturing behind her.

She shook her head, wrapping her hands around her torso in a hug. "You can meet us when we land somewhere," she offered, and something about the way she said it told me it was a lie to make our goodbye easier.

Still, I nodded, then pulled her into my chest, inhaling her sweet scent for the last time.

"I love you so much, Ash. I love you all so much."

"We love you, too, Kyle. But we have to handle this as a family."

As a family. Those words stabbed into my chest like a dull knife.

They were my family. If the roles were reversed, it wouldn't have been a second thought to throw them into the car and head off together. I thought they felt the same way about me, too. But for some reason, in the darkest time of their lives, they decided their blood was thicker. A deeper bond.

I held her until her hands pushed against my stomach. We locked eyes one last time.

This was it. I knew it, but I wouldn't allow myself to believe it.

This isn't what Bonnie would have wanted. Still, I fooled myself into thinking it was the right thing to do, because they believed so deeply that it was.

As she fell into the passenger seat, I leaned down to shake hands with Mason, pulling him into a one-armed hug through the door, whispering in his ear, "I love you, man. Stay safe."

And with one last look in the backseat, at the little girl who we were all doing this for, I stepped away from their car and watched as they drove off, the rising sun lighting their way.

Present

Each time someone was accused of being a Movement Member, the Quarters would have them hauled off into the dungeons beneath their homes. They weren't treated like proper prisoners, though, despite the nasty rumors floating around.

They were provided three gourmet meals, regular showers, comfortable beds, and were free to roam around the underground portion of the property as they pleased. They just couldn't leave, and they couldn't communicate with a single soul outside of those dungeons. There were spells cast to ensure it.

I didn't think they deserved such lavish living conditions for betraying their friends, family, and neighbors by following the gospel of a complete madman, but it wasn't up to me. The Quarters wanted the illusion of corporal punishment without actually having it weigh on their conscious.

"We're still working toward a future where this town trusts us," Lux had said when Enzo and Rhyse complained.

"These are the ones who have already turned on us. We need to make an example out of them, so no one thinks we're weak," Rhyse argued.

"That's why they're hidden away underground. For the illusion."

"Our main objection is to lure Rayner out of hiding and force him to face us without his army of Movement Members," Remy gently reminded them.

"No, my main objective is to show the Movement what happens when you fight the will of the gods," Enzo grumbled. Rhyse grunted and nodded his agreement.

If they had their way, the Movement Members would have been persecuted in the town square, for all to see. They were harboring a rage toward Rayner and the Movement that rivaled my own. They wanted full use of their gifts, and they blamed him for the fact that they still didn't have it. That they still hadn't found their Counter.

They channeled every ounce of frustration over it into the people who chose to side with the Movement. If I didn't already want all of the Movement dead, I'd fear for their lives.

Before they brought them into their homes, the members would wait in a holding cell at the station. I took the opportunity to dig into their minds for any information I could find about where Rayner might be hiding.

I still hadn't told anyone but Blaire about the gift. I knew my time was running out, though. The Quarters would question how I got my information, if I ever got any. But I put that part off, deciding to deal with it when the time came.

It had been two weeks of searching through minds before I caught a tiny breadcrumb. Rayner truly hadn't trusted any of his Movement Members with his whereabouts.

With the exception of Shane Gardener.

A post office employee who had taken over when our old mailman, Doug, retired. He was accused by his neighbor, who overheard him speaking to someone about Rayner in his garage late at night. Coincidentally, his new employment aligned perfectly with the height of Rayner's Movement propaganda.

It took me fifteen minutes to break into his subconscious—a grim and desolate place—and I discovered that he was responsible for bringing Rayner into town undetected in his mail truck.

It was the perfect decoy. No one thought twice about the young mail carrier making multiple trips in and out of town each day.

I wanted to kick myself for not considering it before.

Rayner wasn't one to get his hands dirty. I knew that he mostly used others to do his bidding; I just wasn't sure how he was communicating with them. How had he kept in contact with all these people without being caught? It was the biggest question we had. If we could figure that out, we could cut him off and force him out of his hiding spot.

Shane's thoughts revealed the answer. They were relaying messages to one another through spelled mirrors in their homes.

I probed deeper into his mind for an image of what the mirror looked like and almost lost my lunch. It was identical to the one Blaire had sitting on her vanity. The one we picked up from Dottie Lawson's estate sale.

She must have been a Member without us knowing.

Has he been watching her all this time?

I shook the thought from my mind before my rage could get the best of me. I only had a few more minutes in Shane's mind before he realized I was there. He was already shifting in his spot as I pulled memories forward that he hadn't recalled on his own.

I made one last strike against his subconscious, wading through the useless material for any answers about where Rayner was keeping his victim's bodies. If Shane was trusted with transporting the sadistic leader, he could surely be trusted with that information.

Within seconds, I saw them.

Nearly two dozen girls huddled together, clad in only their undergarments. Their faces blackened with dirt and hollowed out, their bodies made of skin and bones and nothing more. I recognized the ones me and Blaire had made contact with at the police station within the crowd. They were in a small clearing in the woods, surrounded by sprawling elder trees that kept them hidden away.

And every single one of them was still alive.

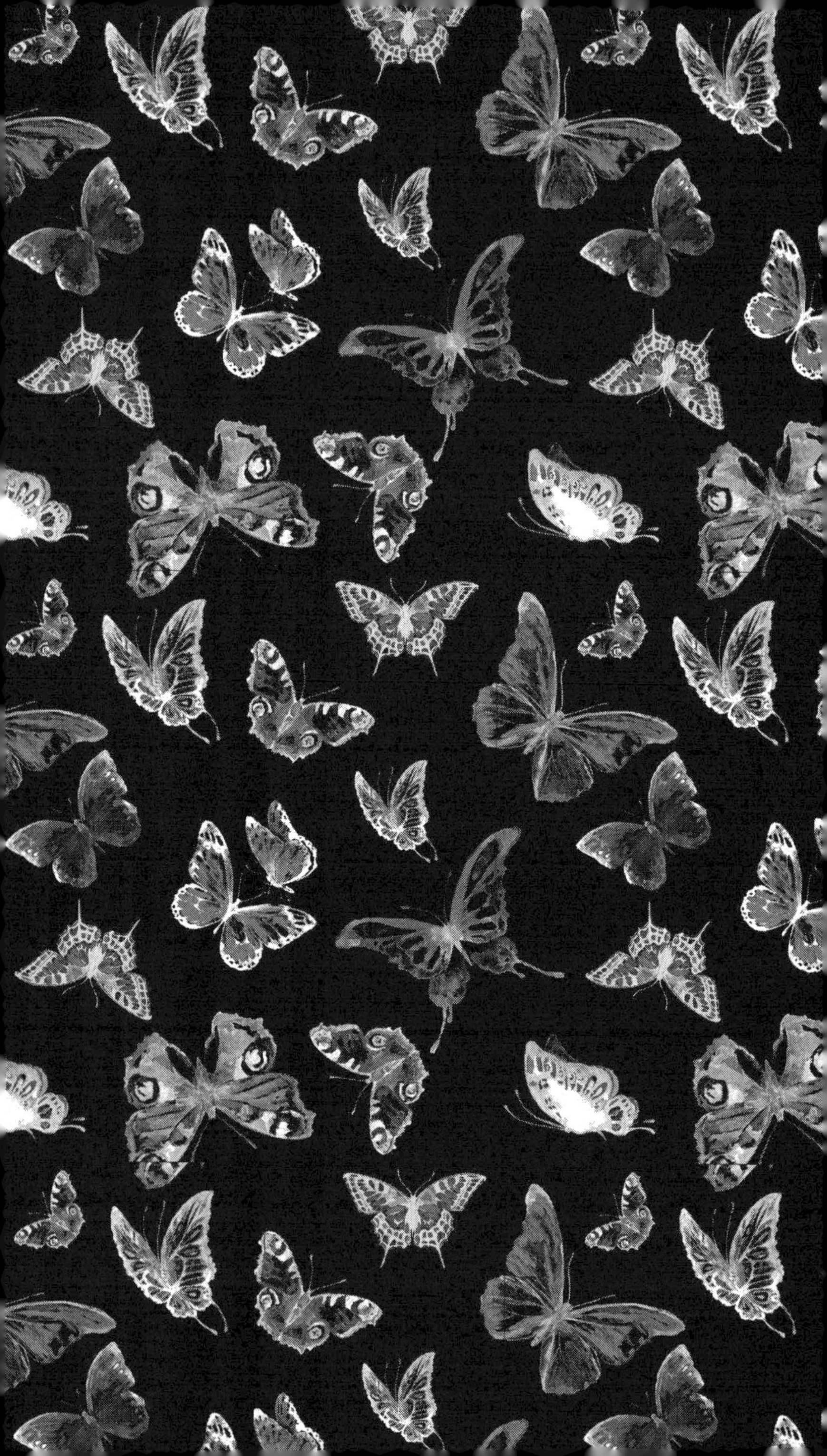

CHAPTER TWENTY-NINE

BLAIRE

"Do you feel anything?"

I looked around at the forestry surrounding us, completely void of emotion. Hailey stood to my left, her ghostly eyes searching for something—anything. But I knew this wasn't it before she had the chance to shake her head.

We were wrong again.

She looked down at the sticks and leaves beneath her feet, unaffected by her misty existence.

"We'll try again," I assured her. I'm not sure why I felt the need to say anything.

I knew this was hard for her. That putting her through this, only to find out we still hadn't gotten it right, was breaking down her will to exist. And neither of us wanted to find out what happened to a spirit that no longer wanted to exist.

"I was sure this was it," Kyle mumbled. He turned around and missed Hailey's sneer at his back.

"We're getting close. I can feel it. There're more spirits nearby."

It was like the buzzing of a beehive. A low vibration deep inside the earth. I wanted to follow it, but each time I tried, I ended up empty-handed and walking in circles.

Hailey didn't bother answering. She fizzled out and disappeared before I could ask her to stop. To help.

I blew out a breath, and Kyle scratched his head.

"I wish you'd stop calling them spirits," he grumbled as he walked over to one of the elder oak trees and looked around its base.

"It doesn't make sense for me to be seeing them if they're alive," I argued for the hundredth time.

He had it in his head that after seeing the girls still alive in Shane's memory, they were out here, in some sort of world in-between worlds.

"I think they're stuck in a fold," he said again, giving up on looking around the trees.

"Or they're buried underground."

He shot me an irritated look. "This is right where they were. I confirmed it in Shane's mind. This is where they were waiting."

His brows scrunched together. "There's got to be something wrong."

"Maybe they took them somewhere else since then," I offered.

"They didn't. I saw them all, Blaire..." He cleared his throat, finding it difficult to speak his next words. "I watched them huddle together in terror right here, like sheep awaiting slaughter."

I instantly felt guilty for giving him such a hard time. Even if it didn't seem plausible to me, it was worth exploring. That was why I admired him so much.

He was willing to go insane trying to find the truth.

"We'll find a different way. This is too hard for all of us. If there's a blockage or a shield, we won't get through it—not alone."

We walked beside each other distractedly, when Kyle nudged my arm, silently communicating for me to take a left. I obliged, and we walked another fifty feet before we reached an oddly shaped weeping willow. Its trunk curved this way and that, refusing to conform and grow into a straight line like the trees surrounding it.

A break in the woods revealed a meadow of tall grass surrounding a spring. The water was a deep blue with small, white wisps of steam dancing off the surface.

Such a small piece of heaven buried in the thickest part of the woods.

"How did you know this was here?"

Storie and I had obsessively studied maps of Beacon Grove when she was looking for answers about her family and we never came across anything like this. I would have remembered.

He looked around with the same amazement I felt. "Mason and Bonnie found it. We would skip school and come out here to hide out."

We strolled over to the creek, and I peered inside, shocked to find the water so clear I could see straight to the rocky bottom. When I turned back to Kyle, he was staring at me with an easy, boyish grin on his lips.

"What?" I asked, self-consciously tugging on my braid.

He laughed, and for the first time, he actually looked relaxed. No longer the tense sheriff responsible for the town's safety. Out here, he was free of it all, and the difference in his physical appearance was almost jarring. I had the fleeting thought about what he must have been like as a teen out here.

"I haven't made this trek in a long time. I'm glad I brought you with me."

A shy smile was my only response before I turned back to the water and dipped my hand in. It was deliciously warm, practically calling for me to slip inside.

My eyes found him again, still rooted in the same spot.

"Can we swim in it?" I asked.

He slipped his hands into his pockets and shrugged. "Usually. But I think we forgot bathing suits."

An idea sprang into my mind, and I smirked at him, toeing the tennis shoes off my feet. He knew what I was doing before I could explain, already having read my thoughts.

Still, his eyes widened as I slipped my fingers into the sides of my shorts and slid them down, exposing the blue lace thong I thanked the gods I chose to wear today. I kept my gaze locked on his as I reached for the bottom of my shirt, lifting it over my head with less grace than I intended.

The matching bra was on full display now, and Kyle looked like he wanted to pounce on me. He remained still, though; those steely blue eyes the only thing moving as they followed me to the edge of the spring. Before hesitation could slow me down, I slunk down into the warm water.

I inhaled a deep breath and focused on gaining my footing on the rocks at the bottom. When I was standing straight again, I lifted my eyes and found Kyle peering over me from the edge of the spring, a heady expression marring his face.

"Join me," I purred with a coy smile.

He didn't hesitate another moment.

In a flash, his shirt was on the ground, exposing the taut muscles I'd grown to love running my tongue over these past few weeks. His shorts came next and before I even had a chance to appreciate his choice of boxer briefs, he was slinking into the water and walking toward me.

I could tell there was so much he wanted to say. So many reasons why we shouldn't do this out here dancing on the tip of his tongue. But this place was too perfect, and we were all alone. The rest of the world didn't matter. So, before he could breathe life into those negative thoughts, I leaned forward and lightly brushed my lips against his.

His body remained still, save for the hand that found my waist in the water, and those long fingers dug in when I opened my mouth to welcome him in. His arousal rubbed against my center, swaying between my legs with the water, only separated by a couple of pieces of fabric.

I knew I had him then.

In one split second, he had my other leg wrapped around his torso, his arms fully encasing me. His teeth dug into my bottom lip. In the next, he was rocking against me, allowing his erection to glide against my sex. His tongue gently soothed the spot he'd just bit, and then slipped inside my mouth, teasing.

A moan filled the air between us. I'm not sure if it was his or mine, though it could have been both. In that moment, our bodies melded together to become one giant piece of abstract art.

This was a union set by the gods—created long ago, before either of us existed as a speck in the universe. Kyle was born to be my mother's Counter, but the gods knew he belonged to me.

And they saved him for me.

There was absolutely no denying that fact as our souls danced together to our bodies' rhythm.

The sopping wet, sticky clothing between us disappeared, a barrier neither of us could stand any longer. He reached his hand around my backside and his fingers teased me, sending shock waves through my body without hardly touching me.

He chuckled at the breath that hissed through my teeth, and then pushed a finger inside me with a devious grin.

When I adjusted to one finger, he pushed a second one in and I jerked forward with a yelp. The water caught me, and its soft embrace tugged me back into him. He wrapped his other arm around my waist to hold me steadily in place and continued moving his fingers inside of me. His teeth nibbled on my earlobe and as his breaths hit the back of my neck, I came undone in his arms.

My cries of pleasure echoed off the trees surrounding us. Bird wings flapped in panic as they flew away, startled by the noise. He snickered in my ear as I writhed around against his chest, a sensation unlike no other shooting through my arms, legs, chest—everywhere. When the pleasure faded away and he moved his open palm over my lower back, I gazed up at him in pure astonishment.

"Watching you come undone has become my favorite sight to see," he whispered.

I didn't respond. Instead, I used the buoyancy of the water to wrap my legs around his waist and guide his rock-hard erection into me. This time, it wasn't just my cries of pleasure that cleared out the forest.

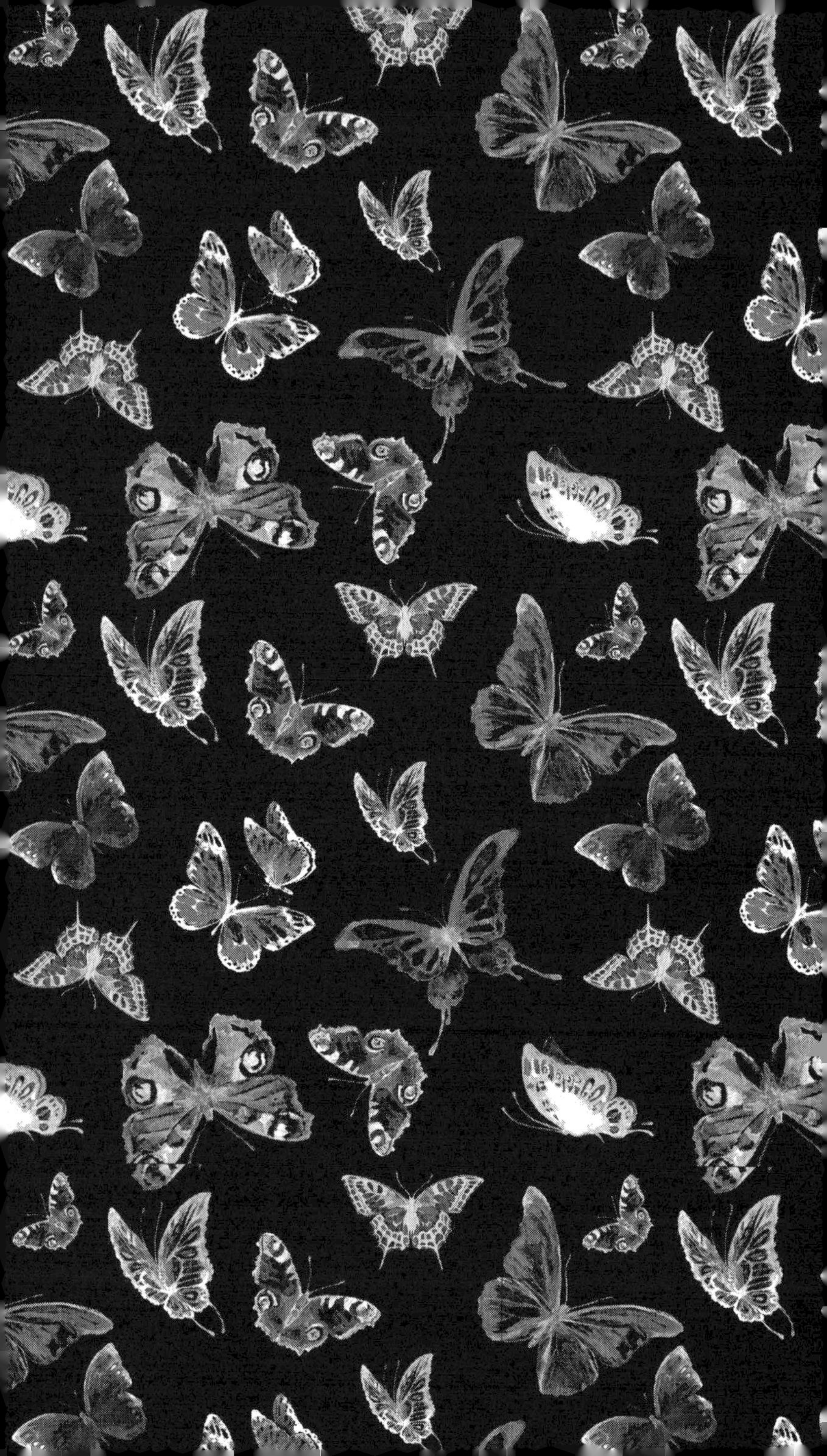

CHAPTER THIRTY

BLAIRE

Grammy temporarily closed the hotel after the covenstead since Mayor Douglas used his last shred of influence over the town to close its borders to any visitors. He claimed it was to stop any Movement Members from leaving or entering, but it only inflamed the conflict within Beacon Grove. Businesses were already being boarded up at an alarming rate due to Members being exposed and detained, and now they wouldn't have the tiny percentage of tourists he was allowing in to help them, either. His ban only put a chokehold on the ones still struggling to survive.

Without work at the hotel to fill my time, I spent most of my days at the cabin, training with the Quarters. There wasn't much else for me to do in town without drawing too much attention toward myself.

So, we continued to train. Every day.

We didn't stop until one of us was worn down or the sun set. Then, I'd run home and Kyle would be waiting for me on the porch, pulling me through his front door before I had a chance to reach for my own.

I hadn't told him what Mom said about being my Counter. Any time I tried, we either got too distracted or I'd lose my nerve. For some reason, putting that label on us made things too real. Too permanent. I was afraid of his reaction when he found out that our connection was one he was stuck with for life, whether he liked it or not.

I decided to ask Storie about it, since she was the only person I knew who had experienced the bond firsthand. Remy had been training with me near the creek for the day and Storie tagged along, as she usually did.

"Isn't that enough for the day?" she complained from her spot on the ground where she'd been watching us manipulate the water in the creek for the past hour. "I want to spend time with my friend."

Remy smiled down at her, then considered me for a moment. "We have to get back to town in a little, anyway. How do you feel?"

I shrugged. "Good. I think I've got the hang of it."

To prove my point, I held up my hand and the water from the creek lifted into the air in thick, round droplets. It hung there, defying all gravity and logic, until I flicked my wrist and sent it flying against the trees beside us.

Remy nodded his approval. "Just make sure you're focusing hard on the destination. That was a little sloppy."

My response was a splash of water in his face. Storie's laugh erupted behind us and Remy wiped his eyes, which were crinkled in amusement.

"Better."

He leaned down and placed a kiss on Storie's lips before disappearing inside the cabin to give us privacy, never allowing too much distance to come between them. Not after last year. Storie claimed they were working on their separation anxieties, but it still seemed like neither one was motivated to stray too far from the other.

"I wanted to ask you something," I began when he disappeared behind the door, jumping right in before I lost my nerve.

She patted the spot on the blanket beside her, and I fell onto it.

"Shoot."

"First, I have to tell you something. I'm not sure how you're going to feel about it, though."

Storie and the Quarters tolerated Kyle whenever he was around, but they still hadn't made much of an effort to include him in their group—not the way they had done for me. I figured it was his age that wedged the gap between us all, but I knew there was a history between Kyle and Storie that neither of them was willing to face.

"My mom told me something interesting about Kyle..." I began nervously. Then, I rolled my eyes, annoyed with my nerves. This was Storie. She understood me better than anyone else.

She stayed quiet, patiently waiting for me to steel myself.

"She said she thinks he's my Counter."

There. I ripped the band aid off.

Those odd, violet eyes widened, blond brows raising into her forehead. "But... he... he wasn't born the same day as you. Or even the same year."

"You mean he's old," I teased, easing the tension behind her words.

She smiled sheepishly and looked down at a speck of lint on the blanket, allowing her hair to fall between us as a curtain.

"I know. That was my first thought, but something happened with these gifts we've been given. Something disrupted them. And as you know, Mom never inherited hers."

Storie nodded.

"So, while our birthdays aren't aligned, he and Mom were born exactly twelve hours apart."

"You inherited your mom's Counter? Why wouldn't the gods just give you your own?"

I shrugged. "It doesn't make a lot of sense. But when I'm around him... I don't know. I wanted to ask you what it was like with you and Remy, when you realized you were bonded."

Her back straightened as the memory returned, and she winced.

It wasn't a positive experience. I knew because I felt it. Fear, fury, regret... it all moved through me like a tidal wave.

Storie was completely unaware of the effect she had on me. I still hadn't told her that I could feel other people's emotions. Admitting it to her now felt like an invasion of her privacy, though. Because while she was feeling these enormous emotions, she managed to school her expression into a mask of indifference. I realized then that there wasn't a lot I *had* told my friend in the past few months. Especially since the Fire Festival. Since we've been so busy.

"It was so intense," her voice finally said. It temporarily distracted me from feeling her. "We could both feel it—physically and emotionally. Whenever I was near him, it was like my body was buzzing... like it was sending signals to his that we were close."

I thought about Kyle. How we had this undeniable connection between us. It happened almost immediately. Like, we instantly knew we could trust one another with our lives—with our darkest secrets.

But as far as I knew, there was nothing insanely physical about our bond outside of when we had sex. No vibrating. No pain. Nothing of that sort. When I told Storie as much, she shrugged.

"Remy has this theory that ours was so intense because his gift is the water element and we, as humans, are made up of sixty percent water. He thinks it was our gifts reacting to one another."

When I blinked at her owlishly, she chuckled. "We've been waiting for one of the others to find their Counter, so we could compare."

"None of this makes me feel any better."

"Your souls have been tied together somehow. It's not something that can be evaluated or studied, or even understood. You just kind of *know*. And if you're sitting here, talking to me about it, then you must know."

"How did you get past the permanence of it? What if things don't work out for us romantically and we're stuck bonded for life?" That was the part that scared me the most.

She barked out a laugh, then rested her chin in her hand. "Isn't that how every relationship begins? You never know. There's just something different about it all."

"I guess we'll see what he thinks." I picked at the blanket.

"You haven't talked about it yet?!" She slapped her knee.

"I'm afraid of what he'll do."

"Give him a chance to react before you make up scenarios in your head, Blaire."

Kyle was waiting for me as I walked up to the house. My nerves flared up upon seeing his warm, welcoming face. He looked worn and tired from the day, yet still managed to smile when he saw me. Still extended his arms toward me, pulling me into his chest when I walked into them.

It was the salve to my burning anticipation.

I hooked my fingers in his and let him lead me through my door and up the stairs. Let him wrap me in his arms and kiss me.

"I have something to tell you," I said between kisses.

His teeth nipped at my lower lip, penalizing me for breaking the spell we were under.

"Can it wait?"

Large hands snaked around my sides and slid down to cup my butt, tightly squeezing when I tried to pull away again. A sigh escaped my lips, and I finally relented, deepening the kiss. I wrapped my legs around his waist, climbing up until we were equal height.

His tongue brushed against my lips, teasing. I raked my fingers against his scalp and tugged on his roots, tilting my head to allow him access to my neck.

He carried us into my bedroom and gently laid me down, only breaking contact long enough to pull his shirt off before he wedged his knee between my legs and leaned over me.

"I've missed you," he said breathlessly against my lips, and I hummed. "Today was shit."

My fingers glided up his torso, then followed the same path downward, slipping under the waistband of his jeans. He hissed out a breath when they gripped his erection, gently tugging. He hopped back off the bed and made quick work of slipping his jeans and briefs off at once, and I watched him spring upward when the constraints were removed.

I pulled my bottom lip into my mouth, smiling shyly as he returned to me and pushed my shirt over my breasts. In one long, slow stroke, his tongue traced a line from my belly button to my sternum.

My hand went back to his erection, gently squeezing as I pumped up and down. He hovered on top of me, arms braced on either side of my head as I stroked him over my stomach. When I began feeling his familiar twitch, he backed out of my grip and leaned down to nibble my ear.

"Not yet," he whispered, then climbed off the bed and flipped me over onto my stomach.

I felt his erection move against my crack before he gave my ass a hard smack that had me yelping. Then, his hand caressed the spot he had just assaulted and slid down to my thighs, spreading my legs. A knee came up onto the bed just before the mattress sunk under his weight, rolling me closer toward him.

I felt him teasing my opening, and then he was slowly slipping inside of me. A moan escaped my lips as he filled me, then slowly began rocking against my thighs. The position had me rubbing against the bed in the most delicious way. That, combined with the sensation of Kyle's hands squeezing my hips to keep them steady as he drilled into me, had my orgasm building up within minutes. Kyle continued as I pulsed around him with stars in my eyes, this time reaching a whole new level of pleasure. It happened another two times before I felt his hot liquid spilling inside of me as he reached his own release.

When we each finished, I sat up in bed and crossed my legs and Kyle remained lounging on his side, his head propped up by his hand.

"I really do have to talk to you about something."

"Sorry, I got carried away."

He smirked, reaching his hand between us to tickle my inner thighs. The move had me ready to jump onto his lap and go another round with him, but I stopped myself.

I took a calming breath, and then looked directly into his eyes as I said, "Grammy and my mom think you're my Counter. I agree with them."

He stilled, face twisted in shock. I could see the different thoughts passing through his mind as they shifted from doubt to disbelief to understanding. I could feel them, too. They whipped through my chest like a deck of cards.

It went against all logic, yet it made complete sense.

He opened his mouth to speak, but stopped as if he'd just remembered something. His head snapped toward the mirror on my dresser, at the reflection of us sitting on the bed together, and he let out a string of cuss words. Before I could stop him, he was hopping off the bed and snatching up his discarded shorts from the floor.

I watched in confusion as he ripped the mirror off the top of my dresser, knocking my things onto the floor, and then lifted it over his shoulder and walked out of the room.

"What are you doing?"

I grabbed my robe and wrapped it tightly around my naked body, then followed him. He was already halfway down the stairs by the time I made it out of my room, and he didn't appear to be stopping.

We crossed the front lawn and Kyle slammed the mirror down against the curb. Shattered pieces bounced around the grass and the street, covering his bare feet. He didn't seem to care.

Not when he finally turned back toward me with a terror-stricken look, and said, "I made a mistake, and now he knows."

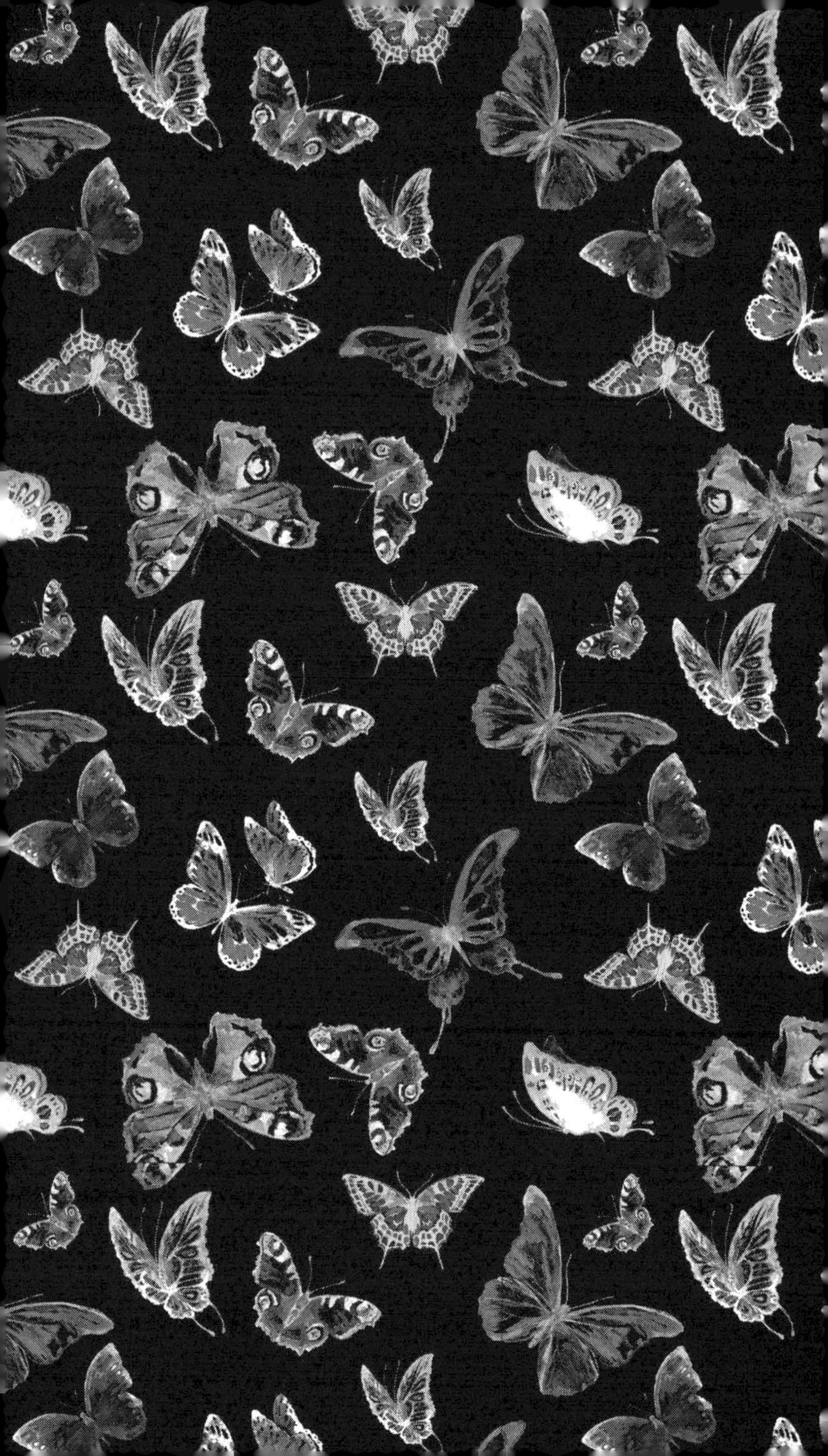

CHAPTER THIRTY-ONE

BLAIRE

In all the time I'd known her, Grammy never apologized.

Not once.

Even if she knew she was wrong, she'd somehow find a way to make the other person apologize. Which was part of the reason I was able to hold my ground about moving away from her.

Why I was able to stay away.

Because when you can't apologize, you ignore the problem altogether. And that was exactly what she'd been doing for the past few weeks.

Pretending.

But her need to keep me under her control outweighed her pride, and while the two fought against each other every time we found ourselves in the same room, it was control that won out in the end.

"I've been watching you with the Quarter boys," she began one day when we were both at the cabin. She had come during one of my training sessions with Rhyse and Enzo to bring something to Lux.

I don't know what they were still searching those books for anymore. Didn't we have all the answers we needed? Rayner was obviously using a magic that went deeper and darker than anything our records showed.

"You manage to hold your own pretty well out there," she awkwardly remarked.

"Thank you."

"I'm not surprised. You're as stubborn as a mule." The smile that accompanied the backhanded comment told me it was meant to be a compliment.

"I get it from you," I quickly countered, and she tilted her head back and howled a laugh, the way I always saw Rhyse do.

"Fair enough. I'll give you that one, but you better keep the rest of your thoughts to yourself unless you want a full tongue lashing."

My smirk told her I didn't give a damn about her tongue lashing, which earned an eye roll from her.

"I'm proud of the woman you've become in such a short amount of time. And I'm... I'm sorry that I ever doubted your ability to handle all of this."

I couldn't mask my surprise at her words.

"Your mother and I made a lot of mistakes raising you. You'd think I could have gotten it right the second time around, but I guess I'll never learn. Now, all I've got to show for it is two grown women who resent me."

She looked down at her feet in a rare moment of insecurity.

I had no idea what to say. If we weren't arguing or avoiding each other, I wasn't sure what to do with her anymore.

"I don't resent you," I finally landed on.

At least, not anymore. I did, though. Before Kyle showed me how fleeting life could be. I didn't want to waste any more of the time we had together on this planet arguing with her. I just couldn't figure out how to tell her that.

"You wouldn't be wrong if you did."

My eyes scanned her face, searching for any sign of mockery or jest, but came up short.

"You know," I started, and my voice broke. I almost lost my nerve to say my next words—to speak them into existence—but pushed my shoulders back and continued.

"Storie came here as an orphan, searching for answers about her family. She didn't know anything about Beacon Grove. And

I felt like such a sham all that time for helping her collect little breadcrumbs when I've got this wealth of information standing right before me and I was squandering it."

Grammy's eyebrows scrunched together. "You weren't squandering anything. You were a child."

I gave her an incredulous look, tilting my head. "I'm no younger than she is, Grammy. I wasn't a child. You were just treating me like one."

She opened her mouth to object, but stopped when I held my hand up in front of her face, a move I'd learned from her.

"My point is that I don't know how much time we've got left together in this lifetime, and I'm tired of wasting it. There can't be any more secrets between us. I want to know everything. I need to know all of it, so I don't end up scrambling for answers about myself the way Storie has been."

She released a breath. I knew her instinct would be to argue with me. To list off a million reasons why I wasn't ready. But they were all wrong. If I'd done anything in the past few weeks, it was that I'd proved how capable I was. She couldn't ignore that anymore.

"Fine. If you think you're ready to hear it, then I'll tell you."

"*Fine*. Let's start with where the Grangers fit with the Quarters."

A look of warning. That wasn't where she wanted to begin, but she wasn't calling the shots anymore. I was in possession of the gifts now. It was only right for her to tell me what that entailed.

"I told you, our ancestors received their gifts at the same time. The Grangers had to hide theirs after it became too dangerous for others to know."

"Why do I feel like that's only half the story?"

She rolled her eyes. "That's all that matters. The Quarters are no strangers to corruption and growing hungry for more power than they were blessed with—look at this last generation, for instance. The Grangers were given their gifts with a heaping load of humbleness to go along with it. That's why we're able to harness all the elements, along multiple generation lines at once, and they only get one.

"Unsurprisingly, they weren't happy about that. They wanted the same abilities, and they began hunting Grangers to figure out how they'd managed to 'trick' the gods into doing it. And we had to lie and say we lost our power. It was mortifying for them. They laid down their egos to protect us and were nearly cast out of their homes for doing so. That's why we've kept the secret generations later. To make their sacrifice worth it."

"Why reveal it to them now, then?"

Grammy thought about that for a moment. "This generation is different from the ones that came before it, just as you're vastly different from me. I knew they would take the information and use it for good."

"That was a gamble." I rolled my eyes, remembering how disrespectful they had been upon finding out that I was their fifth Quarter.

"They came around eventually. They're not bad people, Blaire. They've just been raised by them."

"Why did I have to complete that spell with them to activate my gifts? How did you get yours if they were supposed to be kept a secret from them?" That had been bothering me since it happened.

"Yes. Ordinarily, we would complete a spell on the Mabon, when we knew the Quarters would be lifting their own. It was a way to practice alongside them without their knowledge. Now that they know about you, there was no use hiding it from them. No use in waiting."

"Okay, so the secrets are out. We've been training to fight Rayner and the Movement. Why are you and Lux still buried in those books?"

She hesitated, warring with herself over revealing her plans. But we were moving forward, and she couldn't expect me to be on her side when she was working behind my back.

"There're still things we don't understand about the Quarters and their Counters, especially since things got so mixed up. Look at you and Kyle, for example."

She gave me a knowing look, and I blushed. We had yet to broach the subject of him, but now that we were, I realized that maybe she had been keeping him involved in all of this for a reason.

"They haven't been so lucky. I kept my records and had my theories about who their Counters were based on birthdays, but that obviously isn't a hard and fast rule anymore. Lux wants to find their Counters before they take over Watchtower again."

That was unsurprising. Lux hardly spoke to me, but I knew he was fiercely loyal to his brothers. Of course, he'd want them to be at their full potential before they took on such powerful roles.

"There's also the issue of Rayner. We don't know how he's been able to override our wards and spells. How he was able to use that magic to weaken them last year."

"It was black magic, wasn't it? The sacrifice of those girls' lives?"

I thought about Hailey, Toni, and all the other lost souls who had found me throughout the months since Rayner left. But if Kyle is right, maybe they aren't dead after all. Maybe he's using their life force to fuel his power, and that would be a completely different type of dark magic. I wasn't ready to ask her about it yet, though.

"Yes, but it seems like there's more to the story. How was he able to erase a spirit's memory? How did he manipulate the afterlife so heavily without the gifts?"

She was right. This was all so overwhelming. It was a heavy burden to carry on her own, too. It made sense that her and Lux had grown so close over the past year. They each needed someone to lighten the load, and neither one wanted to rely on the people they loved.

"Did you have a Counter?"

Grammy's face immediately fell, and I knew the answer.

She *did*. Past tense.

"You know, it's not typical for Quarters to be romantic with their Counters. In fact, that's one thing your generation has done differently than the rest of us. When I was a girl, it was strictly forbidden."

Her eyes looked far off as she remembered. "Back then, Counters traveled through blood lines, same as Quarters. Generation after generation, we knew who would be our Counter without any doubt. Of course, since we were forbidden from sharing our gifts, our Counters were also burdened with hiding theirs."

"That sounds horrible."

She only nodded. "He lived down the street from us. We grew up inseparable and at first, our families thought it was adorable. But as time went on and our bodies changed, hormones took over and we started exploring our relationship beyond friendship. Our moms noticed the shift and forbade us from seeing each other again. Of course, that only made us want it more. It wasn't long before I fell pregnant."

She smiled sadly at the memory, and I wished I had Kyle's ability to look inside her head and relive whatever moment had popped up into her mind with her. It seemed like a happy one.

"He came up with a whole plan for getting out of Beacon Grove and leaving it all behind. For raising our child as *normal* people. And on the night we planned to leave, his father found his suitcase."

"Oh no," I gasped.

"He beat him to a pulp, and then told my parents about our plans. We had no choice but to tell them about the pregnancy, and they were terrified to find out what that would mean for our gifts. What would become of a child who was born as a Quarter *and* a Counter?"

I thought about Remy and Storie. About me and Kyle. If we ever chose to have children, what *would* become of them? What would they be?

"What happened then?"

"Things were different back then. I was only seventeen at the time—not a legal adult. I kicked and screamed the entire way to the clinic. I wailed at the top of my lungs, gnashing and clawing against the car when they attempted to dig me out of it, hoping someone would hear and save me. They had the nurse come out and inject me with sedatives because I was refusing so severely. I didn't want to give it up. It seemed so senseless.

"There were women out there who genuinely needed those services and didn't have access to them, and here my family was, using their privilege to eliminate an *inconvenience*. The child wasn't at fault for my decisions, and they were a product of love. They deserved a chance at life."

The bitterness still lingered in her voice as she recalled the horrific events that had happened to her. There was still a lot of hurt there.

"I woke up a few hours later, and it had already been done. I left Beacon Grove that night with the clothes on my back and an aching in my womb. I didn't look back for years. By the time I returned with your mother, both of my parents had died. I never even got a chance to say goodbye, but that mourning mother inside of me still resented them too much to care. And my Counter had already moved on with a wife and two kids."

"I'm so sorry, Grammy." I reached over and grabbed her hand in mine. "You shouldn't have had to go through all that."

"When your mother came of age and didn't inherit her gifts, I thought it was my fault. That maybe somehow, by terminating the pregnancy of my firstborn child—the one who was the rightful heir to them—I had ruined it for all the next generations. That was why we didn't tell you about them right away. Because we weren't even sure if they existed anymore."

It made sense. Why bother unloading the burden onto me if there wasn't a reason? But she should have warned me. She should have realized I could handle it all sooner. That I could help her carry that load. That mom could, too.

"I knew you had your gifts when the town began accusing the Quarters of killing those girls and you agreed with them. I had snapped at you over it. I didn't like that you were taking the side of the people who were against the Quarters—against *us*. You looked at me, and your eyes glowed green. Not like how they shine brightly in the sun. No, they actually *glowed*. And you placed your hands on the table and it shook beneath your touch.

"It was so subtle; I don't even think you noticed it. Neither had Storie. But I did. And then, I felt a shift within myself, and I knew it was the gifts. I knew they were transferring at that moment, and all my priorities shifted."

"So, all of this... helping the Quarters, working with Kyle, tracking down Rayner... it's all been for me?"

"Blaire, every single step I take in this life, I take with you and your mother in mind."

I didn't doubt that for a second. I'd always known that Grammy was willing to do whatever it took to keep us safe and protected. That, for some reason, she carried that burden with her every day. I used to think it was silly. There were no threats looming against us, the lowest members of our little society.

But I didn't have the full picture back then. Now that I did, I was so grateful for every single sacrifice she and my ancestors made for the sake of our safety. I had been so angry and ungrateful when they told me about the gifts because I didn't understand any of it. Now, I could only hope that when future generations of Grangers looked back on my tiny blip in the family line, they'll see something worth being proud of.

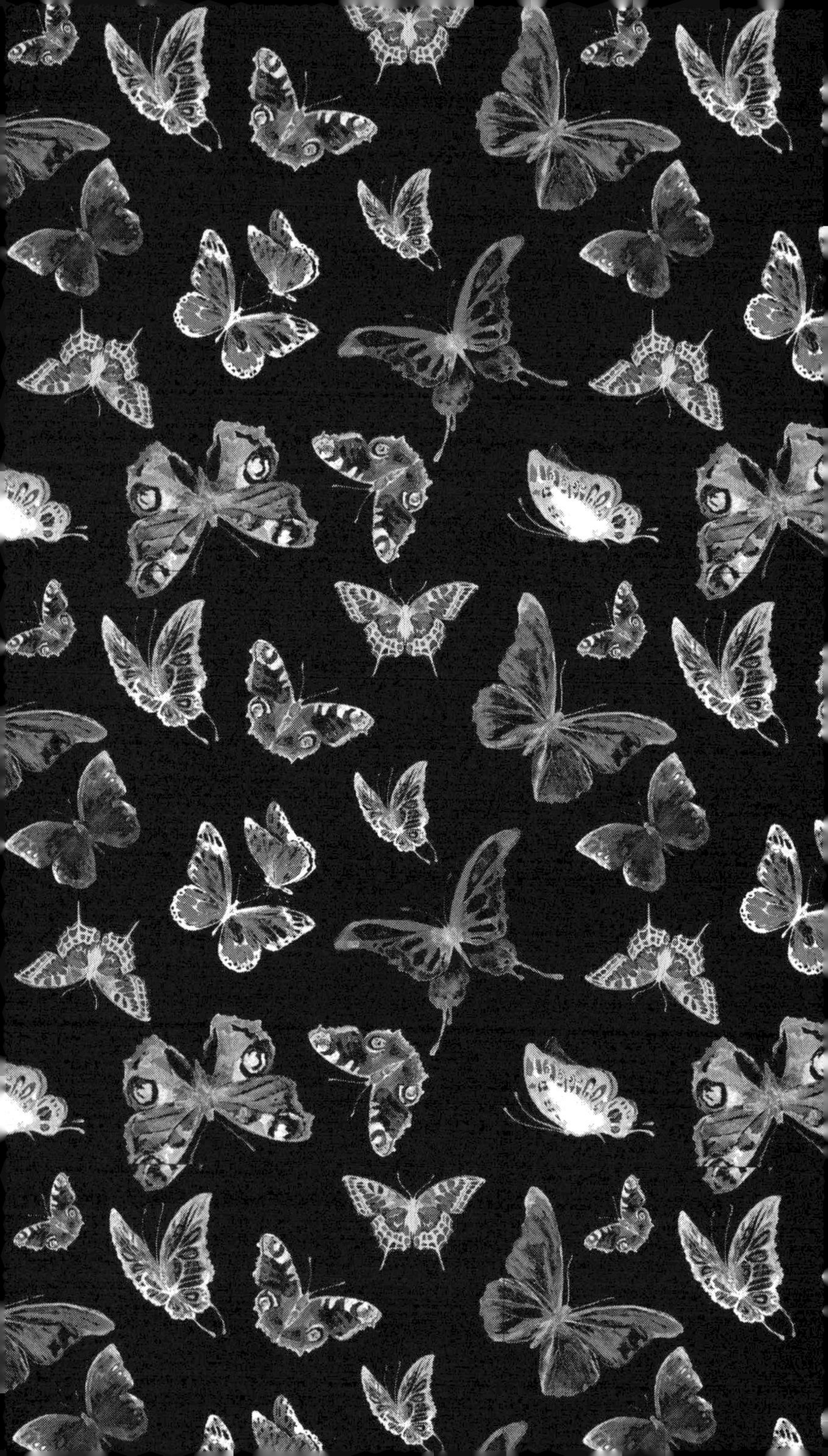

CHAPTER THIRTY-TWO

BLAIRE

Kyle met me in my apartment the following evening. I spent the day on my couch watching mindless TV, wanting to process what Grammy told me in solitude, so I wasn't waiting for him on the porch when he came home from work. As if he could sense that I needed him, he let himself in before even going into his apartment to change and began wordlessly taking off his uniform and gear, letting me know he was here to stay.

I watched him undress in silence with a heated, grateful stare, which he quickly noticed and reciprocated. Once he was down to only his pants and t-shirt, he grabbed my hand and tugged me off the couch, gesturing his head toward my room. As I stood to follow, the light glinted off the silver metal handcuffs peeking out of the discarded police belt. Before I could give it a second thought, I hooked my finger and snatched them out of their case. Unaware, Kyle sat on the edge of my mattress and held his hands out for me to step between his legs.

I sashayed toward him with one of the cuffs dangling from my finger, a sly smile pulling on my lips as his brows shot up.

"What's this?" he rasped.

I grabbed his neck for support as I straddled him on the bed. "I thought we could have some fun," I replied in the sultriest voice I could muster.

His hands wrapped around my backside, fingers digging in when I opened one of the cuffs between us and wrapped the cold metal around my wrist, securing it in place with a loud click.

When he remained quiet and still, I slowly lifted my gaze to meet his, suddenly nervous that I had made a mistake.

What if he wasn't into this sort of thing? What if I had just crossed some weird line between work and play for him and he was trying to figure out a way to let me down easy?

The heated expression on his face immediately erased my doubts.

His silver irises had nearly disappeared behind dilated pupils as his self-restraint dissipated and he grabbed me up, slammed my stomach down onto the bed, and swung my cuffed arm behind my back. My stomach fluttered with excitement, and I turned my head toward the window on the opposite wall, trying and failing to look back at him.

"Some fun?" he ground out in a low voice, reaching for my other arm to line my wrists up.

His body pressed against my back as his lips caressed my ear.

"You're sure about that?" he whispered breathily.

I swallowed hard, then nodded, my face brushing against the sheets.

The other cuff snapped into place on my free wrist, and he backed off me, leaving a cool chill in his wake. I felt his fingers dig into my waistband, and then my leggings were ripped down my legs, exposing my entire backside. He ran his hands in swirls against my bare skin a few times, and then a loud smack echoed off the walls.

I yelped, the sound hitting my ears before the sting even registered. He placed his lips onto the spot he had just assaulted and peppered it with light kisses, then sunk his teeth in.

Moaning, I writhed under him, wanting to turn around and rub my hands all over his body. My fingers itched to rip his clothes off and feel him against me. To be able to reciprocate this game of salty and sweet. The lack of control was already driving me insane, and we'd only just begun.

"I've been trying to figure out a way to punish you for that smart mouth," his gravelly voice cooed from behind, and I heard his zipper come undone before the soft thud of his uniform pants falling to the floor.

It was as if the inability to see him had every other sense heightened. I could smell that musky police station scent much stronger now. Could hear every creak of the bed as his body shifted around it. I tracked him with all my senses, anxiously awaiting his next move.

His hands pushed my shirt up my back, and then trailed down my spine until he hooked a finger onto my thong and pushed it to the side. On instinct, my thighs rubbed together to create a fraction of the friction his touch had me craving. The buildup was torturous.

A light chuckle sounded from behind me before he wedged his hand between my legs to spread them apart, then rubbed his finger along my wet center. My hips lifted to accommodate him better and my hands struggled against the restraints as I instinctually went to push myself off the bed and give him better access.

"Relax," he drawled, rubbing his finger in circles against me.

But I couldn't relax. I had no idea that it would feel so impossible to renounce all my power and allow him to take full control. When I grabbed the handcuffs, I figured we would ease into it. Maybe he'd strap one arm to the headboard while the other could still play. I had no idea I'd have both hands bound. Yet, this was the most turned on I've ever been.

As he continued to work his fingers against me, I felt his weight shift again as I assumed he worked himself out of his briefs. My suspicions were confirmed when I felt his bare erection against my leg as he slipped two fingers inside me, working me up to a climax that exploded out of nowhere. My hips ground against his hand as it lifted me into the sky to dance with the stars. I was hardly over the edge with his name falling from my lips in heavy pants when he began running his erection along my crack, teasing me all over again.

He had no plans to give me a break.

Large, strong hands wrapped around my arms and spun me around on the bed so I was looking up at the ceiling with my hands beneath me. His face hovered over mine with a teasing grin.

"Having fun?" he asked, rolling my left nipple between his fingers. I arched my back and shoved myself farther into his grip, just to defy him.

"I wasn't sure if you'd started yet," I sassed sarcastically, earning another chuckle.

He tightened his grip on my nipple and used the other hand to cup my sex, just barely touching the most sensitive area. The contact was enough to have me pulsing against him all over again.

"If you want me to continue, you have to ask nicely."

I bit back a sneer and raised my brow at him in a challenge, debating if I wanted to play along anymore.

But he sensed the question in my gaze and began backing away from me completely, lifting his hands in the air before him to prove his point. He wasn't going to continue if I didn't play along.

My body instantly reacted to his absence and my hips bucked toward him of their own accord, missing his touch. I laid my head back onto the bed and stared up in defeat, biting my lip.

After a few weighted breaths, I mumbled a quiet, submissive, "Please."

"What was that?"

I sighed, rolling my eyes, then craned my neck to look at him. The cuffs cut into my skin behind my back as the weight of my body pressed against them.

"Please keep going," I said more clearly.

"Good girl," he rasped with a cocky smirk.

Then, he was between my legs again, teasing my center with his rock-hard erection. He gently pushed his tip in and then pulled it out, slowly repeating the motion in a tantalizing pattern.

A small, irritated growl sounded in my throat and my hands fought against the cuffs as I went to reach behind him to pull him into me.

"Succumb to it," he urged in a strained whisper. "Stop trying to control everything."

I took a deep breath and relaxed my muscles. He rewarded me by pushing himself in as far as he could, stopping to give me a moment to adjust. Then, he began pumping inside me in a rhythm I was actually happy with.

It wasn't until I fully loosened up and set aside my pride that I felt the full effect of using his handcuffs. Though I longed to touch his face or rub my fingers along his back, relinquishing control and trusting him fully with my body was a completely different form of intimacy. The metal biting against my skin was the perfect essence of pain to balance out the insane amount of pleasure that came from having him buried inside me, with his hands and mouth all over me, stimulating each of my senses at once.

I fell into another body-racking orgasm, tensing up against him as I followed his advice and succumbed to all the sensations I was feeling. He wasn't far behind, and we were both riding the clouds into euphoria as we moaned each other's names into the air.

Once we were each satiated and the high wore off, Kyle unlocked the handcuffs with a key from his police belt, revealing my raw, reddened skin. There were definitely going to be bruises.

I watched the wave of concern and regret pass over his face as he grabbed my hands up and planted kisses all around my wrists, rubbing them tenderly. I lifted them out of his touch to caress his face and pull him into me, devouring him with a kiss that said there was no room for guilt after the experience he just gave me.

When his fingers still went to caress my welted skin again, I backed away and fell to my knees, determined to repay the favor and make him forget.

"How am I going to get through this?" The pads of his fingers brushed against my cheek.

The morning sun had hardly made its way over the tree line when he rolled over and woke me up with his mouth on my body. We made love slowly and lazily, still exhausted and sore from the night before. Once we finished, neither of us bothered moving from the bed.

"Through what?"

"Rayner wants to end the Quarters. That's been his goal from the beginning."

"Yeah."

"And I've somehow managed to fall in love with one of them."

My eyebrows shot up at the admission. I'd felt it before without him knowing—that gush of adoration as he watched me do the most mundane things. I knew what it was when the stolen sensation found me, because I felt the same for him. But neither of us had outright admitted our feelings yet.

He went on. "It was always only about protecting my town from a madman... about avenging the deaths of the people he already took from me."

My heart, so light and elated at his words from before, fell to the ground, shattering and splintering into a million tiny pieces.

It was in the quiet moments when no one else was around that I felt like he handed himself over to me completely. When we were surrounded by nothing and allowed to feel every thought and emotion fully, without a single outside influence. Those were the moments I was sure we were meant to be.

That I could place my heart into his hands and trust he wouldn't smash it.

Those were the moments that kept me coming back for more.

But conversations like this made me question if that was sustainable.

I knew for certain that I loved him. That revelation came swiftly and powerfully, sweeping me up and carrying me away before I had the chance to object. Even without our bond, I think I would love him.

But if this was what being loved by him was like, was it worth it? Could I spend the rest of my life living in the shadow of Asher Graves? Could I fight beside him in a war, knowing that he was only doing it to avenge *her* death?

"What's wrong?" He shifted to rest his head on his arm as he sat against the wall, his naked body on full display.

I didn't want to give my jealous thoughts a voice just yet, so I lifted my shoulders in a noncommittal shrug and pressed my lips together. A tall, thorny wall came up in my mind, effectively blocking him out. Lux had taught me the trick one afternoon after Kyle finally admitted to them that he had the power to look into other people's minds. It was the only way he could explain to them what he saw in Shane's mind before he was taken to Rhyse's home.

I knew what he'd say, anyway.

Asher was dead. There was no use in allowing her to come between us.

But his love for her kept her alive and well in his heart. Her presence was so large, there were times that I didn't think there was possibly any room for me.

"Talk to me, Blaire."

"I don't know how this is going to work between us if you can't let her go."

Dark brows pinched together, casting a shadow over his eyes. "What? I have let her go. I just told you, I'm in love with *you*."

"And in the same breath, you admitted you were only doing all of this to punish him for taking her from you," I accused.

He leaned forward to sit up beside me, making sure our eyes were level. "You didn't let me finish. I was saying..." His hands came up to cup my face, stopping me from turning away from him as he said, "that's what it was about before—I was doing it for them. But now?"

He shook his head with a humorless laugh. "Now, he's coming after the most precious thing this horrible, treacherous life has offered me. I don't know how I'm going to survive this when I know I'd destroy myself if it meant keeping you safe."

My eyes stung as I fought back the tears that were fighting through my stubborn mask. He tugged me forward by my chin, gently placing kisses in the spots where my tears streamed. I threw myself at him, curling into his lap as he held me, his words lingering in the air between them. And I knew they were genuine. I knew he meant them, and I wanted him to know I felt the same.

That I would rip myself to shreds if it meant saving him, too.

CHAPTER THIRTY-THREE

KYLE — PAST

Later in the day following her death, the news about Bonnie was spread all over town. Rayner had the nerve to act surprised, mourning along with the rest of our neighbors. I was so angry at him.

This was all his fault. All of it. And he stood before our town as if he hadn't killed her himself.

I stared at him from across the town square, watching as he hugged our neighbors and shed fake tears, making a point to question why *anyone* would do such a thing. And I couldn't contain the pure rage that bubbled up in my chest. Before I could second guess myself, my legs cleared the square. Without an ounce of hesitation, I was slamming my fists into him right there, in the middle of the peaceful, mourning crowd.

I couldn't believe he'd betray Bonnie, his own friend, that way. That he'd grown so obsessed with this idea of a movement that he was willing to attack a newborn baby over it to weaken the Quarters. Every punch and kick were a promise that when this was all over, he would pay. He would pay for Bonnie, for Mason, for Storie, for Asher, and for me—for the loss of my family.

It took three large men to pull me off him. By the time they did, he was already unconscious, his bloodied face frozen in shock. As they hauled me away, I spit on him and in the most menacing, *threatening voice I could muster, I promised him this wasn't the end. That I'd happily lose my life if it meant ending his, too.*

It was Officer Cotteral who processed me at the station. We hardly spoke as he filled out the paperwork, lifting his eyes every few minutes. They didn't hold me at the station for long, either. I overheard Cotteral making excuses for me to the Sheriff.

"He's just lost his friend," he mumbled into the old dinosaur's ear just outside my cell. "He clearly hasn't even slept since walking into that house. I'm telling you, it was gruesome. That kind of thing would take a toll on anyone, especially a young man."

I scowled at that, remembering the traumatized faces of the grown men who took Bonnie away. The two men exchanged a few more words, and then the door to the holding cell was unlocked.

"You're free to go. Go home and get some rest, Kyle."

And I did. I slept fitfully for the next forty-eight hours, stuck between the nightmares in my head and the one that was now my reality. Rumor had it that when Rayner came to, it was Cotteral who convinced him not to press charges.

Of course, the town believed it was the Quarters who killed Bonnie, given the tension that was surrounding the new generation being born and the allegations that the Quarters were hunting Counters. They had it all wrong, though, and no one bothered to listen to me as I tried to explain the truth of what really happened.

Rayner took the opportunity to feed that narrative and push his agenda on everyone. And since the Quarters were untouchable, the police overlooked every ounce of evidence Mason and Asher presented them the night before, too afraid to even look deep enough to see that it hadn't been them.

In the weeks following her death, the whispers of Mason being guilty took on a life of their own, until a majority of Beacon Grove believed it was him.

"Why would they leave in the middle of the night like that if they weren't guilty?" I heard the question asked countless times.

Not, "Why would Mason murder the love of his life?"

Despite my protests, the police labeled him and Asher as the primary suspects in the case, while Rayner and the Quarters moved on with their lives. The legal system had failed them—failed all of us.

I tried to track down Mason and Asher two months later. I did everything I could think of to find them based on the loose plans they discussed on the night they left, but always came up short. It was like I was always a step behind them.

After three months of searching, I gave up.

A week later, I drove three hours into the next town and enrolled in the police academy, hellbent on making sure something like this never happened again.

---

*P*resent

Rayner was back in Beacon Grove.

I confirmed it through the thoughts of his Members. He had somehow gotten the signal out to all of them, and every single one that hadn't been caught yet was buzzing with excited anticipation. So many more than we originally thought. Their minds were racing so fast, I couldn't pinpoint who they belonged to.

I only knew that we were surrounded.

That was terrifying, given the fact that their thoughts also revealed what Rayner's plans were.

He wanted war.

And as he marched through the singular road that led into Beacon Grove, his army was preparing to fight for him. To give him just that.

I wasn't sure how I was hearing them so clearly and consistently. It was like he had somehow found out about my gift and tuned his entire Movement into the radio frequency of my brain as some special form of torture. Their internal voices streamed through my head in a distracting, chaotic hum.

I didn't have enough time to warn everyone. The thoughts whirred through me so quickly, so aggressively, they jumbled my own mind.

"We need to get out of here, Blaire," I called up the stairs to her. She had gone up there to shower a few minutes prior. The pipes already creaked from the running water.

She hadn't heard me.

I snatched my phone from my coffee table and ran up the stairs, taking them two at a time as I fumbled through my contacts for Tabitha's number. She'd be able to warn the Quarters while we warned the town.

By the time I got through the bathroom door, revealing a puzzled Blaire peeking from behind her shower curtain, Tabitha answered.

"He's coming," I said breathlessly into the phone and to Blaire. "We need to get everyone together. We need to warn them. *Now*."

Tabitha said something on the other end of the line that I didn't pay attention enough to hear, and then hung up. Blaire was shutting the water off when I walked out of the bathroom and toward her bedroom to pick something for her to wear.

Every second we spent in this apartment was a second we weren't getting things ready. It was a disadvantage.

"Kyle, slow down. We can do this. We've been preparing for it. It's going to be okay," Blaire tried to soothe, but I ignored her.

She hadn't heard what I'd heard. She had no idea.

"He's got so much more support than we thought. They're coming for blood. For *your* blood."

They wanted to end the Quarters once and for all.

I didn't watch her slip into the pants I had laid out on her bed. Instead, I headed for the stairs again. To get outside and warn everyone I could. I didn't care if I had to scream at the top of my lungs in the middle of the street, I wasn't going to let them take my town by surprise.

My mind was in absolute chaos.

Blaire was at my heels, tugging a shirt over her head as we descended the stairs. "You need to take a breath, Kyle. I can feel your panic. It's scaring me."

Rayner wasn't going to slow down, though. And he wasn't going to take my family away from me again.

He wasn't going to touch Blaire.

"Kyle!" Blaire shouted my name from the porch. I had already made it down to the sidewalk before her voice startled me out of my racing thoughts.

"He isn't going to get away from you this time. We're going to help. Just please, stop for a second."

It was the panic lacing her features that had me turning and doubling back over the front lawn. For a moment—just a split second—I allowed myself to take her in. Her green eyes shined in the evening sun, which emphasized the tiny freckles dancing along the top of her nose and spilling onto her cheeks. Her dark ginger hair, usually tied into a tight braid, fell over her shoulders in wild, wet waves. The black shirt and dark jeans she wore hugged her curves in all the right spots.

She was perfect.

She was worth fighting a war for.

"I love you," I breathed out. "And for some reason, he likes to take away the things I love."

Blaire's face fell. "I'm not going anywhere," she promised. Her feet carried her to me, closing the distance between us. "I love you, too."

Her lips were on mine, but she only allowed them to linger for a second. She knew I was in a rush, so she didn't make me push her away. Instead, she stepped back and nodded, ready to move forward.

Ready to fight.

We jogged to my cruiser, and I turned on the sirens, blasting them through the streets the whole drive to the police station. I still wasn't sure how many of my officers I could trust, but I had to try to gather as many as possible.

By the time we left the station and called in as many officers as we could, we drove into town and found that Tabitha and the Quarters had managed to get the majority of their supporters into the square. It was a much smaller group than I'd expected.

I made the terrifying comparison to the Movement's numbers in my head and my heart kicked back up. Blaire sensed my creeping anxiety and her hand found mine at my side, then squeezed reassuringly.

We've got this, she sent the thought into the air between us, and I caught it, offering a stiff nod as response.

I commanded my small police force of about ten officers—only three hadn't answered my call, including Stewart—while the Quarters instructed everyone else on what was expected of them. They handed out weapons to each citizen with grave expressions.

"What did you see?" Tabitha asked once she made her way over to me.

The old woman looked surprisingly fierce, her white hair pulled tightly back in a bun, somehow making her dark skin glow just as bright as those eyes I'd grown to love on her granddaughter. A gun was strapped around her back and two were secured at her sides, just below her bulletproof vest. I had no idea how she got her hands on such things, but she clearly wasn't taking any chances against the Movement Members.

"He's coming up the trail now." I stopped myself.

He should actually be here by now. Where was he?

"Blaire said you think he has an advantage in numbers."

"He does."

I had no idea where he managed to gather so many people from to march with him, or why they chose to enter the town on foot.

Rayner was an exceptional salesman, though. I wouldn't put it past him to have recruited people who had never even heard of Beacon Grove to fight for justice with him. Or his idea of it, anyway. He'd managed to have Mason and Asher killed without ever leaving the town's limits, as far as I knew. He had to have people on the outside.

"The Quarters discovered the entrances to each of their dungeons blown wide open this morning," Tabitha started with a regal expression. Her eyes scanned the crowd of people before us, avoiding contact as she said, "They have no idea how he did it. They swear there were wards against such a thing."

"So, all those Movement Members...?"

I couldn't even say the words. Perhaps it was their voices I heard in my head all morning. That might be a better alternative to what I thought.

"They're likely joining up with him right now."

※

The Movement Members arrived in the town's square minutes after me and Tabitha parted ways, heavily armed and ready to fight. Each one wore stern, battle-ready expressions on their faces.

But something about them was off.

Their eyes—they lacked any sort of life.

And their minds, which had been so disordered before, were completely blank. I tried breaking in and found nothing but radio silence.

Friends and neighbors stood across an invisible line from one another, waiting for the fight to begin. I couldn't understand how it had gotten this far. How one wiry, oddball kid had grown to become such a monster. How that monster managed to influence so many others into fighting his battles.

It felt like just yesterday that I was teasing Rayner for spewing his nonsense to anyone with ears.

How had he managed to take it this far? To turn us all against one another?

Blaire and Tabitha stood in the back of the Quarter Supporters in widened stances, with Callista positioned behind them. Remy and Storie were off to the side, as close to the water as they could get. Lux flanked the opposite side with a calm, bored expression, and Rhyse and Enzo were in front of us all, with me and my police force directly behind them, making up the front line.

Sure enough, all of the people whose names were on the Member Manifest were standing before me, the same dead look behind their eyes as the rest of them.

Rayner was nowhere to be found.

"You've got one last chance to step down. To turn around and let that sick fuck know that you support your Quarters and the will of the gods," Enzo's severe voice growled to the army of people standing before him.

Rhyse shifted on his feet beside him, his hands shaking at his sides as if the flames under his skin were clawing to get out.

No one in Rayner's army responded. Not even a flicker of a reaction came. The two Quarters shared a look, then looked back at Remy and Lux, silently communicating their next move.

Without any sort of warning, Rhyse sent a line of fire before our opponents, temporarily blinding us all as Lux threw an invisible shield of air behind it, catching the bullets that were sent our way. Untrained hands reacted on both sides, sending ammo over the line without bothering to set a target. Luckily, most of them hit the ground or shot through the air without connecting with any flesh. Many others rushed forward and began throwing fists once Lux's shield fell and Rhyse's fire snaked around to the back of Rayner's army, ushering them forward.

Toward us. Into the fight.

I hated this. My oath to protect my town conflicted with my duty to fight for what was right. My eyes kept snapping back to Blaire, who had pushed her way to the front, leaving Callista and Tabitha behind. Her training with Rhyse and Enzo was paying off. She threw her elbow up and caught someone's chin, then threw a force of air against a man who was rushing her. He fell backward onto his ass, and she wrapped vines around his wrists and ankles, shackling him to the ground.

Some time, deep in the fray, when I was worn down and depleted of energy, something shifted in the corner of my eye, on the edge of the woods. I turned to look and was immediately blasted in the side of the head, blood spilling from my mouth. I took my police baton and slammed it into my attacker's knees, then grabbed his neck and threw him to the ground.

My eyes lifted back into the woods, and my heart dropped into my stomach.

Ma and Millie were being dragged through the brush by two burly men I didn't recognize. I took off toward them without a second thought, helplessly watching as they disappeared behind the greenery.

Blaire's voice called to my back, urging me to stop, but I didn't turn.

He set the trap for me, and I fell right in.

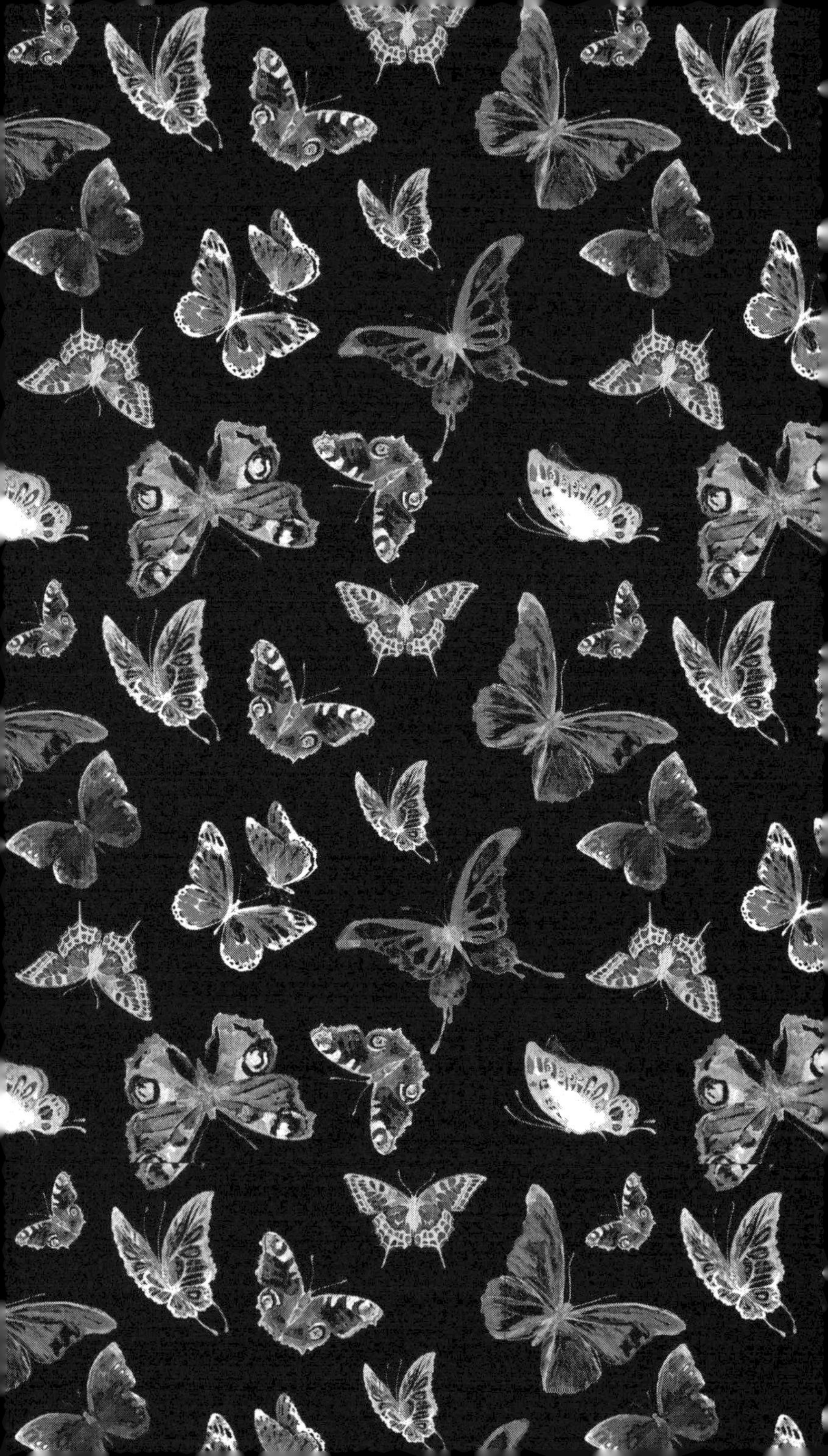

CHAPTER THIRTY-FOUR

BLAIRE

Beacon Grove was mayhem.

Movement Members held the advantage in numbers, but they lacked the gifts we had. They didn't share our passion or devotion, either.

In fact, they appeared to lack any sort of emotion at all. They fought against us like mindless zombies, hardly even reacting to the blows they were given. It was a jarring sight.

Time and time again, I watched them take hard hits—to the face, torso, legs, everywhere—and simply get back up as if nothing happened. As if they were under some kind of war trance, programmed to self-destruct. To run themselves in the ground fighting for Rayner's cause.

But Quarter Supporters fought with spirit and grit.

With their hearts.

I was proud to stand beside my neighbors—my *family*—as we defended our town and coven.

Grammy and Mom hung back, not seeking physical altercations, but taking them on if need be. Storie and Remy worked on the west side, siphoning their powers from the ocean to drown Members where they stood. Lux drew wisps of wind on the east side that knocked groups of them onto their backs, allowing Quarter Supporters to rush in and unarm them.

Rhyse threw flames from his hands on the front line, scorching the earth at their feet to scare them back and burning their skin if they got too close. Enzo fought right beside him, churning up the earth beneath them so they tripped and fell. Vines grew out of nowhere and wrapped around their limbs, holding them down as Quarter Supporters came behind and attacked.

The Quarters may not have been working with the full capacity of their powers, but they were still a deadly opponent.

I harnessed all my gifts—throwing fire, kicking up the earth, splashing water, and pushing air at my opponents as they came. Those who fought beside me were surprised to see such magic come from my fingertips. They paused and gaped at the strange girl, who had always been treated as more of a nuisance than anything, now saving their lives. I didn't stay in one spot long enough for anyone to question me.

The most aggressive Members received the most vicious defense, often resulting in their death.

But we tried our best not to get to that point, especially the Quarters. We were fighting for life—for good. It wasn't lost on us that the enemy consisted of those who were once our friends. The baristas that served our coffee every morning. The chefs that fed us. The police that defended us.

Deep down, we knew they were still in there.

We only wanted to take down one man, and he was too much of a coward to show up and fight for his own cause.

Kyle and his police officers fought beside Rhyse and Enzo, the only ones comfortable enough to wield their weapons. I kept him in my line of sight the entire time, often bobbing or weaving to ensure I could still track him down in the wreckage.

He was fighting this war for Beacon Grove, but he had a past with Rayner that most of us didn't understand. A long history of pain and suffering at the hand of the man who was hellbent on turning our town to rubble.

That was why I knew that when I saw those two men pulling his mother and sister into the woods, it was a trap. One that would lead right to Rayner.

And when I turned toward the man I love and saw his horror-stricken face, I knew he'd fall into it.

I knew he'd take the chance to end it.

I called out to him, screamed and pleaded for him to stop, uncaring of who heard. I loudly begged him to think about what he was doing, to wait for one of us to come with him. But he ignored my screeching, only increasing his pace as the four figures disappeared behind the brush.

And I had no choice but to follow.

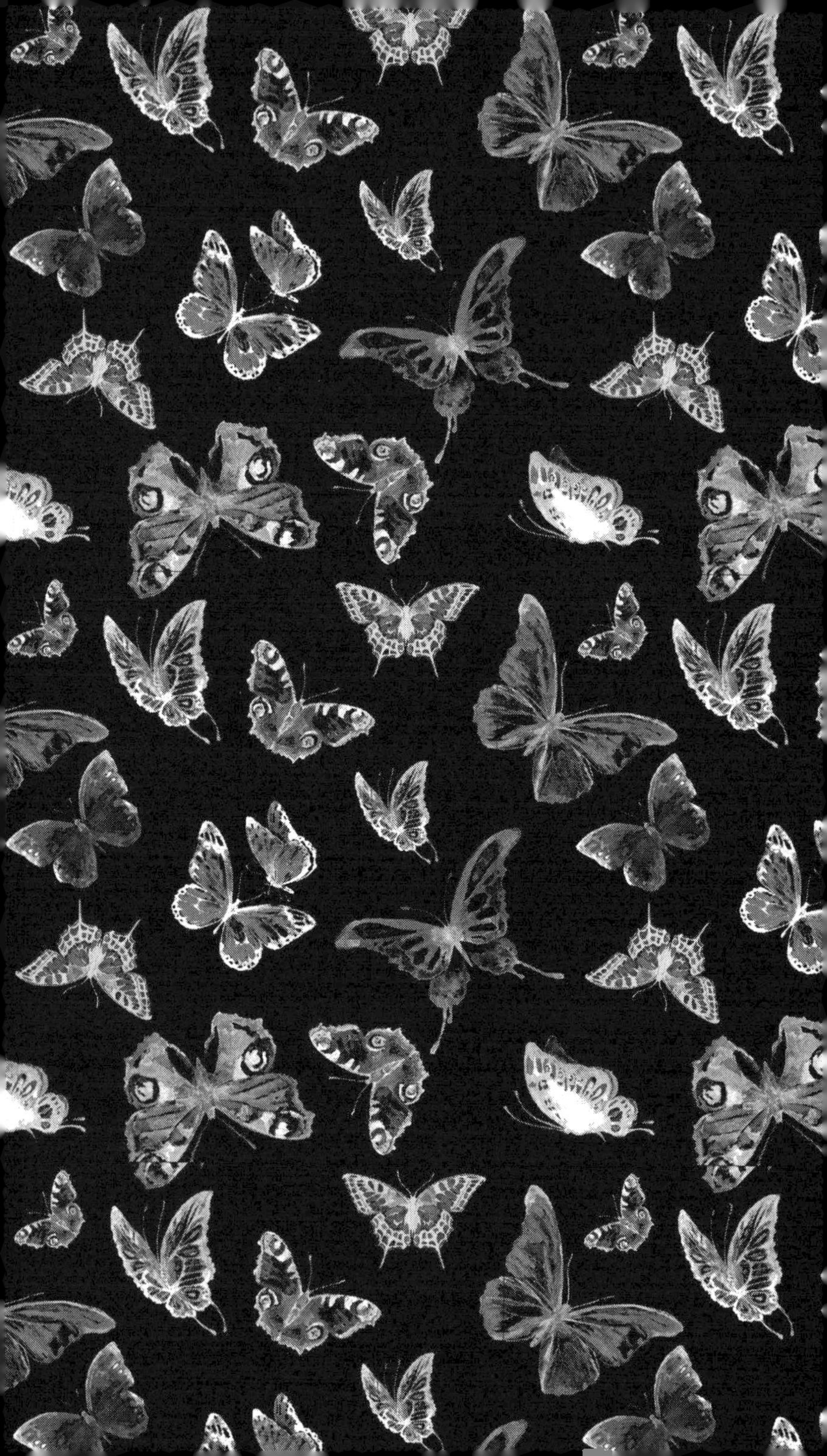

CHAPTER THIRTY-FIVE

KYLE

Rayner already had Millie and Ma tied up and gagged on the edge of mine and Blaire's spring by the time I caught up to them. The men who carried them here were gone. The kids were nowhere to be found, thankfully. Though, I couldn't be sure if that was a good thing.

"You came," his low voice purred from behind me.

I swung around and found him leaning against the willow tree.

He looked different. Even from last year, his face had changed. Any shred of the innocent teenager who was just trying to avenge his father's death was long gone, and in its place was a complete and utter lunatic.

The power had gone to his head. It had already gone to his head on the night he killed Bonnie and walked away as a free man. Back then, I'd wanted to kill him for tearing my family apart. Now, I wanted to do much worse. I wanted him to watch as I destroyed everything he worked toward all these years. I wanted him to pay for threatening the life I built in the wreckage he created.

There was so much history between us, it was hard to nail down the true reason I wanted to tear him apart where he stood. I just knew that I wanted to.

"You didn't leave me much of a choice," I said, extending my hand toward my sister and mom, who had begun thrashing around on the ground at the sound of my voice.

"Ah, yes. I figured I should end this the way it began: with your family. Although, these days, that looks a little different, doesn't it?" He pushed off the tree and strolled toward me. "You truly can't stand the people you were born from, can you? Poor little Kyle, always searching for some way out of the slums."

A malicious laugh erupted from those thin, pale lips, and it floated over toward me, dancing around tauntingly.

"Just let them go, Ray."

"I'm not done with them. Not yet."

"This makes you no better than those Quarter assholes who killed your dad and kidnapped your brother."

Rayner spent most of his life thinking they killed his brother, too. We discovered last year, after Rhyse took over for his father, that Rayner's brother had been Silas Forbes' Counter. He was chained up underground in the Forbes mansion to feed Silas' powers. That was how Rayner got Silas to work with him—he was too afraid to lose his Counter and his gifts.

Even when he was set free, Rayner's brother refused to find him, too disgusted with what he had done in the time he was gone. What he became.

"Yeah, but you have to admit, it works. Look how distracted you are with them flailing around over there."

A wicked laugh, and then he moved his hand to call someone forward. There was a rustling in the foliage off to the left before Doris stepped into the clearing.

I watched in complete horror as she walked over to my family—people who trusted her completely—and shoved her foot into Ma's back.

Ma cried out and Millie threw her body around, trying like hell to slam into Doris and knock her off her feet to release the pressure.

Rayner watched me closely for a reaction that I refused to give. Instead, I remained still on my feet, mentally cataloging every ounce of torture I was going to inflict on these two sadistic assholes when this was all over. I just needed to bide my time until the Quarters came.

"Remember Doris? She worked hard to be the perfect candidate for Mommy's little boy to hire and delegate his moral responsibility onto. You were so desperate not to be around her, you practically begged Doris to help."

Doris lifted her chin and smiled proudly, as if she were accepting an award for her performance. A pet basking in the praise of her owner.

"Oh, cheer up, Kyle. It's all in good fun."

He cocked his head at Doris, silently commanding her to step away. When she did, Millie wormed her way beside our laboring Ma.

"What is your plan, then? Let the whole town kill each other? How do you benefit from that?"

"They won't *all* kill each other. I just need the Quarters out of my way. Then, when they're all gone and there's no one left to save the pathetic people of Beacon Grove, I'll swoop in and offer them refuge."

He looked at his nails distractedly, as if we were having a simple conversation about the weather instead of debating the lives of hundreds of people who were currently fighting against one another. My gaze swung to Ma and Millie, who had temporarily quieted down now that they were left alone.

"Although," Rayner started, stealing my attention back. He truly loved to hear himself talk. "Blaire Granger as a Quarter sure took me as a surprise. She's proven to be quite the girl, eh?"

A devilish smirk appeared. "I suppose what they say about redheads is true, then?"

I couldn't stop the growl that rumbled in my throat, black and red stars filling my vision with my towering rage as he mentioned my Quarter—my *mate*.

"That's the Kyle I know," he beamed.

"They aren't going to let you take them down. They'll rip you to shreds before you're even able to touch them."

His expression darkened, and I knew I had hit a nerve. I supposed it had been a while since anyone spoke against him.

"You know, Asher and Mason had that same smart mouth in the end, too. Is it something you all do to distract yourselves from the fact that you're about to die?"

I stilled at the mention of the Graves. I hadn't lied when I told Blaire that my hatred for him started when he took them away from me—long before he even managed to take their lives. To hear their names on his tongue was like a spoke to my burning rage. It only reminded me why I was standing here in the first place.

"I do wish you could have heard them beg me for mercy in their final moments," he goaded, noticing my restrained reaction. I wasn't aware he was there when they died.

My rage simmered beneath my skin, a monster begging to be released from its cage. But I kept it at bay, conserving its power for when I truly needed it.

When I continued refusing to give him the response he wanted, he clicked his tongue and moved through the clearing toward Ma and Millie, his dark trench coat trailing in the wind behind him like a cape.

"I wonder if you'll have more to say when you're forced to watch me kill your family right in front of you."

"I'm just not playing these games with you. I told you years ago, before any of this began, that it was a bad idea to go against the Quarters. You'll lose every time."

His hands flexed at his sides, the irritation at my words a palpable thing. That ego was going to be the thing that got him killed. I only hoped I could be there when it happened.

"Enough talking, then. Let me just show you the power that now courses through my veins. How easy it will be for me to gut you like a fish. Shall I demonstrate on Mother Dearest first?"

I jumped forward as he lifted his arm and eight long, black arms extended behind his back. Demonic tentacles. The source he was using for his power was taking over his entire body and he was so caught up in the intensity of it, he didn't even care.

He pointed a finger at Ma, and her body jerked as if it were being electrocuted. Her mouth opened, but nothing came out. Millie writhed around beside her with blood-curdling screams, as if whatever magic he had just used on Ma had bounced over to her as well. I shouted for Rayner to stop, but he ignored me. Amusement danced along his wrinkled face as he watched Ma's body flail around, bones breaking with the sheer force of power he was using against her.

Like a cat playing with a mouse.

He didn't stop until her body was mangled and broken, hanging limply in the air as all the life had drained from it. Then, he threw her off to the side and directed his attention toward Millie.

I stepped between them before he could begin the same assault on her, and he smiled in acceptance.

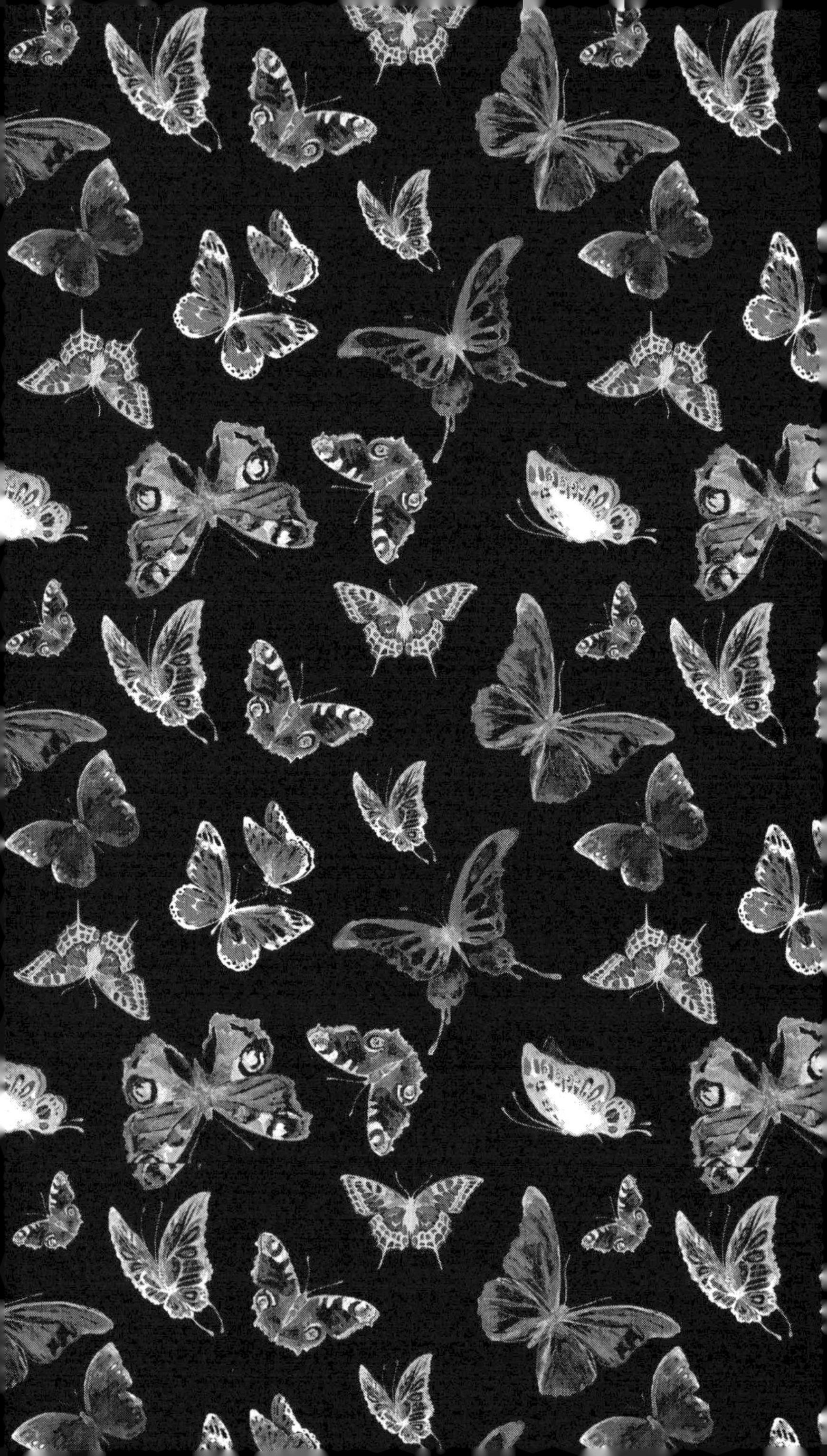

CHAPTER THIRTY-SIX

BLAIRE

My legs couldn't move me fast enough through the dense woods. Trees whirred by, only inches from colliding with me, but never making that connection. Grammy's strained voice called out behind me, pleading for me to stop. To wait for her and the Quarters.

But I wasn't stopping. Not when every second counted.

The earth crunched beneath my feet, obeying the orders I mentally threw at it to shift and get me there. To him.

My hair whipped against my cheeks, my braid loosening from hand-to-hand combat. The wind whistled in my ears, whispering directions. The forest knew where he was. It knew I needed to get to him—my Counter. And my gifts worked seamlessly to bring us together.

His guttural screams grew louder, the aching from before morphed into full-blown agony. I absorbed the pain, hoping it would somehow take some from him. Maybe we could share the burden. Maybe I could buy him some time until I could get there.

I recognized the curved trees that appeared before me. The smell of the wildflowers that bloomed nearby. It made sense that Rayner took him here, to our place. It made sense that the gods would have this be where I saved him. Or where I lost him.

I pushed that thought from my head before it manifested into something real.

"You could have joined me," I heard Rayner's rough voice call out, followed by another grunt. "Mason, too. We could have done so much together, but you two chose *them*. Despite every single time they've wronged us all."

Another groan, and this time, the pain shot through me like a bullet. I rounded the familiar willow tree and broke through the clearing breathlessly. Rayner's head whipped around, his face a vision of pure evil.

I didn't give him more than a second of my attention. Instead, my eyes searched for *him*. For the other half of my soul, which was lying in a heap, nearly completely camouflaged by the overgrown grass.

We locked eyes, and he sent a storybook of images into my mind. And I saw it—all of it. I only risked breaking his stare long enough to find his mom and sister's bodies lying limply near the spring, confirming what he had just shown me.

Rayner was after him this entire time, playing a sick little game to get retribution for things that happened years ago. Before most of us were even thought of.

In a tantrum over the attention not being on him, Rayner let out a loud growl. A wicked smile cursed his lips as he lifted his hand and Kyle's body flew into the air, floating there until he slammed his hand back down, and whatever force of magic he was drawing from dropped him to the ground again. Bones snapped, and Kyle let out an agonizing groan that had me screaming at Rayner to stop. To end this now.

But the sadistic coward turned his attention toward me, and watched my reaction as he repeated the motion all over again. Breaking more bones. Drawing more blood from the man I loved.

My throat was raw from protests. I didn't realize I was screaming. It only seemed to be fueling Rayner, though. Grammy warned me not to go against him without her or the Quarters to support me, but I had no idea how long they'd take to get here. I only knew Kyle couldn't take much more.

I took one step forward and Rayner's smile grew wider, accepting the challenge. But I wasn't focused on him anymore. My eyes fell to Kyle's broken figure lying on the ground between us, his face coated in crimson and his nose going in two different directions. His arms were hugging his torso and his legs were curled up in a fetal position. I swore one of his shins had been broken in half, but I wasn't brave enough to walk around and get a better look.

And his breathing... gurgling sounds were coming from his throat as his lungs wheezed. I was able to feel every ache and pain in my own body through our connection.

It only took a few seconds for me to realize he was now in grave condition. Rayner grew impatient as we stood there, unmoving. He wanted me to take the first shot, but I couldn't risk Kyle getting hurt in the crossfire.

When I didn't act quick enough, he raised his hand again, watching my reaction as he made a fist and Kyle screamed in agony once again.

I felt it, too.

Pain radiated from my head all the way down to my toes. It took everything in me not to fall to the ground beside Kyle and scream with him. I shouted again, commanding him to stop, but Rayner enjoyed our agony too much. He smiled even wider and continued to wield his power against us.

Just as I was about to give up and surrender, everything stopped.

The pain.

Kyle's screaming.

All of it just stopped.

Rayner's face fell as he tightened his fist, and Kyle's body remained limp, no longer straining against the torture. The black tentacles behind his back slinked down to his side.

I realized what had happened and released a long, blood-curling wail.

Fury burned through my body like molten lava, searing the earth beneath my feet as I stepped toward my target with wisps of smoke wrapping around my ankles. The absence of Kyle's pain brought on a wave of power that I'd been holding back.

A force I'd never felt before.

Stay with me, I begged silently, unsure if he could even hear me anymore. The connection we shared felt empty on the other end, but I couldn't give up.

I couldn't let him go.

Hold on for just a little while longer, I tried again, screaming the demand in my head, hoping he'd somehow hear me from wherever he was.

My feet took me to stand right before Rayner, who was somehow pinned to his spot, wide eyes staring at me in complete horror. I glanced down and realized his legs were buried in the earth, vines wrapping around his ankles to secure him into place.

Grammy warned me to wait, but we'd run out of time. The image of my Counter's body—my *mate*—lying on the ground behind me sent my mind into an uncontrolled, feral mode.

There would be no waiting.

Just destroying.

I'm going to make this right, I promised as warm tears coated my face. My heart beckoned for his to hear me. To send out some sort of signal that my worst nightmare hadn't come true.

What is a Quarter without their Counter? I never wanted to find out.

Rayner scrambled for words as I watched him, my stare unwavering despite the crumbling of my heart in my chest.

He did this. He took him away from me.

And while I wanted his death to be swift and powerful, I also wanted him to suffer the unimaginable pain that I now had to live with. I wanted to remind him of every life he'd taken, and incite the same amount of agony onto him as he had done to his victims.

My gifts may be dulled without Kyle, but I was willing to try.

"Blaire," his familiar voice murmured behind me. It was so quiet, yet all-consuming, infiltrating all my senses at once.

I turned around, mentally willing the vines to tighten around Rayner so he couldn't get away.

"You're better than this. Better than him," his ghostly form promised.

I fell to my knees before him, too aware of what this meant for us.

"No, no, no!" I cried out.

Kyle's face crumpled as awareness hit. His translucent body knelt beside me dejectedly. He tried to wrap his arms around my shoulders, but they misted right through me, leaving goosebumps in their wake.

He looked over at his physical form in complete horror. "I tried. It was so damn hard, but I tried," he mumbled, mostly to himself.

"Please come back to me," I begged, tears streaming down my face. I held my hands out toward his lifeless physical body. "There's still time. Just come back, *please*."

"Listen to me. This isn't the end, Blaire. We have lifetimes to go. Wherever we go, whatever happens next, I'll always find you. I love you so much."

He was saying goodbye.

I sobbed into the thin veil between us. "Stop. Don't talk like this. Just come back to me."

I didn't know if Rayner could see Kyle. I didn't care, either. He wouldn't live to speak about this to anyone, anyway.

"Blaire!" Grammy's voice called out from somewhere far away. I didn't lift my head to find her. I didn't call out to tell her where I was.

I just stared at Kyle through swollen, wet eyes, remembering all the stolen moments we shared. Mourning the ones we'd never get. I'd only just gotten him to myself. How was I going to survive an entire lifetime without him?

"Blaire, what's going on?" Grammy was closer now. The earth rustled somewhere behind me, but I still didn't bother to turn.

They were too late.

"No," she breathed, finally close enough to find me. I knew she could see him.

"Get up," she commanded. She hobbled over toward me and tugged at my arms, urging me to stand.

"I don't want to," I cried out, snatching my arms away, refusing to break away from Kyle.

I had no idea when I'd see him again. I wasn't going to waste our last moments arguing with her.

"Blaire, get up! We need to help him."

"He's already gone," I heard myself say. I hated the feel of the words on my tongue.

"We can save him. We can stop this. Hurry up."

She said something to someone beside her when I didn't move, then turned away from me to head toward Kyle's physical body.

"Go with her," he gently urged.

"I can't leave you," I whispered brokenly.

"Give them a chance to help you. To help me."

I stubbornly refused, the tears streaming faster again. He just wanted me to turn away so he could disappear. He had already said his goodbyes, but I wasn't ready.

I'd never be ready.

"Please, baby. Give her a chance. She knows what she's doing."

"I need you," I said frantically, silently begging the gods to bring him back.

"You need to stand up. You need to keep your chin held high. There's still so much work to be done. Don't let them ruin you."

He leaned in close enough to place a ghostly kiss against my cheek without misting through it.

And then, without warning, he was gone.

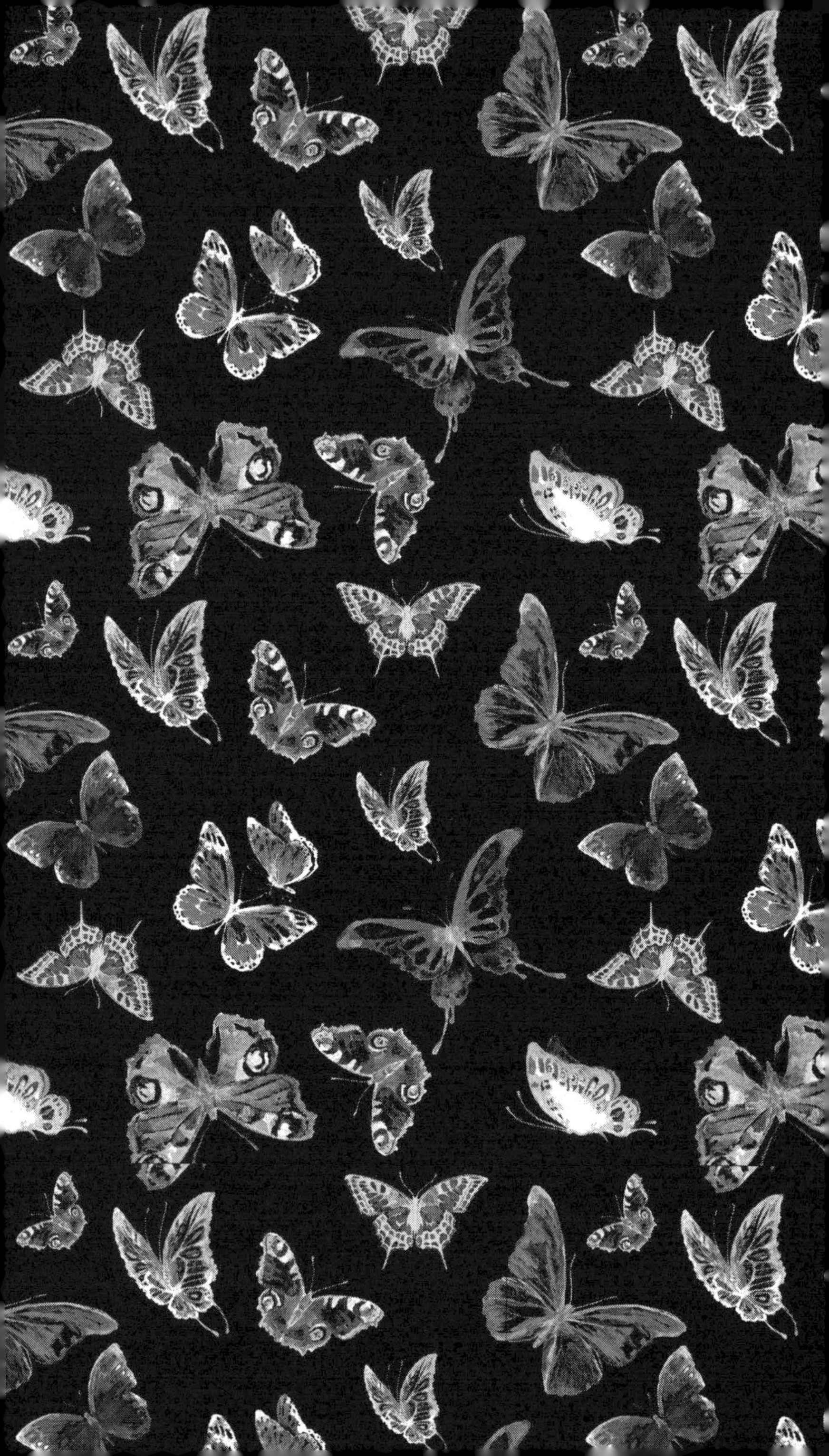

CHAPTER THIRTY-SEVEN

BLAIRE

I finally turned my attention back to Rayner long enough to discover that the restraints I created for him were squeezing so tightly, he had passed out. Or died. I hoped it wasn't the latter because I had plans to make his death long and brutal.

"BLAIRE," Grammy shouted across the clearing.

I steeled myself, glancing one last time at the empty spot that Kyle's spirit had just stood, then walked over to where Grammy waited with Mom and Storie, kneeling beside Kyle's lifeless body. I assumed the Quarters were still fighting Movement Members in town.

How could we bring him back without their gifts?

"Come here." Mom pulled me into her arms and tucked my head under her chin. She held me as my body wracked against hers in quiet, powerful sobs.

Grammy stood up from her spot beside Kyle and grabbed my hand, tugging me out of Mom's grip. I looked down at him and nearly broke apart again. From this close, he appeared ruined beyond repair.

Grammy and Storie had gathered flowers from somewhere and placed them on his chest. She squeezed my hand and held out her other one for Storie to take. Mom completed the circle surrounding my Counter's body, and Grammy began chanting words in the same foreign language she'd used on spells throughout my entire life.

Mom joined in after the first verse of the spell, and Storie closed her eyes. I could feel the Quarters' power radiating off of her, as if she were using herself as a conduit to feed the spell with their gifts.

I hadn't stopped crying. My eyes burned and struggled to focus as I scoured the clearing for Kyle's translucent form. He was nowhere to be found, though. His sister and mother's bodies laid awkwardly beside the spring, and I couldn't tell if they were alive or dead.

Had Rayner wiped out the entire Abbot clan in the short period of time it took me to get to them?

Grammy tugged my hand, pulling my attention back to the spell. I reluctantly obliged, focusing on calling his spirit back toward his body. The effects of the ritual began taking hold of me, siphoning my gifts into the limp body that was before us. My grip on Rayner's restraints weakened as my energy was pulled away from him, and I allowed it, figuring he would remain unconscious long enough for us to complete the ritual.

It was as if my soul stepped outside of my body and into his. The forest surrounding us blurred into a mess of green and brown as a wind picked up and whipped around. I felt like we were standing in the middle of a tornado and the only thing that remained in focus was the face of the man I loved. Yet, I was somehow also looking at myself from his body. Grammy released my hand and urged me to step toward him—to heal him with my touch. So, I did.

I crouched at his side and tested the bond by gently placing my hand against the bruised purple skin on his arm. It instantly turned the same pale shade of white as the rest of his body, completely healed. I moved onto the next wound I saw, slowly making my way toward his torso, where I knew most of the fatal damage had been done.

Grammy, Mom, and Storie held the spell as I worked to heal him completely, erasing any sign of Rayner's wrath. Once I was able to hold my hands above him without sensing any injuries, I dropped my hands onto his chest and looked to Grammy for guidance on what to do next.

She held my gaze while the wind surrounding us picked up speed. Storie's eyes widened in fear as her hair whirled across her face and whatever power she was channeling had strengthened. Grammy and Mom shouted the spell over the roaring tornado spinning around us. As the pressure kicked up, Storie's chest was pushed upward, as if a string was being pulled from the sky to lift her. Violet eyes rolled into the back of her head, and I began to panic.

Grammy glanced at her and spoke even louder—an angry chant. I opened my mouth to beg her to stop, but nothing came out. Storie's feet began lifting off the ground until only the tips of her shoes were making contact with the earth. She hung in the air by the invisible string, nearly unconscious.

I tried again to make them stop. I wanted Kyle back, but I couldn't risk losing all of them in the process.

Maybe it was too late.

But just as I went to bring my hands up to grab onto Storie and pull her back down, Kyle's lungs filled with air beneath them.

His chest rose with the force of it, and then fell completely. I looked to Grammy once more, and she smiled triumphantly around the words of the spell, continuing her chanting until his chest rose and fell again with steady breaths.

We did it.

He was alive.

I leaned over him and grabbed his face in my hands, watching in complete disbelief as his eyes fluttered open, revealing those uniquely silver irises. My mouth was instantly on his.

I kissed him as the wind slowed around us and the trees came back into focus. As Storie's body returned to the ground and she fell onto her knees with a thud. As Grammy and Mom hugged each other in victory.

And I only pulled away when I heard the Quarters' voices getting closer. Remy knelt down beside Storie, holding her in his arms as he revived her depleted energy.

"Where's Rayner?" Rhyse asked.

My eyes found the spot I had him pinned to minutes before. Withered vines lay in a heap on the grass, the only evidence he left behind.

And we all stared in shock as we realized what a grave mistake we had made by leaving him unguarded.

He was gone.

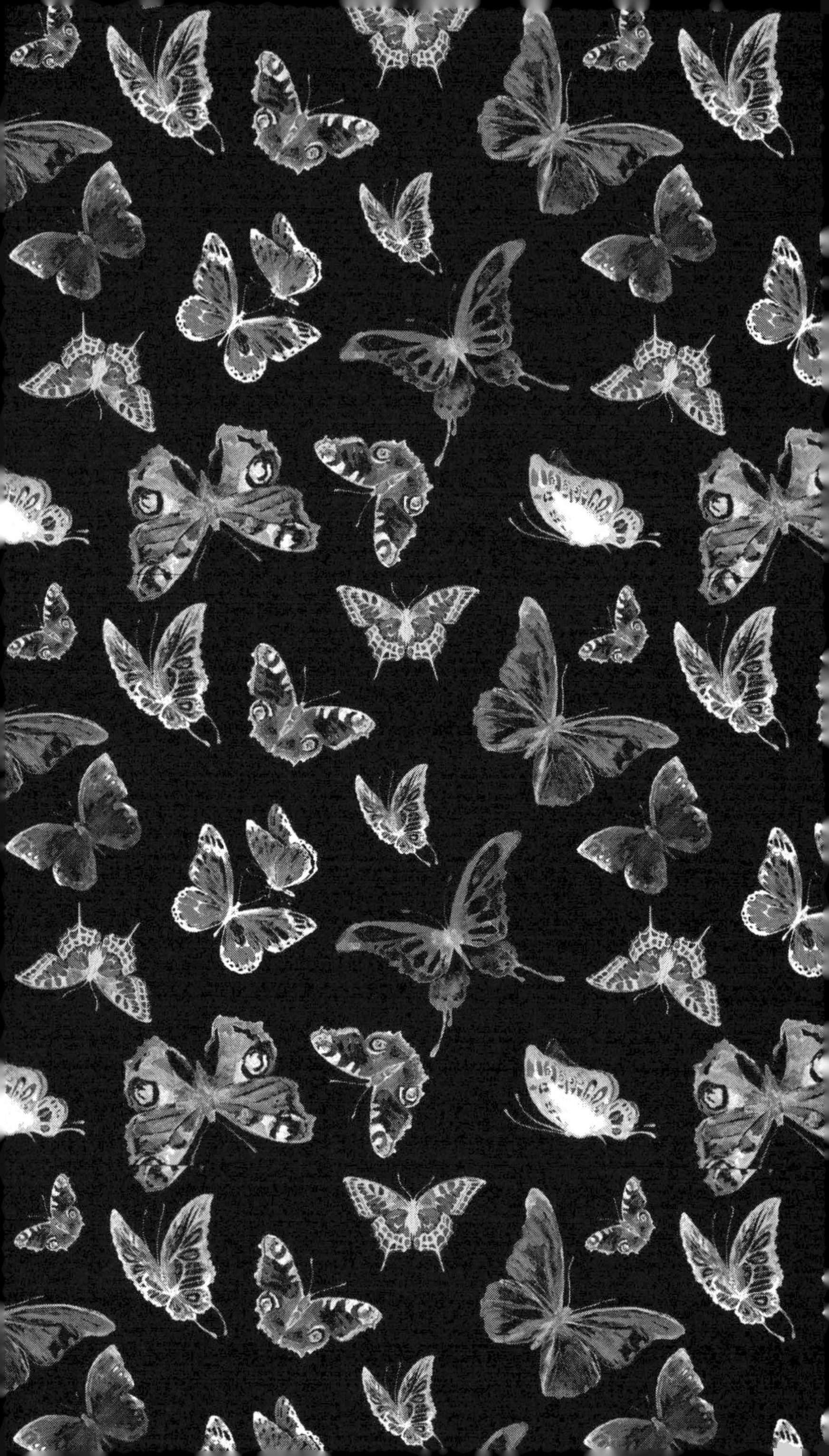

EPILOGUE

KYLE

The war in Beacon Grove resulted in more casualties on both sides than we could have ever expected. Rayner's Movement Members were too detached to stand down and the Quarter Supporters were too stubborn to let them take over their town any more than they already had.

It ended in a bloody, brutal battle amongst neighbors.

At the loss of my mother and many other innocent souls. Millie had just barely managed to escape death at Rayner's hands, though she had yet to wake up from her coma.

Carnage scattered around the sacred grounds that the original thirteen worked and sacrificed to build.

The Quarters explained through painful expressions that they took on the brunt of the fighting after Blaire and I left them to find Rayner, though the others were equally dedicated. They said they battled long and hard, up until Members began randomly moving out.

"It was the oddest thing, watching them drop their weapons and stumble off toward the woods with blank stares," Remy had mused when I asked him about it.

We later learned that was due to whatever communication Rayner made with them after he escaped Blaire's restraints. The haunting image of those black tentacles stretched from his back flashed through my mind as they explained the scene in bewilderment. Whatever entities he was working with were ancient and dynamic. I don't doubt that he used them to get into his Members' heads to possess them to do such horrific things and control their movements.

Quarter Supporters quickly switched gears and mustered their last bit of strength to stop their enemy from leaving Beacon Grove's town limits. They managed to capture the majority of Movement Members who were attempting to leave and sent them back to Quarter prisons.

This time, they were left to rot in their cells until their fate could be decided.

It was archaic and brutal and against everything I knew as a police officer, but things in Beacon Grove had gone so far out of touch with the world, it was hard to defend them. They had long since left my jurisdiction and none of the Granger women had allowed me to leave my house to step in for days, anyway.

"You were dead a few days ago," Blaire crassly reminded me when I complained that as the town's sheriff, I should have been helping rebuild, not sitting in my bed listening to her hash out the gossip from the day.

It was just as important for me to be standing beside them through such a transitional time as it was for her. I could only imagine what they were saying, especially given that the rest of the leaders of Beacon Grove had proven to be enemies.

Had they even told them that I was Blaire's Counter?

Mayor Douglas and his ancient council members were nowhere to be found when the war broke out, and no one had seen them since. It was expected for them to sit out the fight since they were elderly and out of shape, though it was rumored that the townspeople were fully expecting the announcement of a town meeting in the days following that never came.

It was an unsurprising turn of events, given that the remains of Mark Tackle, editor of The Beacon, were likely still scattered across the street of Beacon Grove. He was one of the first Movement Members to be taken down before my eyes. The paper was still scrambling to find someone to replace him, though there wasn't much use for it at the moment. Anyone still remaining in the town could be found in the town's square, clearing away evidence of the horrific war. If word needed to get out, it could be done so immediately.

As for the mayor and the council, no one knew where they disappeared to, but it was clear that they picked a side and made their allegiances known.

"And you healed me completely," I argued, grateful for the bond we shared and our ability to heal one another. Without it, I would surely still be on the other side. Rayner took a great deal of pride in his ability to destroy me.

I grabbed a random shirt from the laundry pile on the floor and tugged it over my head, determined to leave. Staring at the same four walls wasn't doing anything for my mental health.

She huffed out a breath and moved to stand in the doorway, arms crossed over her puffed chest.

I lowered my voice to a gentler tone. "You have to let me leave sometime. I have a duty to protect them, too."

Her freckled features fell as the defensive mask melted away, revealing the insecure, terrified side of her that she'd been trying like hell to hide. I only noticed it in the rare moments we were alone and she thought I wasn't looking. And in the nightmares that kept her thrashing around in the sheets each night, but I doubted she realized it.

"It's not safe for you while he's still out there."

The images of Rayner slinging my body around the woods like a rag doll infiltrated my mind, and I knew they were coming from her. Of course, that was why she was so protective over me. I would probably be worse had the roles been reversed. But I didn't need her worrying about me.

"He's not coming back." At least, not until he had a plan in place.

"I don't want to risk it. There's no way to know who we can trust anymore. Especially now that everyone knows what we are to each other. I can't lose you again over this." Her gaze fell to the floor as her voice broke on the last word.

I closed the distance between us and wrapped her hands in mine, pulling them up to my chest to remind her that I was still here. That we lived through the nightmare and made it out the other side.

"If anything, this experience has proved that nothing can come between us, Blaire. Not even death herself. And all those people out there have more than proven their loyalty toward the Quarters and Watchtower when they fought beside us against their own friends and family. Rayner's Members can't hide in the shadows anymore."

When a single tear rolled down her cheek, I tipped her chin up with my finger and brushed a kiss against her lips, whispering assurances that we were safe. She didn't have a response, but stepped out of my way and silently followed me out the front door.

The most terrifying part about Rayner getting away was that now he knew all of our secrets and would most likely use them against us. We no longer had an element of surprise against him.

Blaire was angry with herself for losing him. In those moments after I was brought back, once the ecstatic relief over bringing me back settled, she quickly realized the mistake she had made in loosening her grip on him. She and the other Quarters screamed their frustrations into the empty forest, and I'll never forget the sound of their despair echoing off the trees all around us as Tabitha, Callista, Storie, and I watched helplessly. The image of the five of them covered in the blood of the people they were tasked by the gods with protecting would be burned into memory as well.

They were angry at the choice to bring me back instead of sending Rayner through the veil right behind me.

And while I know I would have made the same choice for Blaire—for *my Quarter*—I wanted to scream right along with them. Because we were so close to ending this suffering, and we let it slip right through our fingers.

Where Blaire's anger was quiet and self-deprecating in the days following, Rhyse and Enzo's fury were palpable, living things, roaring to life as more time went on without any sign of him. When Tabitha came to check in on me the next day while Blaire was caught up in a Quarter meeting, she explained that they scoured every inch of Beacon Grove, to no avail. It was as if he disappeared into thin air.

Along with the girls whose souls he was drawing his power from.

I hadn't told Blaire yet, but I saw them. When I was stuck in the veil between life and death, they were all there. Not quite on either side, but somehow woven into the veil itself, floating in some in-between place, just as I suspected. Their souls were crushed, and their energy was depleted, but none of them were fully dead.

Though, they were dangerously close.

It only raised more questions about what magic Rayner was working with and I didn't want to add that to her already-full plate.

Things looked different for me after being on the other side. As if the lens I once looked through was warped or scratched. The world was more grim and a lot less appealing. Problems that held so much weight before seemed so miniscule.

I was happy to be back with Blaire, but it was like a part of me had stayed behind. Like I'd forgotten something and couldn't figure out what it was.

And while we all had reason to be joyous over our victory in the small war that broke out in our town, none of Beacon Grove was feeling very celebratory. They were left to clean up a mess and rebuild from the ground up. To clean the remains of our friends and neighbors who fought both beside us and against us and honor their lives, regardless.

It was a celebration of life for the deceased on both sides. Of course, there was discord about whether the Movement Members should have been included in the service. It was the first issue that all five Quarters had to make a final decision on. In the end, it was decided that they were once our friends and neighbors. They still had surviving family members who fought as Quarter Supporters and deserved to have closure.

Given that Watchtower was still without a High Priest and Priestess, the Quarters led the funeral ceremonies together as a unit.

All five of them.

Blaire was terrified.

"You don't get it," she had said the night before when I tried to assure her it would be fine. It had been two days since our standoff in my room over me leaving my house to help around town. She still hadn't left my side unless absolutely necessary, too afraid that we might find this was all some sort of dream.

We were lying in her bed together and the only light filling the room came from the moon shining through her open window. She turned in my arms to face me as she further explained.

"Watchtower has never treated the Grangers like true members, especially after what Grammy did with the Counters when they were born. How are they going to react when the one family they ostracized and ignored for *centuries* ends up being filled with the most powerful women they've ever met?"

I laid my palm over her leg and gently squeezed. "You don't owe them anything, Blaire. Not an explanation, not an apology, and certainly not your peace. They saw what you did for them against the Movement, and they're grateful for it. If anyone has a problem, they can take it up with the gods."

She didn't seem convinced, but still dropped it. She did a lot of that recently—letting go of issues that she would usually dig her heels in about. It worried me to see her feisty side disappear behind this meek facade. I tucked my concern into the back of my mind, making note to revisit it another day, when things were more settled.

I wished I could find a better way to assure her that she was worthy of every ounce of power she was given, of every gift the gods bestowed upon her. That maybe they always treated her so poorly because they could sense it vibrating beneath her skin, and they weren't sure what to make of it.

The next morning, she stood alongside the Quarters and owned the role that she was so certain no one would accept her in. Instead of being gawked at and ignored in the way she predicted, she was honored and praised.

The five of them recited ancient prayers to the goddess, asking her to guide the fallen souls from both sides back home. The bodies were wrapped in cloth and placed into the earth, and then the townspeople and coven members spoke. They shared stories and inside jokes. They laughed together and cried together. And when it was all said and done, the bond that held Beacon Grove together through such a tumultuous time was secured even stronger.

And they didn't only accept their new Quarter, they worshiped her.

There was a reception held in the community center following the funeral for the fallen members of Beacon Grove. It was the only public place that wasn't still littered with debris from the war that took place only days ago.

I beamed from a distance as they formed a procession before her to offer their thanks and blessings. It wasn't long before an anxiousness settled over me when I realized nothing would be the same. Suddenly, Blaire's protectiveness over me and her insistence on staying locked away in my home made a lot more sense. It wasn't about control or fear.

The small safe haven that we've shared the past few months was now infiltrated, and I'd have to share her with the rest of the town as they came to know the amazing woman who stole my heart. She must have felt the same way about being around all these people.

※

B^{laire}

I was convinced standing in front of what remained of Watchtower coven and Beacon Grove—of my past bullies and abusers—that they'd reject me as one of their leaders. The coven had *four* Quarters. That was how it had always been, and they weren't too keen on change, especially in the wake of such a traumatic event.

But to my surprise—and apparently no one else's—they accepted me without hesitation. Remy, Lux, Enzo, and Rhyse made a point of keeping their expressions neutral and stern as they explained my role to the coven to ensure they knew there was no room for argument. Lux informed me of the tactic only minutes before we were supposed to perform the ritual, *just in case*.

Of course, the five of us had to come to a decision a few days ago about including Movement Members in the ceremonies, but that was done behind closed doors. Standing before my town and owning all the power I'd spent the better half of a year resenting was a completely different story.

"You're one of us, Blaire. Whether anyone likes it or not," Lux gently soothed.

His presence was always so calming. I wondered if my ability to control emotions may have been shared with him the same way I could control water like Remy or the earth like Enzo. In the chaos of everything, I hadn't ever found a chance to ask him what else he could do with the wind element, aside from the obvious.

And when everyone accepted the news without complaint, a weight lifted from my shoulders.

Centuries of anger and resentment—of hiding away and cowering down—to get to this moment. To see the members of my coven accept me as a Quarter, and for the Quarters to accept me as an equal. To see Grammy finally watch me with a smile on her face and pride in her expressive eyes. For Mom to remain present long enough to watch me lead our town into the future.

Still, I had trouble deciding if any of it was worth the trouble.

The anger I'd been harboring for the past year whispered vicious thoughts into my head, reminding me how it felt to be ostracized and isolated and flat out abused. The sorrow connected to the lives lost in a fight that I couldn't even end when I had the opportunity also dug its claws in. Neither feeling would release its grip on me long enough to allow me to submerge myself fully into the ecstatic high of winning the war and being accepted by my peers.

It all left me feeling uneasy and on edge. Paired with my constant fear for my Counter's safety, I was rarely able to relax. It almost felt as if there was a false sense of calm blanketing Beacon Grove and in our weakest and most distracted moments, the Movement would strike.

Everyone assured me that I was wrong. That Rayner was too calculated to attempt another attack when all his Members were locked away in the dungeons and his odd, dark power was exposed.

But something told me that even if it wasn't what Rayner wanted, he was no longer in control. The source of his magic was potent and unknown. Those tentacles clearly came from some ancient, black magic that had likely been dormant for centuries. There was no way for us to predict what might happen if it were to take over and truly use Rayner's body as the vessel he likely agreed to be.

One thing I was learning about the gifts I'd been given was that they were accompanied by a strong intuition. One that was rarely wrong.

The spirits that once haunted me had gone utterly silent since the war. I wasn't sure if it was from some kind of block that I unconsciously put on them after communicating with Kyle, or if they were no longer able to reach me from wherever Rayner was holding them. For the first time ever, I was actually missing their chaos. Maybe if I could conjure one of them up, I'd get some insight into where the snake was hiding out.

I admitted to Kyle that I hadn't seen them the night before and he was oddly hesitant to share that he had seen them when he crossed over. That Rayner had them stuck between realms to siphon their power without resistance. The lack of communication from them either meant that he had completely depleted them to make his escape, or he had somehow found out that I could talk to them and was keeping them away from me. Either way, it would take a significant amount of power to get to them, but it would be worth it to bring them back home to what remained of their families.

For once, Kyle agreed.

"You did amazing," he breathed into my ear from behind before his hand snaked around my waist and he spun me to face him.

I forced a tight smile and linked my hands behind his neck, leaning into his chest. I finally understood the anxiety that Storie and Remy felt from being apart from one another. The unease that filled me and turned my stomach any time he wasn't in the same room as me was nearly crippling in those first few days. I was so afraid that I'd walk through his front door and find his body lifeless once again. I had nightmares that his translucent form would wisp out of my grip and disappear before I had a chance to even speak.

After a few days passed, the debilitating fear faded into a nervous ache that only dulled when I was near him. It had me running back to him every chance I got, just for some sense of relief.

"They didn't leave much room for argument." I rolled my eyes over to the three Quarters standing across the street from us. Rhyse had quickly excused himself from the group after the ceremonies with a vague excuse about dealing with one of the Members that was locked up under his home.

"Even if they had, there wouldn't be any."

He kissed my cheek and my eyes found Lisa Golden, owner of the Watchtower Tavern, watching us with a shocked and jealous expression. Before I could question it, he grabbed my hand and tugged me in the opposite direction, toward our house.

"Will this feeling ever go away?" I asked him, placing my hand over my chest.

He knew what I meant.

The tense disquietude that whispered warnings into my ear as each person and building passed by. It reminded me that the monsters I feared most had been living amongst us all along as wolves in sheep's clothing. That the worst of them had slithered out of our grip and were now circling us like prey. No one could truly be trusted, and we would never be safe.

He shrugged, then wrapped his arm around my shoulders.

"Probably not. But we can't let it steal away all the small moments like this one. The ones where things feel okay. No matter how brief they may be."

"Is it weird that it seems harder to do that now that we know what we're up against?"

He kept his eyes trained ahead of us. "I don't think so. But now, we've been to hell and back. We know what it's like to lose to him—to have our deepest fears come to fruition. I sure as hell am not going to let it happen again."

I understood what he wasn't saying. Even if Rayner tried to come back tomorrow, he wasn't going to let the same thing happen again.

His words didn't ease the storm inside my chest, but we had made it to his front door, and I was determined not to bring the conversation into our safe space. When he walked through the entryway and emptied his pockets, I grabbed his hand and led him back into his bedroom.

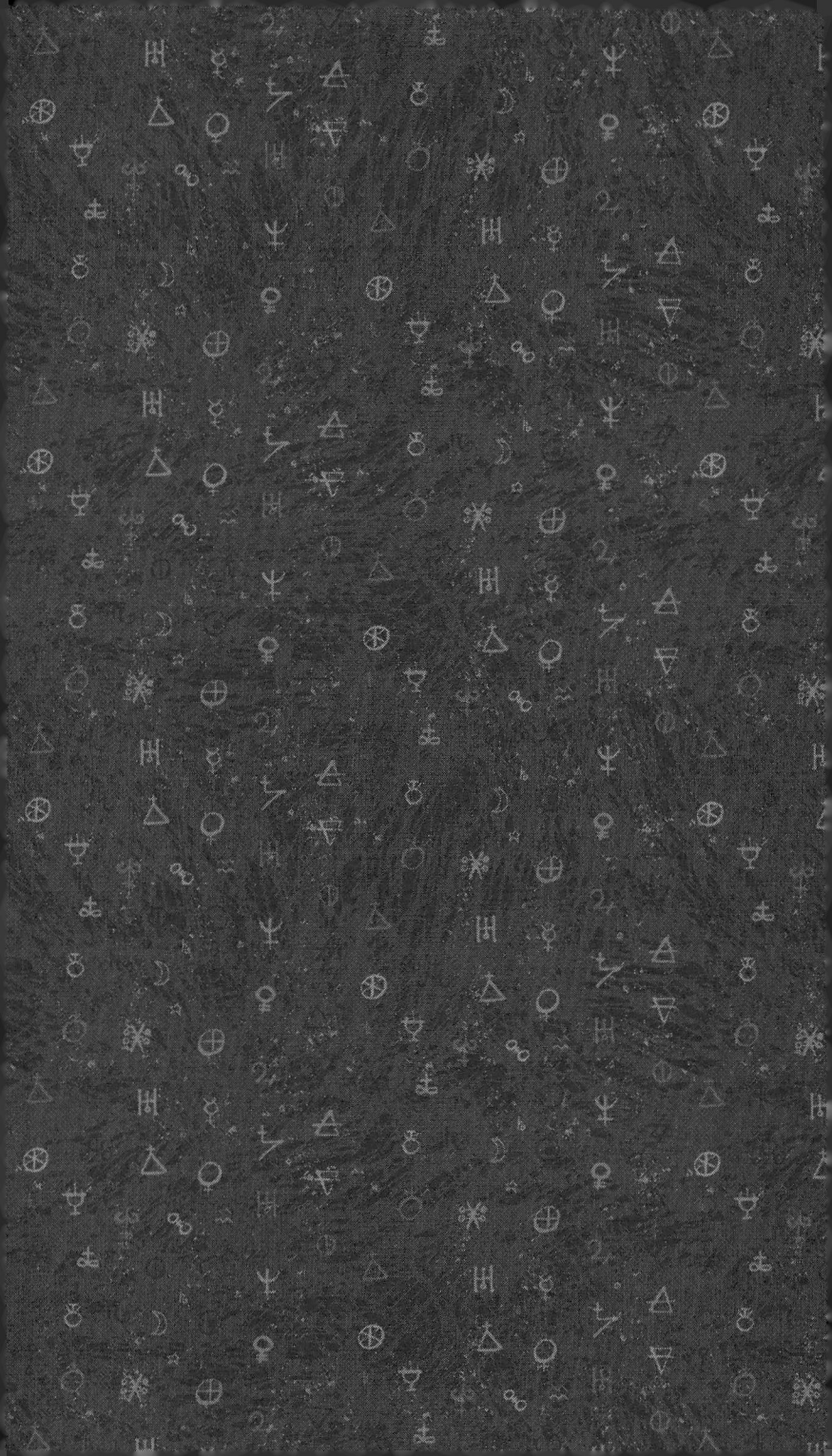

A PREVIEW OF CATCHING QUARTERS

Ready to find out what happens next in Beacon Grove? Flip ahead for a sneek peak into Catching Quarters!
You can read book three for free in Kindle Unlimited today!

BLURB:
I was bred for the Movement.
My parents sculpted me into the perfect companion for their leader, promptly handing me over the instant he showed interest.
He led us into war, and then abandoned us—his devoted followers.
Now, I'm a prisoner, stuck in the dungeon of one of my worst enemies: the fire Quarter of Watchtower coven.
Rhyse Forbes has tried everything to bleed me of information, never wasting an opportunity to use his gifts against me
What he doesn't realize is that I'd sooner rot in this cell than share my family's secrets. I'm positive they'll find me and burn his entire estate to the ground. All I have to do is bide my time.

Only, it's not long before we both feel it: that unmistakable bond between Quarter and Counter. Neither of us wants to admit it, but we can only keep the secret for so long.
I'm forced to face the reality that my family and the man I've dedicated my life to aren't coming to my rescue, and that Rhyse and the bond that ties us is the only thing keeping me alive.

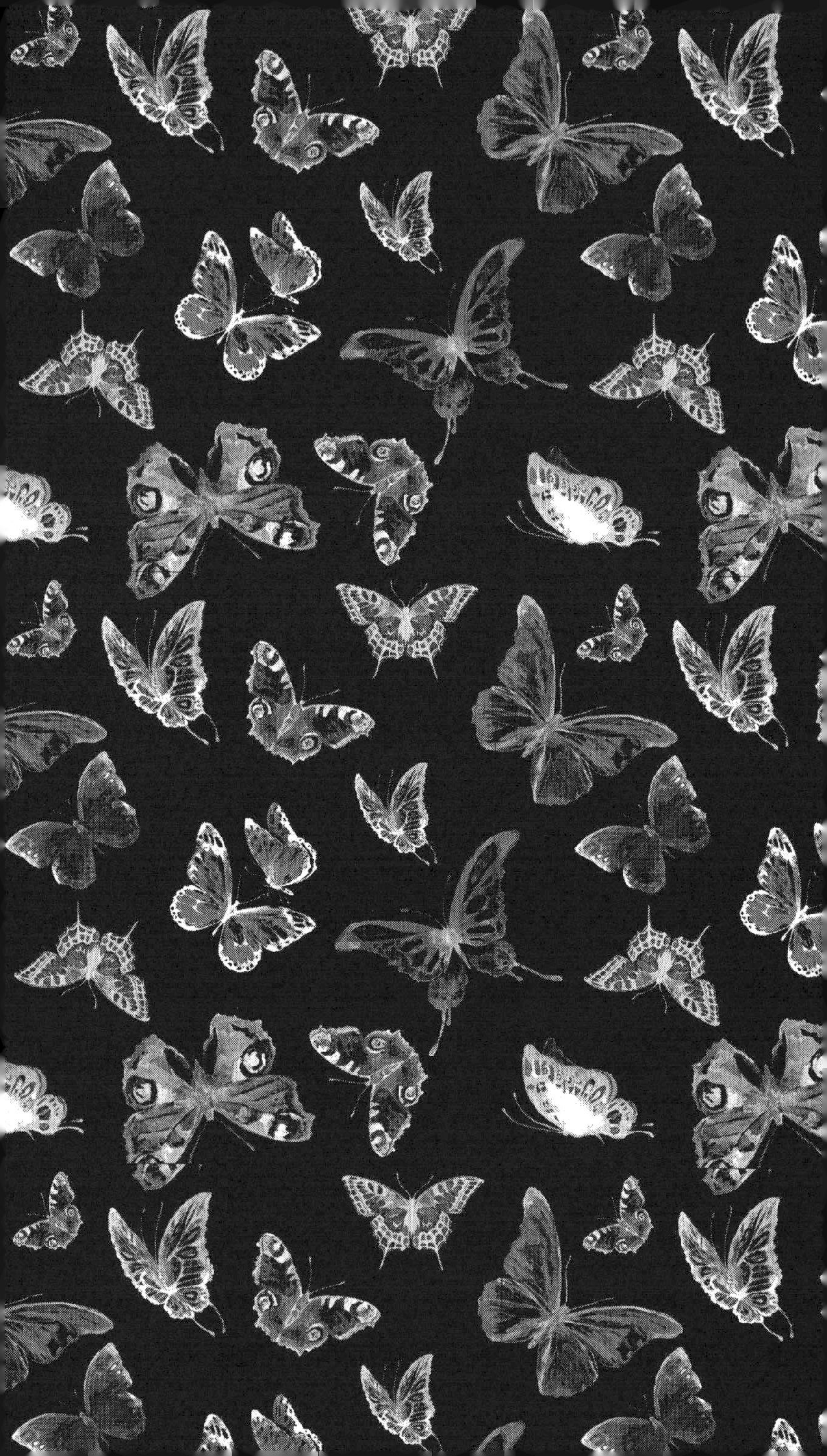

PROLOGUE

In my world, there were two clear-cut sides, separated in stark black and white.

Good and evil.

Right and wrong.

The Movement and the Quarters.

The Quarters of Watchtower Coven were a cancer to my town. They drained us of resources and used the blood, sweat, and tears of the hardworking people of Beacon Grove to fund their lazy, lavish lifestyles. No one dared challenge them in the century they reigned. At least, not until Rayner and the Movement came along. But we were met with malice and violence when we attempted to speak out about the supposed heroes.

My secret role as the second-in-command to our Movement came to a quick and fiery end as we were imprisoned by the Quarters following the war, and our leader—the man who once loved me—left us for dead.

Illusions were cleared and veils were lifted in the cold, wet dungeon below the Forbes' estate.

Revealing that all along, I had been the very thing I despised most.

This isn't a love story.

This is a story of shifted allegiances, severed relationships, and a soul connection far beyond the physical realm.

About Jen

Jen Stevens was born and raised in Michigan, where she enjoys the weather of all four seasons in a single day. After obtaining her Bachelor's degree, she quickly realized the corporate world wasn't for her and instead took on the daunting role as her children's snack maid. Reading has been an obsession for a long as she could remember, while writing has always been an escape. Jen could quote The Office word-for-word and proudly refers to herself as a romance junkie. She could live off anything made of sugar and has recently obtained the title of Lady. Most of all, she loves connecting with readers!

Check out Jen's website and socials for the most up to date publishing information: www.jenstevenswrites.com
Socials: @authorjenstevens

JOIN MY COVEN!

Join Jen's Coven of Wicked Little Sunflowers on Facebook today for early looks, exclusive content, and to just hangout! Scan this code:

Also by Jen Stevens

Check out all Jen Books!

Dark Romance:
- Ugly Truths (Grimville Reapers Book One)
- Untold Truths (Grimville Reapers Book Two)

Contemporary Romance:
- Advice from a Sunflower

Urban Fantasy Romance:
- Calling Quarters (Beacon Grove Book One)
- Counting Quarters (Beacon Grove Book Two)

Made in the USA
Columbia, SC
24 June 2024